HIDDEN SIN

Also by the same author

JULIE SHAW

HIDDEN SIN

THE PAST WILL ALWAYS HAUNT YOU

HARPER
element

Certain details in this story, including names, places and dates, have been changed to protect the family's privacy.

HarperElement
An imprint of HarperCollins*Publishers*
1 London Bridge Street
London SE1 9GF

www.harpercollins.co.uk

First published by HarperElement 2018

1 3 5 7 9 10 8 6 4 2

© Julie Shaw and Lynne Barrett-Lee 2018

Julie Shaw and Lynne Barrett-Lee assert the moral right to be identified as the authors of this work

A catalogue record of this book is available from the British Library

ISBN 978-0-00-822848-4

Printed and bound in Great Britain by
CPI Group (UK) Ltd, Croydon

MIX
Paper from
responsible sources
FSC™ C007454

This book is produced from independently certified FSC paper to ensure responsible forest management

For more information visit: www.harpercollins.co.uk/green

This book is simply dedicated to our Alan Taylor.
Rest in peace, Alan – you fought with every last breath
to stay as long as you could with my lovely little cousin,
Sue, AKA our Nipper, and your girls, Penny, Lou
and Lindsay. They all did you proud, Alan, and
always will do. You were everything a man
should be and you'll be sadly missed. x

*'Behold, I was brought forth in iniquity, and in
sin my mother did conceive me.'*

Psalm 51:5

Prologue

Bradford, June 1997

Mo took a slow look around him and sniffed the air. Nothing had changed, he realised. The Sun Inn still delivered: its familiar cocktail of stale beer, cheap perfume and sweat. Did it feel good to be back? He wasn't sure yet.

On balance, though, yes. Because he knew he still had it. Knew from the ripples of reaction that seemed to flow out when he moved. The odd stare. The covert nudge. The inevitable whispered conversations. Conversations that he knew were taking place in his wake. So on balance, yes. Yes, the weather was shit, *obviously*, but for the most part it felt good to be home.

He swayed – he couldn't help it – to the rhythm of the music. A young band. Loud and fast. A little raw, but pretty good, currently banging out Blondie's 'Picture This'. He leaned in towards Irish Pete – well, as close as his nose allowed, anyway. 'These are good, man,' he shouted at his friend above the noise. 'What they called?'

'Parallel Lines,' Pete said. 'Blondie tribute band.'

'I think I got that much.'

'And that blonde tart's a dead ringer for Debbie Harry, is she not? I know what I'd fucking like to do to her, too!' Pete grabbed at his crotch and thrust his hips forward. 'She wouldn't have to picture this, eh? She'd get the whole ten fucking inches!'

Mo eyed his old friend with distaste. One thing he'd forgotten during his long years on the oh-so-much more civilised (well, at least in that sense) Spanish Costas was that the Petes of this world never changed. Dirty-tongued, always. And dirty-mouthed, too. The recipient of some very expensive dental work recently, Mo was the proud owner of a gleaming new set of teeth, which only served to highlight what a sewer Pete's own mouth had become since he'd gone away. It stank like one every time he opened it, however sweet the words that issued forth, the rank-smelling interior fenced in by uneven rows of yellowy-brown, misshapen teeth.

'In your dreams, Pete,' he said, turning sideways to avoid the stench. 'Ten fucking inches, my arse.' He nodded back to the stage. 'Seriously, you know anything about them? I'm on the lookout for some talent for when me and Nico's place gets sorted. Decent house band. Something with a bit of class.'

And they did seem to have that. That sense of knowing their own worth. The blonde at the front, in particular – she had enough attitude to start a war. And the kid on the drums. There was definitely something special about him. Muscular. Mixed-race. Maybe twenty. Possibly younger. A whir of mesmerising movement beneath a cloud of chocolate curls, his hands moving in an expert blur across the whole drum kit.

'Not sure about "class",' Pete was saying. 'The bird's Josie McKellan's kid.' He nudged Mo. 'You know? Paula? Don't you recognise her? Tidy wee fucker she's turned out to be, eh?'

Mo looked more closely at the girl belting out the Blondie track. Of course. He'd been fooled by the bleached hair. If you took the peroxide out of the equation it was immediately obvious. That same familiar Hudson look. She was very like her mother. Taller than Josie, yes – hardly difficult, to be fair – but the same cocky expression. And a stark reminder of how times had changed in this particular corner of Bradford – like The Sun, which had reinvented itself from spit-and-sawdust to what was now obviously the thing: coloured-glass Tiffany light shades, lots of polished wood, dark, patterned carpets – like a migraine on the floor. He made a mental note, filing the look away for his latest venture.

The people had changed too. It no longer seemed such a man's world. Not like Spain – well, his bit of it – which still clung to the old order. Where men were the bosses and women were mostly meek. He could hardly believe the amount of skirt that seemed to be out partying unaccompanied – and none of them seemed to look as if they cared less.

A fresh rum and Coke appeared in front of him. 'Here you go, mate,' said his friend Nico. 'Lot to take in, isn't it? A bit different to how it was when we were banged up, eh, my friend?'

Nico laughed – a big booming laugh that might grate if you didn't know him. Ditto his usual moniker – the ridiculously unimaginative 'Nic the Greek'. Still, it had served him well enough in prison, Mo decided, greasy Greek fucker that he was. And it was serving him well now. They'd do all right together in this new version of Bradford. Even if Nico couldn't quite get his head around why Mo had wanted to return to it. After all, he'd been living the high life in Marbella since he'd come out of the nick, hadn't he? But the pull had always been there. Even though sometimes Mo didn't really understand why himself.

And he'd come back at the right time, with cash in his pockets, half of which he'd already invested in a house on Oak Lane's 'millionaire's row'. And now the club – into which they'd both now invested a ton of money; Nico's from the stash he'd managed to hang onto from the armed robbery that he'd done nine years for, and Mo from what he'd saved from his various business ventures while in Spain: the lease on a huge nightclub in Bradford city centre.

He sipped his drink, taking stock. All on track. Things looked good.

Pete was tugging at his sleeve. 'And you know who he is, don't you?' he said, following this announcement with a fetid burp.

'*Who* is?' Nico asked, irritably fanning the air in front of him. He had yet to see the benefits of Irish Pete, Mo conceded.

'Yes, who is?' Mo asked, annoyed that Pete was pissed already, and already so incongruous among the mostly youthful, attractive crowd.

'Joey Parker,' Pete persisted. 'I *knew* I recognised him. Joey *Parker*.'

'Yes, I got that bit,' Mo said. 'And I'm supposed to know him, am I?'

And even as Pete's mouth formed the shapes to say the next bit, the penny dropped, and Mo made the connection in his head.

'*Christine* Parker's lad, Mo.' Pete nodded towards the stage. 'As in –' He faltered now. Nervous about saying it. 'You know?'

As in – could it be? *Really?* Mo looked again, much more carefully. Considered. Checked the dates out. Could it be? Yes, it could.

The track having come to an end, the Debbie Harry bird – Paula – was doing her frontwoman bit, telling the audience that they were having a break and would return in fifteen minutes. Seconds later, some tinny shit from a CD started up, half drowned out by what seemed like genuinely rapturous applause. So they already had a bit of a following, which was a plus point, Mo noted.

And that drummer. Still in place, while the rest left the stage.

He put down his rum and Coke and motioned to the skinny barmaid to pull a pint for him.

And once in hand, he held it aloft to make his way

through the chattering, sweaty crowd. Which parted to allow him through as if he was fucking Moses or something. He grinned as he sauntered. Still got it. That presence. That respect. That fear.

The young drummer was oblivious, fiddling with some component on one of his cymbals. No fear here, obviously. Mo cleared his throat.

The lad looked up finally. Big innocent eyes.

Mo smiled. 'You look like you could use this,' he said.

The boy's face and neck were slick with sweat. He now looked wary. As was to be expected, Mo conceded. The young Mo would be wary if approached by the older Mo too.

'Go on,' he persisted. 'It's on me, dude. Great set. And it's Joey, right? You're good. You'll go far.'

The boy glanced around. Not eighteen yet, by Mo's quick calculations. But then thirst got the better of his evident concern about the landlord and, after eyeing it thirstily, he took the cold beer. And in two Adam's-apple bobbing gulps had half of it downed.

'Thanks,' he said, surfacing. 'Er …?'

Mo held his hand out to shake. Big, dark and manicured.

'Macario,' he said, surprising himself. He never told anyone his real name.

The boy nodded as he took it. 'Okay. Macario. Right, cool.'

Knocked off-guard by a jolt of unexpected emotion, Mo crushed the smaller, paler hand with more force than he'd intended. But the boy held his gaze. Didn't flinch. Squeezed right back, with powerful drummer's hands.

He winked. 'Hey, but you just call me Mo.'

Chapter I

For as long as he could remember, Joey had always made music. Right from the start, it had always been a part of him. From the foggy memories of his early childhood, of wielding a wooden spoon and saucepan while his mam belted out songs off the radio, to being in the percussion corner – always – in primary school productions, right up to learning the recorder, then trying the trumpet (a short-lived excursion, that one) to the point where he was allowed to try the battered high-school drum kit, music, particularly rhythm, had been in his blood. He'd more than once wondered (his mam and step-dad always having been so tight-lipped about it) what kind of man had put the curl in his hair. A musician. It just had to be a musician.

And here he was now. Making music. And getting paid for it, however little. Playing to an actual audience, who seemed to like him, as well. And in one case – he quickly downed the rest of the pint, in case the landlord clocked him – even being given drinks by complete strangers.

He watched the man who'd just spoken to him – a giant of a man, too – weave his way back round the scattered tables to the bar. Was this what it was like, then? Being in

1

a band? Being famous? Well, not so much famous – that would be pushing it. It was the band people had come for. It was Paula they *really* came for. And he got that completely. He'd come to watch her sing here a few times himself. First as an old mate he'd rediscovered – their mams had been really close once – and then because, well, because the band were pretty good. And Paula herself … Well, who *wouldn't* want to watch her sing?

He watched her laughing with some friends of hers at the side of the stage. And for too long, as well; she caught his eye and must have realised he'd been staring, because she flicked her hair at him in a way that made it clear she'd read his thoughts. She gave him a thumbs up before turning back to her friends, and he felt his cheeks flush. Was he imagining it, or did she like him as well?

Joey lowered his gaze, flustered, and went back to his high hat, checking the nuts, touching the cymbals, pumping his foot on the pedals, and all the while still not quite believing – or feeling quite deserving of – his luck. It was his second gig with Parallel Lines now, and he'd been told that if things went well, there would be more. But he didn't like to think too much about it, in case it was all taken away from him. He'd been brought up to understand that you didn't count on anything. So counting on this might be tantamount to jinxing it.

He knew the beer might have something to do with it, but for the first time since leaving school he felt a welling of proper pride, even so. Pride in having achieved his own ambition, the first rung on a ladder that was a world away, or at least could be, from the one he inhabited doing the rounds on his window-cleaning cart. Not that he wasn't proud of that too. Of course he was. A gift from his dad, on the day he'd left school two years back, the window-cleaning round he'd inherited from him had always been a precious means to an end.

His mum and dad might not have believed it, but his own belief had never wavered. If he worked hard and saved hard – and he'd been good at doing both – he'd known from the outset that it could provide him with his chosen future. The means to practise in the short term – once he'd paid his keep, every spare penny went on kit – but, longer term, to make him a more viable commodity. A drummer with his own drum kit was more desirable than one without; it was at least half the reason the band had given him a try-out when their regular drummer, whose wife had just had a kid, had decided to call it a day. The trick now was to prove his talent and commitment, both of which he knew he had in spades.

He risked glancing up again. Paula had gone now. Presumably to the loo, before they began their second set.

But apparently not.

'Boo!' came a voice. Joey swivelled on his stool. Paula was behind him, in a cloud of musky fragrance, presumably having just returned from the ladies'. She nodded towards the bar, which was still rammed with people getting their drinks in before they started. 'Who was that?' she asked, as she tucked her bag down behind him. Her hair brushed his shoulder as she did so.

'That black guy? Dunno,' he said. 'He said his name was Mac-something. Nice bloke. Bought me a pint.'

'I noticed.' She looked across to the bar again, where the man was half-hidden in the crush. Except he wasn't crushed. It was like he had some sort of force field around him. He also stood a whole head above the men gathered around him, none of which Joey recognised either. He looked for his uncle Nicky, who'd brought him and his kit down here in his battered van earlier. He might only just be out of prison but he seemed to know everyone. But there was no sign of him and Joey realised he'd probably not returned yet from where he'd gone once they'd brought the stuff in, to 'see a man about a dog'.

'But I'll be back before you're finished,' he'd promised. 'Help you pack up and take you home and that.' And though Joey didn't doubt it, he couldn't help wondering what exactly the man and the dog bit was actually all about. His mam had spent fifteen years visiting his uncle Nicky in prison – VOs as regular as clockwork, and she never missed one – but now he was home, Joey couldn't fail to notice how tense she seemed about her brother. Did she worry he'd end up in the nick again? But she and his dad were as tight-lipped about that as about everything. Drugs. That he did know. Though he'd gone down for murder. *But he's not a wrong 'un, love, trust me* – how many times had he heard his mam say that? And on the evidence of the few weeks he'd been stopping at theirs Joey was inclined to believe her.

'So who d'you reckon he is?' Paula was asking him now. 'He looks like he owns the place, doesn't he? Well, acts like it, anyway. D'you reckon he's someone in the music business or something? Did you cop the designer threads he's got on?'

Joey nodded. 'That jacket. Must have cost a bit. A *good* bit.' He reached for his drum sticks. 'Macario,' he said, remembering. 'That's his real name. Macario. But he said to call him Mo.'

'Macario. Strange name,' she mused. 'No wonder he likes to shorten it. Hey –' she nudged Joey. 'D'you think he might be a producer or something? Or an A&R man? Oh my God, can you imagine? I mean, it's not outside the bounds of possibility, is it? I mean, like, out scouting – that's what they do. They go round all the pubs and clubs. What was that band … Oh, it'll come to me … Used to play down the Devonshire Arms? That's what happened to them. They got spotted by an A&R man and invited to send a demo in to some record company – don't remember which, but, God, he *could* be. He looks the part, doesn't he? That bloke with him as well. The one with the hair. Macario. We'll have to ask around. I wonder if Matt knows him. Matt!' she said, raising her voice and beckoning towards the approaching lead guitarist. 'That black guy at the bar – the one who was talking to Joey.'

'What about him?' Matt, the lead guitarist, was also the unofficial leader of the band. He was in his mid-twenties and had the air of a guy who'd been everywhere and done everything. Though he seemed a decent guy (not least because he was gay and obviously had no designs on Paula) Joey felt very young and naïve in his presence.

'Do you know who he is?' Paula was saying. 'He's not a regular, is he? We were wondering if he might be in the business.'

Even Matt's normally furrowed eyebrows lifted at this.

'He's called Macario,' Joey supplied. 'Mo. He seemed impressed with the band.'

Matt peered across at the bar, but the man had his back to them now. 'Don't think I recognise him,' he said. 'Or those other blokes he's chatting to. Not seen them in here before.' He spread his palms. 'So you never know. He might be.' He grabbed the neck of his guitar and ducked his head beneath the strap, settling the instrument against his stomach. 'Actually I do know of a Mo, come to think of it,' he said, pulling the plectrum from where he'd slipped it between the frets. 'Wasn't that the name of that drug dealer people used to talk about? You know, back yonks ago when we were kids? Wasn't he called Mo or something?'

'Not that I've ever heard of,' Paula said. 'Anyway, he looks more like an off-duty solicitor than a drug dealer. Well, maybe not a solicitor. Not with the dreadlocks. But someone in the business, definitely. You remember that bloke, don't you? The one who –'

'Wish away, Paulz.' Matt said. 'Anyway, who's to say he isn't both? It's been known.' He laughed. 'Did he try and slip you anything, Joey? Anyway, here's Dan,' he added, as the bass player ambled over. 'Christ, man, get a move on!'

'And he's staying for the second half by the looks of it,' Joey said, looking back across to the bar. The man Mo

– former drug dealer, record scout, solicitor, whatever – caught his eye, lifted a tumbler and smiled.

Joey raised a drumstick and smiled back. He couldn't help it.

Chapter 2

Brian peered out of the front-room window and cursed his brother-in-law. Yes, on the whole, Nicky was a sound bloke these days, and he'd be the first to leap to his aid in a fight, but he couldn't seem to quash the constant hum of anxiety when he was in any way left in charge of Joey. He might be Joey's kin – biologically, he was, where Brian wasn't, which sort of rankled – but he wasn't a dad and he didn't understand. He just wasn't reliable enough.

He turned back to where Christine, curled in an 'S' at the far end of the sofa, was apparently engrossed in her new Jackie Collins novel. How could she remain so unconcerned? 'I swear, Chris,' he said irritably, 'if your Nick's forgotten to pick our Joey up, I'll fucking swing for him, I really will! I warned him not to go on the piss if he was driving, and now it's –'

'Not even that *late*,' Christine said, tenting her open book on the sofa. 'Stop worrying. He said he would and he will. Have a little faith, love,' she added. 'They'll get here.'

'Since when was gone midnight "not that late"?' Brian huffed.

'Since for ever,' Christine said. 'Bri, he's almost eighteen. You can't keep him wrapped in cotton wool for ever.

Think about it. They've been playing. They've got a lot of gear to sort out. If anything it'll be our Joey holding Nicky up. All excited. All that adrenaline. And it's not like they're going to just unplug their amps and bugger off, is it? There'll be the pub to empty out, the clearing up, the loading up … And they'll probably have stopped to have a drink with the landlord and everything – you know how it goes. Love, they'll *be* here.' She picked up her book again, the conversation apparently over, and Brian continued his vigil at the front-room window.

That was the main problem. That he *did* know how it was. Not as someone in a band – he never was, never had it in him – but he certainly knew all about pubs. Not to mention lock-ins, and the sort of people who hung around for lock-ins. And how being in a band meant spending a lot of time in pubs, with exactly the sort of people that he used to be. And what about the lad's window round in the morning?

'Fucking poncing about in a band,' he muttered. 'I really don't like the idea. He's a grafter, that lad, not some pie-in-the-sky wannabe with ridiculous ideas. He should be home in bed.' He waggled a finger in Christine's general direction. 'He's going to be too tired to get up for the windows tomorrow, just you wait.'

Christine gave him a look that he'd come to know well. Because Christine, who he'd been with since Joey was still a toddler, knew him so well – so uncomfortably well. She knew exactly why he was so hard on poor Joey; it was simply because he was terrified. He'd completely wasted his own youth – in a booze- and heroin-filled oblivion, much of it alongside her brother – and couldn't even begin to contemplate the prospect of that kind of life for his son. Worse than that, they'd even lost him for a bit – well, Christine had, anyway – to social services, when he was just a baby. And he'd been complicit. Involved. A central part of the problem. Had even stood, albeit off his face, and watched the social taking Joey away – he could recall his frightened screams like it was yesterday. And Christine howling like she was dying. Because it was almost like she had been. It had been a long wretched road to get him back again.

But you know what's going to happen, Bri? For God's sake! Can't you see it? You're going to be the one that drives him to it! Christine's words, spoken in anger after one of their interminable 'differences of opinion' about Joey – what he could and couldn't do, where he could and couldn't go – were never far from Brian's mind. Because a part of him knew she was right. But if he didn't look out for him, who fucking would?

He lowered the heavy green curtain and managed a conciliatory smile in the face of her tutting. 'Stop fretting, love,' she told him. 'Joey knows where his bread's buttered. He won't give up the windows. He knows that would be mad. It's doing that round that's enabled him to buy the bloody crap he needs in the first place.'

Which wasn't exactly why Brian had passed his window round on to Joey. It was supposed to be his living – a proper, stable, decent living. Not just a stopgap till he 'made it' as a bloody pop star! No, it wasn't charity – Brian had been only too happy to accept a job at Beechwood Brushes, not least so he could drop Chris off at work, and bring her home again – but he'd done so with the intention of giving his son a future. One he was constantly anxious that Joey might at any moment throw away.

Brian glanced out again, sensing a light in the street. *Finally.* 'Oh, thank fuck for that! They're back,' he said, feeling the tension drain from him. Sometimes he felt like he was going on eighty rather than forty. 'And judging by the way your Nicky's parking that bleeding van, he is pissed. For definite, the knobhead.'

'Come away from that *bloody* window, Bri,' Christine snapped. 'The frigging neighbours'll be wondering what's going on. Honestly! Nowt like drawing attention to us, is there?'

Though there was little chance of avoiding it, given the way Nicky was sauntering up the path – not to mention the way he was singing at the top of his voice, despite Joey's fruitless attempts to shut him up.

'The kid did good!' Nicky bellowed, once they'd both clattered in, slinging his keys on to the coffee table where they immediately overshot and skittered down to the rug. Joey rolled his eyes as he followed him into the front room.

'Er, what about the stuff?' he said, sounding plaintive, and looking hopefully at Brian. 'No way am I leaving it all out there to get nicked.'

'Patience, lad,' Nicky said. 'All in good time. At least give me a chance to have a fucking slash!' Upon which he burped loudly and flung himself down on the sofa, giving

Christine just enough time to save her book from being crushed.

Brian shook his head but decided not to say anything. He and Joey could deal with the kit between them once Nicky had gone to bed. He knew how anxious Joey would be at the prospect of Nicky dropping something precious like his snare drum or something. He also looked happy, and Brian didn't want to spoil that.

'So you had a good night, son?' he asked, as Joey sloughed off his denim jacket. 'You must be buzzing, mate. Did you get plenty of claps and all that?'

Joey's caramel-coloured eyes shone with pride. 'It was mint, Dad! I swear the punters loved us. *Really* loved us.' He was pacing in front of the gas fire. 'And I swear down, Paula's brilliant. I mean, really, *really* brilliant. You'd never know it wasn't Debbie Harry – just you wait till you see her yourselves. And, like, we all fit together' – he meshed his hands – 'so *incredibly* well. You know, if I could bottle this buzz, I'd make a fortune!'

Christine laughed. 'Well, my boy, you never know, do you? If they can clone a sheep can't be long till they can bottle buzz too, can it? How difficult can it be, after all?' she smiled. 'Trust me, I can feel it from here.'

Brian smiled too, caught up, as he always was, in pride for his stepson. 'You and Paula still getting on alright then?' he asked, just about managing not to wink. Paula's name had been coming up such a lot lately that he and Christine had both picked up on it independently – and both agreed they knew why, as well.

'*Dad!*' Joey said, his cheeks darkening immediately. 'Course we are. We have to. We're working together, aren't we?'

'And she's a lovely lass,' Brian pointed out.

'She's fucking *fit*,' Nicky added.

'And you could do a lot worse,' Christine said, standing up. 'Me and your dad were only saying the other day, weren't we, love? You and her would make a lovely-looking couple.'

'Whoah, whoah, whoah,' Joey said, looking suddenly aggrieved. 'Have you heard *yourself*? Nowt's happened yet, Mam, so you and Dad can just keep your nosy snouts out. Last thing I need is you two showing me up if she calls round.'

'Ooh, calling round, is she?' Nicky said. 'You're well in there, son. Lucky bugger. Anyway, is anyone going to make a brew, or am I going to have to do it?'

Brian reached for his pouch of baccy. 'What do you think?' he said.

Nicky roused himself and Brian followed him out into the kitchen anyway, leaving Joey to tell Christine all about the evening, the words 'I've got a permanent place in the band now' following his progress down the hall. He was pleased to see Joey happy – how could he ever not be? – but he couldn't shake the nagging anxiety that increasingly accompanied it. Things were changing and he wasn't sure he liked it.

Dreams were one thing but real life was a very different matter. And it seemed to him that Joey's dreams, however talented he might be, were surely destined to end in disappointment. Maybe not now, not right away, but eventually they would. He wasn't stupid – half the bleeding pubs in Bradford made it so obvious; how many of them had bands in, scratching out a meagre living, day to day, from one badly paid gig to the next? What were the chances of it ever really amounting to anything? Whereas with the windows, if he knuckled down and extended the round onto another estate, the world would be his oyster in no time. He'd be able to buy his own van, too. A van meant for ladders, buckets and chamois leathers, not frigging speakers, amps and drum kits. Why was Joey always so restless? Always looking for something more? Why wasn't his life – which was a *good* life – enough for him?

Brian rolled his ciggie and lit it, then helped Nicky with the tea, tuning out from his pissed ramblings. He also made a mental note that next time Joey needed a lift, it would be him and not his uncle who took him, even if taking the drum kit meant two trips. He also made a mental note that he'd need to say something to Christine. He was happy enough putting Nicky up in the short term – least they could do, given the extent of the sacrifice Nicky had made for his sister – but not for too long. He was too bad an influence on Joey. But it seemed it wasn't just Nicky in pole position for turning Joey's head.

'So I think he might have been some kind of record producer or something,' Joey was saying to his mam when they returned. He glanced across at Nick. 'Did you see him, Uncle Nicky?'

Nicky grunted as he put the mugs down. 'See who?'

'The man who came and spoke to me. I think you might have already left by then, actually. But he was there till the end. And you wouldn't have missed him if you had seen him. Big black guy. Posh clobber.'

'Didn't he say who he was?' Christine asked. 'Give you a business card or anything?'

Joey shook his head. 'No. I just told you, Mam – he just came up and said how good he thought we were. And bought me a pint.'

'So what makes you think he was a record producer then?'

'Just the way he was, Mam. We all thought so. Just the way he looked and the way he acted. I dunno.' He spread his hands. 'He just seemed sort of professional, you know? Not someone you'd expect to see in The Sun. He stuck out like a sore thumb. But in a good way,' he added, leaning down to grab a mug of tea.

Brian was properly listening now. This was what he had been afraid of as well – of his son being taken advantage of by some fly-by-night agent. Of him being exploited in some way. Joey wasn't exactly naïve but he was definitely still a bit wet behind the ears. And you heard about it all the time, didn't you? 'Well, did he have a name, this guy?' he asked. 'And did you see him, Nicky?'

'See who?' Nicky said again.

Joey shook his head. 'He couldn't have done. But his name was Macario.'

'Macario?' Brian said. 'Odd name.'

15

But ringing a bell, strangely. And soon not at all strangely, with Joey's next, damning, utterance. 'Yeah, it is, isn't it? But he said I should call him Mo.'

The name hit Brian like a physical whump in the chest. And he didn't need to look to know the colour would be draining from Christine's face. And when she spoke it was little more than a whisper. 'Mo?' she said. 'You *sure*? A big man? A black man? Definitely called Mo?'

Joey nodded. 'Massive dreadlocks.' He fluffed up his own substantial head of hair to illustrate. 'Like, *huge*.'

Brian felt cold, despite the tea, which was now scalding his hands. 'Why?' Joey asked, smiling happily. 'Do you *know* him?'

Brian didn't dare look at Christine, because he knew his mask might slip. Masks tended to do that when long-buried secrets threatened to come out.

'Think I'm thinking of someone else,' he finally plumped for.

Chapter 3

So this was the moment, was it? Come to get her? The moment she had always known might come, but had wished so hard never would. Christine folded her arms across her chest and buried her hands in her armpits so that Joey wouldn't see that they were shaking.

It took a couple of heartbeats before Brian met her eye. He opened his mouth and then closed it.

'Anyway,' she said. 'So what did he look like, this Mo, then?' Her voice hadn't betrayed her but she knew her burning cheeks might. She was grateful for the gloom in the room. 'Older guy, was he?'

Joey gave her a strange look. Or perhaps she was being paranoid. 'I don't know, Mam,' he said. 'Not old. Forties? Big bloke. Really smart. Seemed to know what he was on about, you know?'

It figured. 'So did he say anything else to you? Ask your name?'

Joey shook his head. 'He already knew my name. He called me Joey when he came over, so I supposed he must have already asked someone about us. About *me*. About the band and that. Exciting or what?'

17

He seemed completely irrepressible. Smitten even, God help them all. Christine glanced helplessly at Brian, who cleared his throat noisily. 'Well, you never know, son,' he said, clapping Joey on the back. 'But right now, it's nearly one and we need to get that stuff inside.' He looked down at Nicky, who was well away now, and beginning to snore. How did he do that? Christine wondered. Just be awake one minute and then spark out the next? Fifteen years in the nick, she thought grimly. 'Let's you and me go and get it in, eh?' Brian was saying to Joey. 'This one looks fit for nothing. And then bed.'

He reached down for the discarded car keys and, dismissing Christine's offer to help as well, followed Joey back outside to the van. *Don't panic.* He mouthed the words at her as he went.

Christine grabbed her pack of Benson & Hedges and lit one with shaky fingers. How could it *be*? But then again, why would it *not* be? She'd covered her brother with a blanket and smoked a second cigarette to the tip before the kit was all back in the house. 'Up you go, love,' she said to Joey when he'd stacked the last of it in the tiny hallway. 'No sense taking it up till the morning, is there? Just head up to bed,' she added, stretching up to plant a kiss on his cold cheek. 'We'll be up once we're all straight down here.'

As if they could ever be straight with her brother camping out in the front room. But Joey seemed happy enough, clearly too excited to clock the tension in her voice, and remembering to give Brian a grateful hug before he left them. Such a big lad now but still so much their baby. So loving – never afraid to hug his dad, even in public. God, the thought of that bastard Mo so much as sharing his airspace made her want to punch a wall.

She went into the kitchen, her legs leaden. It *was* Mo. She just knew it. How many men of his description could possibly exist in the world? But back in Bradford? For fuck's sake, *why*? And after all this time? What could possibly be here for him? Well, apart from his kids – and there were a few of them knocking about; that much she knew for sure. And not one of which, as far as she knew, had ever had anything to do with him. He spawned them and discarded them. That was what he had always been best at. So why approach her Joey? Surely to God he wouldn't want to know Joey now? Not after all that had happened. Surely to God that would be that very *last* thing he'd do?

She shivered as she put the kettle on, an action that was automatic. God, she wished her mam was still alive and doing it for her. Taking charge. Because she knew Mam would know what to do. Despite all her faults – and they'd been legion, no question – her mam had never been scared of anyone. Specially Mo. The man she'd loved. The man who had let her down so badly. The man who'd made such a calculated move on her own teenage daughter. On *her*. And she'd … God. It was no good. She couldn't even bear to let the thought take shape. She grabbed the cigarettes again and lit another.

'Look, love, I know what you're thinking –'

Christine turned around. Under the strip light, Brian's face was pinched and grey.

'I bet you don't,' she said, keeping her voice as low as his was. 'I'm thinking how much I'd like to plunge a knife into his gut. It's him, Bri. I know it is. It *must* be.'

'Not necessarily,' Brian said. 'Come on. He can't have been the only Mo in Bradford.'

She stubbed out the cigarette. 'A big black guy, called Mo? That would be one fucking massive coincidence.'

'What about Paki Mo? Remember him?'

'Mo, as in *Mohammed*. He said *black*, Brian, with dreadlocks. It's him. It *has* to be. Trust me, I can feel it in my bones.'

Brian went to put his arms around her, but she shrugged him off. She felt like glass. All sharp edges. Too fragile to be touched. 'What will we *do*, Bri? What the fuck does he want with us after all these years?'

She leaned heavily against the kitchen counter, feeling all the strength going from her legs. Brian took a step, pulled her towards him again, and this time she didn't stop him.

'I don't think we should panic,' he said eventually, speaking into her hair. 'Even if it *was* Mo, we don't know that he knows for definite who Joey is, do we? And even if he had an inkling, or someone told him, it could be that he was just curious. You know, to get a look at him or something.'

'But *who'd* tell him? It's not like anyone in their right mind would bring it up, is it? It's not like he's ever wanted anyone to know about it, is it?'

She knew that for a fact. It had been the exact opposite. If she remembered right – though there was so much she'd been at pains to forget – he'd denied it outright, with contempt. *I don't have a son. At least, not with you, girl. Who in their right mind would ever lay down with a fucking tramp like you?*

'So maybe no one *has* told him,' Brian was saying. 'Maybe he has no idea. And even if he's worked it out, come on, love – he's hardly Father of the Year, is he? What on earth has he to gain by suddenly claiming a grown-up son who he's never paid fuck-all for all his life? Christ, Chris, he's never even acknowledged his *existence*. Seriously, I know you're upset, but let's not go off on one about this. I think we should just see how all this pans out before worrying about things that might not even happen.'

Christine tried hard to pull the brake on her galloping thoughts. Brian was right. She was running away with herself. Panicking. Being paranoid. But how could she not, when she had so much to be paranoid about?

She stood up straight again, and reached for her cigarettes on the kitchen counter. The silky smooth wooden counter top Brian had made for her so lovingly. That got to her sometimes, the way he loved her. The way he cared for her. The way he loved her Joey as if he was his own. Christ, he *was* his own. And now this.

There was a noise then, of something banging heavily against furniture. No. Some*one*. Her brother staggered into the kitchen. 'Wassup?' he asked, looking from one to the other as he headed towards the sink. 'Where's our Joey? Don't we need to get the drums in?'

He turned the tap on, too hard, and water fountained off a plate in the washing-up bowl.

'For fuck's sake, Nick!' Christine hissed. 'And will you fucking pipe down?'

'*What?*' Nicky whined. 'Keep your hair on. You making tea?'

'Make a brew, love,' Brian suggested. 'I think we could all use another one.' Then he turned to Nick. 'So did you see him?'

'See who?'

'Fucking Mo!' Christine snapped. 'Rasta Mo – *hello?* In The Sun?'

'That was Rasta Mo?' Christine could almost hear the cogs whirring in her brother's head. 'That's who it was, was it? That our Joey was banging on about? Fuck me.'

'So you didn't?' Brian asked.

Nicky shook his head. 'Nah, by the time I got back it was just the last stragglers. The band and that. And just a couple of the usual alkies. So it was him spoke to Joey?' He looked from one to the other. 'So, what – you going to tell him, or what?'

Booze or no booze, Christine couldn't believe her brother had even asked the question, let alone that Brian was now looking at her as if it was an entirely reasonable one to ask.

'No, I'm fucking not!' she said. 'And you make sure you don't say anything either. Not to Joey. Not to anyone.' She pushed a finger into Nicky's chest. 'But I need you to help me. I want you to try and find out what he's doing back here –'

'Assuming it even is him,' Brian pointed out.

'Round the pubs and that,' she went on, ignoring him. 'What he's up to. Why he's here. I need to know what he's come back for. And do it discreetly. He mustn't know –'

'As if he *wouldn't* know,' Nicky countered. 'If it *is* him, that is. But if it is, then what about Joey? Shouldn't *he* know who he is?'

Brian raised his hands. 'Hold up,' he said. 'Stop running away with all this. He's just turned up in a pub and bought the lad a pint, that's all. That's *all*,' he said, grabbing Christine's hand and squeezing it. 'That's all that's happened. For all we know, Joey's never going to see him again. We could be getting stirred up over nothing here. Seriously, love, this could all just be a coincidence. He's in the pub, Joey's playing … End of.'

'And even if he does,' Nicky said, accepting a mug of tea. 'He might have seemed like Mister Smooth, but our Joey's not daft. If he does show up again, Joey'll soon find out who he is. He'll hear the talk, about who he is, who he was – and *what* he was, more to the point – and even if he doesn't, it won't be two minutes before he makes his own mind up, will it? You've brought him up better than that, sis. He's not daft, that kid. He'll drop him like a bag of shit once he realises what a cunt he is.' He slurped the tea. 'Trust me. You'll see.'

Karma. The word came into Christine's head unbidden. Hung above her as she stared up, sleepless, at the bedroom ceiling. Karma. The spiritual righter of all wrongs. *Leave it to karma.* Wasn't that what people said when you were bent on revenge for something someone had done to you? And her mam. Almost on her death bed. So young. So ridiculously young. Hadn't she banged on about karma then too?

A patient bastard, that's what she'd called it. Biding its time before coming to claim her. With cancer. To pay her back for being a shit mum, a loser, a waste of space of a person. And Christine had tried so hard to soothe and reassure her. 'It's just life, being life, Mam.' She'd repeated that so often. Doling out death whenever it felt like it. No concern for any notions about the unfairness of things. And Christine believed it, too, because the good died young all the time, didn't they?

Mally, for instance. The man – the man-child – she had killed. Not wittingly – God, *never* – but time hadn't helped her learn to live with it. Hadn't lessened her guilt, and would never absolve her, because she'd still done it – her hand, hers alone, had been the one on the knife. One life gone, by her hand, and another one ruined. She could try to atone all she liked, but she knew it would never be enough; the one thing she could never give her brother were the years of his life back. Years that *she'd* had. With Joey. Yes, it might have been Nicky's choice – as he'd pointed out, endlessly – but time hadn't buffered her guilt about that either. It was done, and it could never be undone.

So perhaps her mam had been right. Karma was indeed a patient bastard. Lying in wait till she'd finally found happiness before pouncing, its claws ripping at her conscience, piercing her heart, stealing her soul.

Which she knew she had long since sold to the devil.

Chapter 4

Joey's window-cleaning cart had been a labour of love. And proof positive that, though seemingly pointless at the time (who really needed a spinning MDF spice dispenser anyway?), his years toiling at GCSE woodwork had not, in the end, been in vain.

It had also been forged in friendship, him and his best mate, Dicky Turner, having built it between them, with a bit of help from his dad and a lot of scavenging round Canterbury Estate. The wheels, in their past life, had graced an abandoned (no doubt stolen) racing bike, and the base was a reclaimed front door.

Trundling it along Dawnay Road, shirtless, because of the warm summer sunshine, Joey felt a sudden pang of guilt. He often felt bad when he thought about his dad these days, particularly when he was out doing his round. It was while working at the job his dad had virtually handed on a plate to him that he felt the distance that was opening up between them most keenly.

It wasn't that he wasn't happy doing his window-cleaning round, because he was. On days like these, as jobs went, it was pretty hard to beat. He was answerable to no one – and how many lads of his age could say that? He worked in the fresh air, out of doors, too, doing hours to suit himself. Wasn't a slave to a time-clock, cooped up in some factory, clocking in and out, like his mam and dad did. It was also sociable – a little *too* sociable sometimes, admittedly – and, best of all, he had only himself to fall back on. The harder he worked, the more he could earn. And he'd never been afraid of hard work.

But it wasn't everything. He knew he should be grateful, and he was, but it wasn't all he wanted. And, just lately, that truth – never out-and-out spoken – seemed to be driving a wedge between him and his dad. Like, despite his grafting, he was becoming a source of unease.

He lowered the cart handles gently, so as not to slop the bucket of warm suds. How many times, in the last couple of weeks alone, had he heard the same thing? *You're a lucky lad. You've got it made. Good solid prospects. Set for life, son.* And how many times, just like always, had he agreed that he was? And he *was* – that was the worst of it – if that *was* all he wanted. But it wasn't all he wanted. Why couldn't his dad see that?

Which wasn't to diss him. God, that was the last thing he'd do. His mum and dad had done everything for him and he'd never forget that. But there were only so many times he could nod – like a bloody puppet – when inside all he wanted was for his dad to acknowledge that he understood that Joey wanted *more*. To contemplate the possibility that he might even get it – that he was good at what he did. That – for something other than the bloody window round – didn't mean the instant end of the world.

And now his mum seemed to be at it, too, which troubled Joey greatly. It was almost like she wasn't happy that he'd got the job with the band. His mum! Who'd always encouraged him and supported him with his music – it was like, now he'd actually got a place in a proper band, she'd been infected by the same virus. The 'don't get ideas above your station, son' virus, that he'd heard over and over again, both at home and at school, if he ever so much as hinted that he might like to do music for a career.

The 'nice, steady job' disease – that's how Dicky had once put it. That constant 'knuckle down, have some security, shape up' line of nagging. It was one of the main reasons Dicky no longer lived with his mam. No, Dicky wasn't exactly working his socks off at anything – he'd been a labourer since leaving school, here and there, on and off, getting work as and when it came around. And maybe he wouldn't ever be anything else either. He cut his cloth to suit his choices, and he had rent to pay. But Joey sometimes envied his friend his complete independence to do – and be – whatever he liked, without being constantly held to account.

He bent to unhook his ladder, conscious of a noise coming from behind. He turned around, squinting against the sunlight, to see the silhouetted form of a trio of girls, teetering their way towards him on the far side of the road.

Then a wolf whistle. 'You can give me a wash down any time you like,' one of them called out suggestively, causing the others to throw their heads back and roar with laughter.

Normally he'd have blushed, but today he puffed his chest out. 'Sorry, girls,' he said, hefting the ladder up as they passed him. 'I'm already spoken for, otherwise I might have just helped you out.'

The girls duly giggled, and he basked in their approval for a moment. But that was another thing, wasn't it? What was going on with Paula? No sooner had he asked her out than his mam and dad were all anxious about it. His mum and dad, who (he'd been at great pains to remind them of this only yesterday) had been the ones to say what a lovely couple they would make. Yet now they were an item (well, sort of – they'd only been out the three times so far) there was this weird kind of tension in the air. Which made no sense – yes, she was older than him, but not *that* much older. And her mam and Paula's mam had once been really good friends. Till they'd drifted apart, when Paula's mam and dad had moved to a different part of Bradford, they'd apparently been best friends for, like, years. Since before he'd been born, in fact. God, he and Paula had even played together when they were little. He was still trying to get his head around that. That the girl he'd seen – and couldn't drag his eyes away from – belting out Blondie in her band was the same girl who'd once played with him in their back garden. If he'd been the sentimental type, he'd have thought it was destiny. But he wasn't. It was just bloody amazing.

Perhaps that was it, though. That they both saw what he did. That Paula *got* him. That, unlike them, she really understood his ambitions. Of course she did, because she shared them. And though she didn't know it – and there was no way he'd be admitting it any time soon – she made him even more ambitious to be more than he currently was. He knew his mum and dad worried that it was an uncertain business (they'd told him that a lot too), and perhaps him being in the band now, however much they liked Paula, made them anxious that he'd throw the whole window round in. As if he was really that naïve – that fucking stupid.

'Penny for them.' A chuckle. 'Well, if they're decent, that is.'

He turned towards the house. Mrs Hanley was standing on her path, holding out a mug of steaming tea. She nodded to where his admirers had just disappeared round the corner.

Joey leaned his ladder carefully against the front wall and took the hot mug. In truth, he'd rather have had a glass of water, but he took the tea with good grace. The second of several, no doubt – he'd already had his first from Mrs Atkins at number 17 – because dispensing mugs of tea was what most of his regulars liked to do, not to mention ply him with biscuits, like they were fattening up a golden calf; it was a wonder that he wasn't as fat as one too. Perhaps one day he would be, he thought, if he kept on accepting them.

He leaned down to kiss her whiskery cheek. 'Always,' he said. 'And thanks, Mrs Hanley. I'm ready for this.' He gave her his best smile – his mam always said he had a way with the pensioners. 'This is just what I need.' He leaned a little closer. 'Here, and don't tell my mam, but you make a much better cuppa than she does.'

Mrs Hanley gave him a friendly slap on the backside. 'Cheeky bugger, she'll have your guts for garters if she hears you saying that. How is she, love? Coping?'

For which, read '… with your uncle Nicky,' Joey thought. Was there anyone who didn't know about his uncle? 'Oh you know, plodding on,' he said, taking a slurp of the tea. 'Bit stressed at the minute, what with my uncle Nicky staying for a bit – it's a bit cramped and you know what mam's like about the house. And he's not the tidiest of blokes, if you know what I mean.'

Mrs Hanley made a good stab at looking surprised to hear this. 'Oh, so he's out of the big house, is he, then?'

Joey nodded. 'Yes, he is.'

'Well, I have to say, your nan would be pleased to know that, God rest her soul.' She made a sign of the cross as she spoke. 'Terrible business, him being locked up for so long. Terrible. Terrible thing to die knowing your flesh and blood's banged up …' She shook her head. 'God rest her soul,' she said again. 'Would have almost been better if she'd gone not knowing, wouldn't it? If she was going to go, that is, if you get my meaning. She was a fine woman, your nan.' She made another sign of the cross.

Joey nodded. That was another thing. Everyone seemed to know his nan as well. Bar him, that was. His mam hardly ever said anything about her. Never had. Only that she'd died of cancer, very young, and that for the short time she'd known him, she'd doted on Joey. But the little she had said, she'd always said in that way she had which made it clear that that was all you needed to know. That there wasn't more to come. She could be tight-lipped, like that, could his mam. 'Still, he's out now,' Mrs Hanley was saying. 'Has he got any plans?'

Joey decided that 'getting pissed and seeing men about dogs' perhaps wasn't quite the thing. 'Oh, this and that,' he said instead. 'Right now he's just finding his feet. Anyway, I'd better get on, hadn't I?' he added, placing the half-finished mug of tea at the edge of the doorstep. She promptly picked it up. 'I'll make you fresh for when you're done,' she said.

Not more tea. 'Honestly,' he said. 'There's no need.'

'There's every need,' Mrs Hanley said firmly. 'Oh, and one thing, love,' she added, glancing up and down the street. 'Word to the wise. You take care around that uncle of yours, okay? Make sure you stay on the straight and narrow. Don't be led. Between you and me, that uncle Nicky of yours can be a bit of a bugger.'

Something else Joey had heard at least a dozen times before. Mud sticks, he decided. And after all, it was probably fair enough, because his uncle *was* a convicted murderer. But with mitigating circumstances, as his mum had always told him. A good man who had once, long ago, done a bad thing, by accident. Joey had lived with it so long that it ceased to feel shocking. It was something from the distant past, done and dusted, forgotten. He'd served his time for what he'd done, and was apparently very sorry. What more was to be said? His mam loved

Nicky, and his dad loved Nicky. And that was good enough for Joey.

But perhaps, when it came down to it, his uncle Nicky *was* the problem. For all that they loved him, perhaps his mam and dad were scared that he might lead Joey astray. Not the music. Not Paula. Just his plain old uncle Nicky. Perhaps *that* was it. 'Oh, don't you worry about me, Mrs Hanley,' he said. 'I'm good as gold, I am. Pure as the driven snow.'

Mrs Hanley considered him for a moment. Then she winked. 'Well, whoever she is, make sure you hang on to her,' she answered. And had gone back in to boil the kettle before Joey had even digested what she'd said.

Then it clicked. I intend to, he thought.

Chapter 5

Paula stepped out into the street and gaped. '*Really*, Dad?' she squeaked, not quite able to believe what she was seeing. 'You mean I can have it now? *Seriously*? Oh my *God!*'

Christmas, it seemed, had come early. After a long lie-in – the band had been rehearsing till late the night before, and she'd lingered a bit, with Joey – she'd come down to find an unlikely silence. Her dad was out somewhere, her younger brothers too, the latter being an extremely rare occurrence for a Saturday morning, as they were usually glued to some rubbish on the TV. And her little sister Louise had been in a decidedly funny mood. Which wasn't *that* unusual – Louise had just turned thirteen and become the family diva overnight – but there was definitely something going on in the house that she wasn't party to.

And now, out in the street, winking diamonds of sunshine at her, was the reason. Parked at the kerb was a beautiful red Mini. Christmas had come *very* early.

Her dad, Eddie, stood proudly by the open driver's door.

'*Yes*. I just *told* you. So, come on, lass, don't just sit there gawping at it,' he urged, as her brothers tumbled out of the passenger side door.

'You deserve it, baby,' her mam said, appearing at her side and shunting her forwards to take a closer look.

'But I didn't even know you'd *got* it,' she said to her dad, touching the gleaming paintwork. 'God, Dad, it's beautiful. It looks brand spanking new!'

'Well, she's definitely not that,' her father told her. 'She's a middle-aged lady. Needed a fair bit of TLC to coax her into showing her best side, I can tell you. Bit like your mother.' He quickly ducked to avoid a whipping with Josie's furled tea-towel. 'Inside and out, mind – there's been a lot going on under that bonnet. Reconditioned engine, new gearbox, new clutch, bit of a paint job.' He stuck his hands out, which were a mass of cuts and scrapes and bruises. 'As my poor porkies can testify.'

Paula didn't doubt it. Her dad was a legend. He could do anything. Make anything. Fix anything. Everything. And he was a fine, fine mechanic. Everyone said so. And had clearly been beavering away in secret for weeks – maybe months. She felt tearful all of a sudden. What had she ever done to deserve a mam and dad like she had? She cleared her throat – she wasn't a crier – and hoicked a thumb at her youngest brother, Tommy, who was sliding his grubby hands over the bumper. 'Oi!' she said. 'Get your grubby mitts off, Tommo! Out of bounds, you hear? No touching!'

He stuck out his tongue. As did his older brother, Sam.

'Off inside and make your beds, you two,' her mam said. 'And clear your bedroom up while you're at it. So you like it, love?' she said to Paula as her brothers thundered back indoors. 'We've been that excited to show it to you.'

'It's just –' she was struck dumb again. 'It's just incredible, Mam. I can't believe it's really mine. It's so – so *pretty*.'

'Just like you,' her dad chuckled. 'Anyway, now you're so famous, me and your mam felt you ought to have the car to go with it. Besides, no point leaving it mouldering in the lock-up for six months, is there? All the gadding about you do these days – or rather nights – you need your own set of wheels, don't you? Just don't be drink-driving, okay? Not even one. I know what it's like when you're doing shows in pubs. All too easy to get caught up when everyone else is drinking, and –'

'Gigs, Dad,' Paula pointed out, laughing. 'They're not shows, they're called gigs. I'm not a bloody ballerina! I'm an artiste.'

Eddie rolled his eyes. 'Oh, *artist* is it now? I thought they painted pictures. Anyway, whatever you call yourself, just don't be a piss-artist, okay?'

'Ha ha, very funny I don't think,' Paula told him. 'Oh, God, it's just amazing.' She showered both her parents in kisses. 'Can I take it tonight? Round to show Joey? To the gig? Is it all insured and that?'

'Insured. MOT. You're good to go. Want to try it? I reckon we ought to take it for a run-out together first anyway – been a while since you passed your test now.'

'Oh my *God*!' They all turned around to see Lou had by now appeared. Not yet two in the afternoon and she was already done up like she was off to an all-night party. They were good kids, her siblings, and with the age gap (at fifteen, Tommy, the next eldest, was still five years her junior) she felt like a second mum to them sometimes. And she was, much of the time, because her mam worked long days at the factory, and together they could be a right handful. And Lou especially, now she'd discovered boys and UB40 as well as her and her mam's make-up – a potentially lethal combination round their way. She was definitely going to need some watching over from now on. 'Yeah, and good plan, sis,' she was saying to Paula now. 'You could drop me off at the youthy, couldn't you? I am going to look *way* cool turning up there in that.'

'Not looking like that,' her mam said. 'You're going nowhere till you change out of that skirt and put some jeans on or something.'

'As long as the "or something" *is* jeans,' her father added sternly.

It only took a couple of circuits round the neighbourhood before Paula's dad pronounced her safe to venture out alone in her new toy. To see her toy-boy, as her mam had joked when she and her dad had returned home. She'd seemed as tickled by their fledgling romance as Paula herself had been surprised by it. Joey was two years her junior, and a world away from her last boyfriend, after all. But that had been a good thing, not least because her last boyfriend, she'd discovered, had been an ignorant oaf, and as her mam had pointed out, age was only a number – and because Joey had had such a rough start in life, he had a very old head on his shoulders. Not to mention a very handsome one, she thought to herself as she sorted out her mic stand.

She and Joey, his uncle Nicky having dropped his kit off earlier, were now back in The Sun with the rest of the band, setting up for what was already looking like being a sell-out performance. Well, or would have been, had the audience had to pay to come and see them, anyway. And, just perhaps, one day, they would.

She glanced across at Joey, bent over his various stands and pedals, feeling a flush of attraction rise up through her stomach. She was going back to his tonight, as his mam and dad were going to be out late, and though nothing had been said as such, she knew there was a possibility that she might end up staying over. Though they had his uncle staying, on the sofa, Joey had also mentioned there being a little box room the other night. Perhaps to persuade her that his intentions were honourable? She smiled at the thought. Not *too* honourable, she hoped, but for the moment, because she really liked him, she was keen to take that side of things slowly.

And now she had her car, she had the precious gift of independence. She'd see how it went. How well she'd be able to resist him …

For the moment, however, her mind was mostly focussed. 'Can you believe it?' she said to Matt as he jumped up on stage. 'I've never seen so many people here at this time before. God,' she added, a thought having suddenly hit here. 'We're going to have to do the soundcheck in front of them!'

'You'll be fine, babe,' Matt reassured her, in his usual chilled style. 'They'll know it's a soundcheck. What's the problem?'

'Hey, and look who's just come in?' Joey said, pointing across towards the bar. 'That bloke.'

'What bloke?' Matt asked.

'The one I told you about? The one I reckon might be in the music business. Spoke to me last week.'

Matt shielded his eyes. 'Hmm. So that's him, is it? Hmm …' he said again. 'Don't hold your breath,' he said finally.

'Why – d'you think you know him?' Paula asked.

'Never seen him before,' Matt said. 'Or those other blokes with him either. But if I had a fiver for every time someone told me some big-time scout was going to be in, I'd be a lot fucking richer than I am, trust me.'

'Yeah, but don't you want to be?' Dan, the bassist chipped in. Though, in Paula's estimation, Dan was about as interested in making the big time as he was in knitting. Which was to say, not at all.

'Well, whatever,' she said, feeling the nerves begin to kick in as the man turned and stuck a thumb up in their direction. He could surely tell they were discussing him. 'You never know,' she said brightly. 'Tonight might just be that night. Come on, let's get this soundcheck done. I still need to get changed yet.'

'Never change, babe,' Matt told her, grinning. 'Stay as sweet as you are.' And there was something about the way he said it that made her pause – was she imagining it? Made her think they weren't perhaps on the same page any more.

The applause as they finished the first set was rapturous. Almost the whole pub had been dancing and singing along with them. It was, Paula thought, the very best feeling ever. She was buzzing as she grabbed Joey and tugged him through the crowd – many of whom were cheering and whooping and slapping them on the back, like they'd just got married or something. 'Come on, Joey,' she yelled as she dragged him through the reluctantly parting mass. 'Let's go chat up this mystery man of yours, shall we?'

The man's expression when they reached him seemed to hint that he'd been expecting them to as well.

'Joey,' he said, moving along the bar to make room for them. He was standing apart from the group of men he'd been watching the set with. Paula noticed how, despite the rush of people anxious to get a drink in, no one seemed to dare invade his space.

Joey nodded. 'Mo, isn't it?' He held a hand out. The big black man shook it. Joey then put his other hand on Paula's back and edged her forwards. 'Nice to see you again. And this is my girlfriend, Paula.'

Mo raised his eyebrows. 'Girlfriend?' he said. He trained his dark eyes on Paula. Assessing. 'Well, it's very nice to meet you, young lady.'

Paula felt irritated to realise she was blushing as she shook his hand. Even more so that she also had an almost overwhelming – and completely ridiculous – urge to curtsy.

'Nice to meet you too,' she said, squaring her shoulders instead. 'You from round here?'

Mo smiled, flashing his perfect white teeth at her. 'Oak Lane,' he said smoothly. 'Do you know it?'

Paula had to stop herself from gaping. That meant serious money. Oak Lane was very much where the 'other half' lived. Well, if it was true, which they didn't know yet. Nor where his apparent wealth came from. She nodded, sensing he was challenging her. 'Sort of,' she said. 'I once worked as a receptionist at an insurance company up there. Been pulled down now, though. It's a mosque now, I think.'

The big man grinned. 'Aren't they all, love? Aren't they all?' he said. 'More mosques in Bradford than greengrocers these days, eh? Anyway, I'm glad you've come over. I have something to ask you. More of a proposition, in fact.' He glanced at Joey. 'That's if you're both interested.'

Joey was grinning like the proverbial Cheshire cat, Paula noticed. Perhaps he'd been right. And Matt wrong. Maybe this man *was* some sort of talent scout or something. Perhaps her natural suspicion of anyone with his sort of confidence said more about the Hudson genes in her than anything. Suspicion of anyone who wasn't a Hudson was a Hudson family trait. Oak Lane. He was something big, at any rate.

'Course we're interested,' Joey said. 'Shall I get us all a drink?'

Mo politely declined. 'But I'll buy you both one if you'd like one.'

'I'm cool,' Paula said, conscious of her dad's comment earlier. She never liked to drink when she was performing anyway. 'But if you'd like –' she turned to Joey, whose face was sheeny with perspiration.

'I'm cool too,' he said. 'I'll just grab a water.'

The man raised a hand, mouthed the word, and a glass of water appeared in an instant. Another reason to believe that he was someone with influence. The queue for drinks now was five deep and the barmaids were struggling to cope. But clearly what this man asked for he got. Right away. 'I've just bought a nightclub in town,' he explained, as he pushed the brimming pint glass in Joey's direction. 'Silks. You probably know it? Or of it, anyway. And my business partner Nico and I' – he nodded towards the swarthy Greek man standing a few feet away, who had his back to them currently – 'well, we're on the hunt for talent. A decent house band.' He paused. Paula saw Joey's eyes widen. 'So we were thinking that we'd like to offer you a provisional residency there, if you're interested. One night a week to start with. See how it goes before making it permanent, obviously. Do you think you might be interested? The pay's good, of course. It'll be more than you get here. And we would need you to finish here because it'll be Saturday nights we'd want you. Now,' he said, looking at Paula. 'Do you need time to think about it? Discuss it with your bandmates?'

Paula wavered. Taking in that he wasn't a record company scout was a bit disappointing, and now her reticence took precedence again. Yes, it sounded good, but the strings attached – dropping The Sun gig – needed thinking about. It seemed a bit unfair to drop The Sun, especially after they'd been so good to them. It had been The Sun, after all, that had given them their first real start. Regular work too. Which wasn't something you turned your back on lightly.

And what did they really know about these characters? Only what this Mo guy had told them. And wasn't it true that nightclubs opened up and closed down again all the time? Silks hadn't always been Silks. It had been lots of things before that. Like many a nightclub, its history was littered with the corpses of many an ambitious business-man's shattered dreams. Money pits – wasn't that what her dad had once told her? And she'd no business agreeing to anything without consulting Matt, not to mention Dan first. It was Matt who'd given *her* a start, after all.

'Can we get back to you?' she said, causing Joey to look at her like she was mad. 'Only we do need to speak with the rest of the band before making a decision like that. How about you give us your number and we ring you after the weekend?'

Mo nodded, his expression cool. Then pulled out a business card from his wallet. She slid a thumb over its surface as she took it. Embossed. Expensive-looking. 'Suit yourself,' he said. 'But I'm willing to pay well, as I say. Say, £225 per gig? So don't leave it too long making your minds up, will you?'

Paula tried not to gape. That was more than double they were currently getting paid by The Sun. She tried not to let her surprise show on her face.

'Sure,' she said. 'We'll be rehearsing tomorrow anyway. Will Monday morning be okay?'

'I don't do mornings, sweetheart,' the man said. 'Bit of a creature of the night, me. Monday afternoon would be better.' He nodded towards the stage, where Matt and Dan, presumably returned from sharing a joint out the back, were getting ready for the second set. 'Anyway, looks like you're on again.' He winked at her. 'And we'll be here watching.'

And there was something about the way he said it – something she couldn't put her finger on – that made a flicker of uneasiness edge into her brain. She pushed it aside. Just force of habit, she told herself. Bound to be hard to break.

Their second set, if anything, was even wilder than the first. They even got thunderous applause when they performed a couple of their own numbers, which she knew would make Matt, who'd composed them, ecstatic. Perhaps the chance to play in a nightclub really could launch them to another level. But Matt was so naturally cautious – it was in his nature – and she wasn't sure how he'd react to the idea of dumping The Sun, who could get another band in just like that, on the strength of an offer from a complete stranger, to play in a shut-down nightclub that hadn't actually re-opened yet. Not least because she knew Matt really didn't share her ambitions. He'd been gigging a few years now and though he loved writing music, she suspected he liked his life just as it was. Couple of gigs a week, plenty of downtime and a healthy weed habit. For which he had more than enough in his pockets, because he also played with a showband, doing weddings and birthdays, where he banged out the usual staples for a decent wodge of cash. He was a pragmatist. There were definitely no stars in his eyes.

And as it turned out, there was little opportunity to sit down and discuss things anyway, by the time they'd finished. The mysterious Mo and his cronies had slipped away before they'd done, and Matt was anxious to pack up and get his gear home as he and Dan were off to a party. Perhaps, on balance, they should wait till rehearsal tomorrow anyway. Discuss it properly then.

'Not that I'm sure what there is to discuss,' Joey observed, once he'd loaded his kit onto Matt's van – he was taking it back to his place ready to take to the rehearsal – and he and Paula were in the mini and about to head off to his. 'I mean, it's miles more money, a bigger venue, and a chance to be heard by thousands. What's the problem?'

To be fair, Paula thought, Joey didn't know Matt and Dan like she did. Didn't really know them at all yet. And he had that irrepressible way about him – that eagerness, that puppyish enthusiasm that so appealed to her. Was that why she liked him so much? Because he reminded her so much of her father? Though wrapped up in a package that was a million miles from her father. Tall, dark and … well, it was a heady combination.

'It's not a problem, exactly,' she told him now, as she fiddled about looking for the headlamp switch. Joey leaned across her and turned it. He smelled appealingly of fresh sweat and some kind of woody aftershave. 'It's just that I think we should maybe proceed with caution – as my old driving instructor used to say. Just that we should make sure it's the right thing for all of us before committing. I mean, what if this Mo is a fly-by-night? He might be talking bollocks about owning Silks, mightn't he? I mean, you've seen the size of that place. Well, I suppose you might not have,' she corrected herself, remembering his age. 'But it's huge. Only someone seriously rich – or seriously stupid – could afford to take on a place like that. I mean, the rent on it must be massive.'

'But to what end? I mean, why would he do that? Why would he say he was looking for a band if he wasn't?'

'I know, but if we pull out of The Sun we might lose it permanently, mightn't we? In fact, I'd say that was probably a cert. And, don't forget, it's the only regular slot we have.'

'Well, it's not for me to say anyway,' Joey said. 'I've only been in the band five bloody minutes. So whatever you reckon, I'm cool with that. It's your call, completely, Paula. I'm just so bloody happy to be part of it – be it in The Sun or anywhere else. Anyway, we don't have to say now, do we? Whatever this Mo says. In fact, why don't we tell the lads that we're going to check the place out for ourselves first? And if it all seems genuine – and everyone's happy – we give it a go. Proceed with caution, like you said.'

Paula reached to switch on the engine. 'I reckon that's best,' she said. Though despite her concerns, her automatic need to analyse, she was still buzzing from the response to their final set, the adrenaline still pumping. Whatever else was true, the world suddenly felt full of possibilities. New car, new recognition for the band, new boyfriend … She smiled at him coyly. 'Still, however it pans out, exciting times, or what?'

She then blinked as two passing cars flashed their lights at them, one after another. 'Whoah! Am I on full beam or something?' she said, rootling around again in the darkness to try and find how to dip the lights. 'I really need to sit down properly with the manual for this, don't I? Anyway, how come you know where everything is anyway?'

Joey tapped his nose. 'Comprehensive education, me.' He didn't elaborate. Instead he leaned across her and this time he doused the lights completely.

'What you doing?' she asked.

He grinned and snaked his other arm around her, twisting round, pulling her against him. She could feel the hardness of his bicep against her shoulder. His hair tickling her cheek. 'Just proceeding with caution,' he said.

Chapter 6

Paula woke up and couldn't work out where she was. She looked around her; lemon walls, a pile of boxes and bin bags full of clothing, a small window, where a net hung, flowers dancing along its border and the scent of a lavender air freshener strong in her nose.

The Parkers' box room. It filtered through then. And in the smallest of single beds. If she stretched out – she did now, her bent legs protesting – she could touch the far wall with her toes. No wonder Joey's uncle preferred to kip on the sofa downstairs.

It was cosy, though, and she lay still with her eyes closed for a minute, realising it must still be quite early. She wondered if Joey was up yet, or still stretched out, lean and sleepy, on the other side of the wall. She felt good in a way that she hadn't in a long time. Though she'd resisted the urge to take things where she might have last night – admittedly with some difficulty – the feelings he'd stirred in her were unfamiliar and rather thrilling. Was this how falling in love felt? She was hesitant to even think it. They'd only been together five bloody minutes. And she was as far from a swooning heroine as it was possible to be, after all. But if the cap fitted ... and it wasn't as if they were

47

complete strangers, was it? They shared a common past, wanted a common future. *Christ, Paula, listen to yourself*, she thought. She let her mind drift then, where it fancied, and dozed a little more.

She was woken again, both by her bladder, which was by now protesting, and by the unmistakable rumble of voices from below. Not raised voices, quite, but with a definite edge. Was that Joey's she could make out? She thought so.

Further evidence presented itself as she padded out onto the little landing, clutching her handbag (containing spare undies – a moment of sensible foresight) and her bundle of clothes – just her stage dress and a cardi. Feeling like a fallen woman, even if she wasn't, in one of Joey's T-shirts, she hoped she wouldn't bump into any of the family till she was dressed.

Unlike Paula's own home – full of messy teenagers – the house was small and uncluttered, and she could see Joey's empty bed through his open bedroom door. The bathroom was just opposite, so she dived into it gratefully, and it was only once in there that the voices properly revealed themselves, coming up directly from the kitchen below. And then she heard her name spoken, by Joey's mam, and, her interest piqued now, she strained to listen. And moving closer to the propped-open bathroom quarter light – the back door was clearly open – she found she could hear pretty clearly.

'I'm not saying *that*,' Joey's mam was now saying. *What? What was 'that'?* 'I'm just telling you to be sensible. That's all. It's all very well you being pie-eyed over her, and I'm not saying you shouldn't be. It's just that she's –'

'For fuck's sake, Mam!' Joey's voice. 'Will you just shut up going on like that? I'm not a kid, for God's sake!'

'No, you're not.' His mam's voice again. 'But you don't know what you're getting into with this group of hers. And you know *nothing* about this … this man. About *any* of them, come to that. And when your head's turned by –'

'My head's *not* fucking turned. Just how stupid d'you think I am, Mam?'

Then a deep shushing noise. Soothing. Maybe Joey's dad was there too?'

'Alright,' Joey's mam again. 'Love, I'm not saying you *are*. I'm just saying you need to think hard about what you might be getting into with this group.'

'Band,' Joey corrected. 'And it's just a *gig*, Mam. Christ, we're not being sold into bloody slavery! Just the chance of some gigs at a new place – a *bigger* place. A better place. Honestly, anyone would think you didn't *want* me to be successful. Is that it?' A long pause. 'Jesus, Mam! *Stop* it.' Then another. Paula imagined Joey putting his hands on his mam's shoulders. She didn't know why, but she could just see it. 'Look, stop *worrying*, okay?' he said again. 'We're just going to go and meet up with him, and –'

'Where?' She was snapping now.

'At his *club*. Where else? And it's not like we've even *agreed* to anything yet. *Christ*.'

'Son.' Definitely his dad's voice. 'Calm down, okay? Your mam's just concerned, that's all. As she has every right to be. These people … this whole … *business* …'

'It's just a *band*, Dad. Not a vice den.'

'Yes, but …' Joey's father seemed to flounder to find the words. 'You've got a solid, reliable job, son. We just don't want you running away with ideas that might …'

'For fuck's *sake*!' Paula heard a door opening. And she could now hear Joey – she assumed at least – thumping up the stairs.

Paula stayed in the bathroom a good while longer. Washed her hands and face. Did what she could with what was left of her make-up rather than scraping it all off and starting again. Washed as well as she could before slipping back into her clothes. Brushed her hair – bloody hell, her roots needed doing – and only then, dressed and decent, did she open the door.

Joey was dressed too, pacing in his room, obviously waiting for her.

She felt a frisson of joy seeing him. And the feeling was obviously mutual. No, *that* hadn't happened yet, but something had last night.

'You alright?' he said. He was standing in front of a *Trainspotting* poster that hadn't been there last night, rolling a piece of Blu Tack between his fingers. He didn't look as agitated as she'd expected. But he was clearly keen to go. She glanced at his bedside clock. Nearly ten. So she'd slept on for a good while, then.

'Never better,' she said, sidling up to him and kissing him, on tiptoe.

She placed the T-shirt on his bed, as his arms slipped around her. 'Let's get off, shall we? Maybe go and get some breakfast at the Tuck Inn before rehearsals? What d'you reckon?'

'What I reckon is that I could eat a horse, so that sounds divine.'

He studied her for a moment, not speaking, his gaze travelling over her face.

'*What?*' she said finally.

'It'll keep,' he said. 'Come on. Let's go.'

'So was she alright, you know, your mum?' Paula said as they drove round the corner. The farewells had certainly been fond enough. Joey's mam had been keen to make them bacon sandwiches and reminded Paula to tell hers she hoped for a proper catch-up, very soon. But though Joey seemed himself, she was still anxious about what she'd overheard.

'Yeah, she's cool,' he said. 'She loves you. How couldn't she? You're her oldest best mate's daughter. She's just, you know, Mam.'

Paula didn't know. 'I meant about me staying over.'

'Course she's cool,' he said. 'It's not like we're children, is it? And you slept in the box room anyway –' he turned to grin at her. 'More's the pity.'

And since he didn't seem perturbed, she decided she should leave it. She had to keep remembering he was their only child, and that Christine was probably over-protective. What with Paula being an 'older woman' and all that. She knew what parents could be like anyway. Didn't realise their kids grew up, had ambitions, could think for themselves. Whether they liked it or otherwise.

They headed to hers first, so she could change into jeans and a T-shirt, and with the minimum of fuss – it seemed everyone wanted to make them bacon sarnies this morning – were soon back in her car and on their way to the rehearsal room, their tummies full of a full English apiece instead. Which wasn't a rehearsal room, strictly speaking; it was one of the spare rooms in the Old House at Home pub, generally only used on high days and holidays. Matt knew the landlord's daughter, and when it wasn't needed they let them use the room for nothing. Which was a godsend because it was hard to find places where you could belt music out without running the risk of annoying all the neighbours.

The other lads had both arrived by the time they got there, and were keen to crack on, so it wasn't until they'd run through the four new numbers they'd planned on including in their new set that they took a long enough break for Joey and Paula to run their encounter with Mo by them, and to put forward the proposal he'd made.

'So, no, he's not from a record company,' Paula explained. 'But he certainly seems legit – more than. He lives on Oak Lane.'

'So he says,' Dan pointed out. 'That doesn't mean he actually does.'

'But why would he lie about that?' Joey said reasonably, revisiting what he'd said to Paula before. 'It's not like it's something we couldn't find out soon enough anyway, is it? And why would he ask us to do a gig for him if he *didn't* have a nightclub? The question is whether we're interested in doing it, isn't it?' He spread his palms. 'Though that's obviously up to all of you, not me, man. I'm just glad to be playing gigs at all.'

'And it's a good earner – well, if it *is* that,' Dan said. He, at least, seemed to be up for it.

'So why don't Joey and I check it out?' Paula suggested. 'Call him and tell him we'd like to go down. We're both free to see him tomorrow, if he'll let us. And we've got nothing to lose, have we? Not till we decide we want to do it anyway.'

'No, you're right,' Matt said. 'Do it. Let's try and get ourselves a piece of Cool Britannia, eh?'

As Paula and Joey were both otherwise engaged with their 'proper' jobs – his mam's words on Sunday morning about that still stung, and his anger was still simmering – it was late on Monday afternoon before they could get into town. Though at least by now they'd managed to find out a little more about the mysterious Mo. And mostly good things. Both about him and his business partner, Nico, Mo having apparently just returned from several years doing property development in Spain, and Nico – who apparently was known as 'Nic the Greek' locally – being in the property business too, only in Bradford.

Yes, he'd done time – rumour had it that he'd been a bit of a bad boy in his youth, the mastermind (well, till they caught up with him, anyway) of some big bank job back in the late eighties. But he'd apparently since amassed a legit-imate fortune and was a family man these days – wouldn't harm a fly, as some mate of his uncle Nicky's had described it. And as far as Joey was concerned, that was all water off a duck's back in any case.

'I'm not sure it's quite that,' Paula had said. 'I mean, that still makes him a former bank robber.'

'And my uncle's a convicted murderer, and he's completely sound these days, isn't he? And it's not as if either of us comes from whiter than white families, is it?'

A point which Paula could only concede. Her mam's older brother Vinnie was currently serving a long stretch for robbery himself. And, much as she loved him – well, as much as she really knew him – she admitted that she wouldn't plan on doing business with him any time soon, however much of a hero her mam had always had him down as.

'Two peas in a pod, us,' she'd observed thoughtfully. And Joey agreed they were. And he'd been firm in the belief that had been drummed into him all his life – that you didn't judge people based on what they'd done in a former life. You took them at face value and saw how it went. Because everyone deserved a second chance.

They turned onto the road Mo had told them they'd find the club – not that he'd needed to, because Paula already knew it – and were greeted by the sight of an enormous thick-set man, standing in the entrance, wielding a heavy-looking chainsaw.

'Can I help?' he asked politely, his voice higher than Joey'd expected, while lowering it and kicking a snake of lead out of the way.

'Alright, mate?' Joey said. 'We were hoping to see Mo?'

'He expecting you?' the man said, narrowing his eyes suspiciously, as if he were acting out a line out of a film.

'He should be,' Joey answered brightly. 'Spoke to him on the phone a couple of hours back? Joey Parker and Paula Foster.' He tried not to stand to attention.

The man, who was wearing a regulation yellow hard hat, was dressed in an assortment of baggy clothes – all heavily spattered with various shades of dried paint. He put down the chainsaw just inside the open double doors and wiped his enormous hands on his trouser legs. Then he stuck a hand out. 'I'm Billy,' he said. 'Big Billy.'

He cracked a smile, looking sheepish. Joey took the meaty hand in his and shook it hard.

'But it's just Billy, really,' the man added as Joey released his paw.

Paula shook his hand too. 'Nice to meet you, Billy,' she said, giving him a mega-wattage smile.

'Is he for real?' she whispered to Joey as he lumbered ahead, leading them both inside. 'He's like something off a bloody cartoon!'

They'd stepped into what Joey assumed had once been an impressive high-ceilinged foyer but was currently in the middle of major renovations. Well, what he assumed would be renovations, once they'd put back together all the stuff that had clearly been torn down. The walls were a mess of exposed brick and peeling plasterboard, with wires sprouting listlessly from the remains of sockets, and skeins of power cables hanging like vines from what was left of the ceiling. The floor, too, was a mess of rubble, tools and timber. 'Mind all the shit,' the man shouted back at them over the whine of some nearby drill. 'Watch your step, right? It's this way to Mo's office.'

Joey took Paula's hand – she was in heels ('Dress to impress!' she'd told him) – as they weaved their careful way over mounds of ripped-up carpet and a variety of screws and nails. There seemed no way that this place would be re-opening any time soon. But perhaps that was all to the good. A bit more time to think about the decision before committing. Or, more accurately, persuading Matt that the prospect actually *had* any for them. He'd said he might be up for it but he hadn't seemed *that* enthused.

Their giant host, via a short flight of steps and a long walk down a dark corridor, eventually fetched up in front of a door marked 'strictly private' and beyond that to another – a sturdy door, made out of oak – on which was screwed a brass plate that said 'Manager's Office'.

Billy knocked gently and, without waiting, turned the handle to open the door, upon which Mo's distinctive voice floated out to them. He was talking on the phone. Though it wasn't any phone – it was a mobile. A bloody *mobile*. That, as much as anything about the dark, compelling stranger, seemed to signify he was someone to be reckoned with and maybe be around. Paula obviously thought the same. As Billy ushered them in, she squeezed Joey's hand and nudged him.

'Do you clock that?' she whispered as Mo finished the call.

'Ah, good afternoon,' Mo said warmly. He sat back in his swivel chair, looking amused. 'Come to check us out, then, have you?'

'If that's still alright with you,' Joey answered. 'Looks like you're pretty busy. Lots to do.'

Mo nodded at Big Billy, who was still standing by the door. 'Bill and his team reckon it'll all be ready in seven days, tops, don't you, Billy? So, give or take any problems that crop up unexpectedly, that's when we expect it to be done. Which means opening next Saturday week. Just under a fortnight.' He waved Joey and Paula towards a brace of seats parked on their side of the crowded desk. 'Billy works for Nico, my associate, and he's good at what he does. If he says we'll be ready,' he said, obviously noticing Joey's raised eyebrows, 'then ready is what we'll be. Thanks, Bill. I'll take it from here, mate, if you want to get back.'

The man touched his yellow hard hat deferentially. Another movie. This time a war film, Joey thought. 'Cheers, boss,' he said. 'You want me to give Nico a shout?'

'If you wouldn't mind, Bill, yes. You'll probably find him in the cellar.' He smiled at Joey. 'He's with the brewery guy, probably getting on his nerves trying to better the deal we've already struck with them. All about the numbers,' he added, as Billy left the room.

He went on to explain that a number of other breweries had also approached them, all so eager to get a piece of the pie that they were desperate to throw money at them in order to be the ones to secure a hefty regular beer order. 'It's big money in the long run,' Mo explained, talking to Joey on a level, as if he expected him to understand it all. 'They know they'll make a fortune out of us if we deign to stock their product, so they're bending over backwards, offering to refit the cellar, build us a new bar, provide us with the very best in brass pumps and so on.' He chuckled. 'But *still* Nico tries to squeeze them for a bit more.'

'Can't really blame him,' Joey said. He'd yet to properly meet Nico – bar a nod back in The Sun – but he was already impressed by him. 'Better in your pocket than theirs,' he said.

Mo laughed heartily. '*That's* my boy!' he said. 'I already pegged you as having a good head on your shoulders. Not just a pretty face, this lad of yours, is he?' he added to Paula.

Joey glanced at her, pretty sure he could read her expression. Which, without a doubt, was saying, *Ahem, I'm here too?*

'No, indeed,' she said briskly. But then she softened under Mo's relentless bonhomie. 'So it's looking definite, then? This opening a week Saturday? And you definitely want us? Because we'll have to let The Sun know in time to get another band in for that weekend. I mean, they're ten a penny, as you know.'

'But don't have *you* fronting them,' Mo pointed out. 'Which is why we're prepared to pay top dollar to secure you.'

He couldn't have said it better. Joey could almost feel Paula puffing up. 'That's kind of you to say so,' she said politely. 'But –'

'I only ever speak as I find,' Mo responded. 'As you'll find out for yourself. Anyway, good girl. And, ah, here he is,' as the door again opened. 'Nic, come meet the new talent. Well, two-fifths of them anyway. The *top* two-fifths,' he added, winking at Joey.

The man was wider than Joey remembered. He all but filled the doorway. In his fifties, Joey judged, dressed in an expensive-looking grey suit. He put him in mind of the actor Bob Hoskins, who'd played a gangster in that film his mam and dad loved so much. Though he was tanned, he looked more like an accountant than a nightclub owner – albeit a rather scary one. Joey stood to greet him, grateful that he had the advantage in height.

'Ah, welcome, welcome,' the man said in a deep voice, thickly accented. 'Joey and Paula, yes?' He shook Joey's hand with some force and then, to Joey's surprise, leaned in to kiss Paula hard, on both cheeks. 'You like our little place, no? Come, I will show you the performing area.'

'He means the stage,' Mo added. 'Oh, but hang on.' He yanked a drawer in the desk open and rummaged around in it. 'You should have this, son, before I forget.' He took something out and handed it to Joey. 'It's a pager. You know how to use one?'

Joey was dumbfounded. A pager? He suddenly felt extremely businesslike. 'Well, yeah, I think so,' he said, though he didn't have a clue. 'Well, I'll work it out, but –'

'So we can keep in touch,' Mo said, rising from the desk, and reaching for his mobile phone. 'I have the number,' he explained, 'and when I need you, I can bleep you. Then you go find a phone and then you call me. All very simple. One thing though, it'll be my mobile phone number that comes up. And no one gets that, okay? So no sharing it around. Paula, yes,' he said, turning to her. She was looking distinctly peeved again. 'But other than that, no one, you understand?'

'No, I don't know why he gave it to me and not you, either,' Joey hissed as they followed the two men out of the office and back down the stairs.

Joey was no expert but the club was way bigger than he imagined. It had a capacity of a thousand – Nic explained this to him proudly – and after the first year they had plans to extend even further, and were already in talks about leasing the building next door. 'Been closed up for over two years,' Mo said. 'Used to be a law firm, I think. But what with planning to be gone through, we won't commit yet. So we'll see. Decide whether it's going to be any use to us before committing. A bit like you've done today, eh?' He put a friendly arm around Joey's shoulder, and, again, Joey wondered at him sharing these plans. He was just the drummer in a tribute band, after all.

The dancefloor, too, was massive, as was the DJ booth. As was the space that Nico pointed out as where the stage was being built. 'When you perform here,' the Greek man said, 'we will be the only club in Bradford providing regular live music alongside DJs on the same night. So you'll only need to do the one spot, around forty-five minutes. And that's it, you'll –'

'What?' Paula said. 'Do just the one set? But we were promised a set fee of …'

'And you will receive that,' Mo told her. 'Of course, there might be times when you want to do more. But, yes, a much easier night for you all. You can then stay and enjoy the rest of the evening, or you can go home, as you wish. Up to you, but this is it.' He splayed his arms and did a slow 360-degree turn, taking in what in Joey's mind's eye already transformed itself into the finished article. The thought of playing here, to so many people … he could almost taste his excitement. Mo caught his eye. 'This is our baby,' he said. 'Welcome aboard, kids. Well,' he added, and now he slipped an arm over both of their shoulders, 'assuming your fellow bandmates are interested, of course.'

'Oh, they will be,' Paula assured him.

Chapter 7

Mo had been as good as his word. Silks opened the following Saturday just as he'd promised, the whole place having been transformed. The building site, a place of drills and wires and sawdust, of loud bangs and harsh noises, had become bejewelled and shining, pulsating – almost a living, breathing thing.

There was a sign over the door which, in two-foot-high letters, shouted 'SILKS' in arresting pink neon. Inside, the large foyer was painted in blood-red and black, with blow-ups of black and white photos on the walls, depicting scenes of another Bradford, before any of them had been born: elegant buildings, old buses, horses and carts, factories, lines of stoic-looking men hoping for an honest day's work, gatherings of women, clutching shawls to themselves, skirts billowing. It seemed far removed from the gaudy opulence in which they hung.

Inside, scruffy murk had become sensuous gloom; light fell in pools, which dispersed to the soft shadows, and with the stage and DJ stand forming a natural focal point – more pink neon – the space seemed to fall away, into deeper, darker shadows, where a series of booths, some of which could be hidden behind velvet curtains, suggested the place had no beginning or no end. 'For the VIP set,' Paula had commented, with a knowing wink.

To Joey, who'd not as yet ever managed to talk his way into any proper nightclub, it was jaw-dropping, both in its magnificence and its scale. The best he'd ever managed, in terms of playing or watching music to or with any masses, had been the school hall, when he'd competed in a battle-of-the-bands competition, and the local youthy, in which 'glamour' meant someone turning off the big fluorescent strip lights, so the battered chairs and tables looked that little bit less ratty, and someone lighting joss sticks, in a vain effort at creating a nicer atmosphere than that in there by default as a result of the kitchen chip fryer.

And it was a transformation that had even extended to the gentle giant they'd met, Big Billy, who'd now swapped his splattered overalls and hard hat for a black suit, snow-white shirt and bow tie, and had ushered them into the club with a small reverential bow and shown them to the place where they could stash their coats.

It was ten now, and the place was full to capacity and, according to Matt, who'd nipped out to pick up the forgotten set list from his van, there was also a queue stretching almost as far down as Manor Row.

'Get a grip, Joey,' Paula giggled, seeing his expression of shock and awe. 'It'll just be like doing The Sun. Just take a deep breath and remember to picture the crowd naked, like I said.'

Joey frowned. He couldn't quite believe they were here. In this place. Much less that they were actually going to play for them. So many people, so much expectation and anticipation. He was now rechecking the parts of his drum kit to calm his nerves as much as anything. 'That'll just put me right off,' he said, his nerves beginning to jangle. 'I don't think I'd know where to look,' he added, trying to keep a lid on them. 'I'd just be scanning the room for the bird with the biggest tits!'

'Is that right?' Paula asked, playfully punching him on the shoulder. She looked burnished in the coloured light; as if she'd sprinkled herself in glitter. Whereas he just felt like a rookie, and a bit of a dork. But she was still Paula. He rubbed his shoulder. 'Well then,' she said. 'They'd have no problem spotting the guy with the tiniest prick, at least, because if I catch you eyeing anyone's tits up, I'll chop it off, do you hear me?'

They shared a look that made him smile, and helped settle his nerves down. Because they'd shared something else – something bloody amazing – last night too. He wondered if his mam had clocked it when he'd returned home this morning, but shook the thought away, because it detracted from the memory of the pleasure. Her expression had been knowing, and odd and unreadable. Like, what did she expect? It was none of her business, anyway.

There was still almost an hour before they took to the stage, and, though he was beginning to feel the adrenaline, he was anxious about performing well too. So despite his general adversity to drinking before playing, when Matt suggested they grab a drink, he decided to have a half;

adrenaline was great, but nerves he could do without. Nerves invariably found their way to his fingers.

They made their way over to the spot by the end of the lengthy bar, where a sign hung saying 'No service – staff only'. They had a good view of the side of the stage here, and the DJ, a young good-looking Asian guy, who seemed in a world of his own, busy spinning and mixing his vinyl. The whole place was jumping – people were definitely in party mood this evening, not least due to a free welcome drink to celebrate the opening.

The band got their drinks free as well – another perk Mo had thrown in at the last minute. Of Mo himself, though – not to mention Nico – there was currently no sign. Since Joey had last looked, they seemed to have disappeared.

He picked up his half, and nearly spilt half of it straight down his front, as Paula nudged him sharply in the ribs. She was looking so much in character, in her shift dress and stilettos – a fat streak of eyeliner slicked across her eyelids, above false lashes as big as butterfly wings. He was dating fucking Debbie Harry! He could see blokes ogling enviously. He found it hard to take his eyes off her as well.

Her own eyes were now looking past him. She grabbed Matt as well. 'Those guys over there,' she said, raising her voice over the thump of the music. 'They look a bit shifty, don't they? Who'd d'you think they are? The police? They must be over fifty if they're a day.'

Joey looked. And agreed – they looked exactly like plain-clothes policemen. God, was the club being raided or something? Already? Another of his mam's comments about the gig they'd accepted came to Joey; that the night-club – in the days before it was Silks obviously – was a place that was raided all the time by the police, and why did he imagine it was ever going to be any different? That they should open their eyes, and were better off out of it – and yadda, yadda, yadda – lots more in the same vein. But then she would. If she had her way he'd never bloody go anywhere.

'Nah, don't worry. They're reporters,' Matt said. 'Seen them before.'

'Reporters?' asked Joey. 'What, to check us out or something?'

'Probably,' said Matt. 'New club opening up – they're bound to be here, aren't they? They'll want something for the paper – they're from the *Telegraph and Argus*, I think.'

'Bloody hell,' Paula said. 'Glad I put my best frock on. One's got a camera. See? And it looks like they're headed over here.'

They were. It took a while, but the men finally got to them, the one without the camera pulling out a battered notebook and a pen.

'Parallel Lines?' he said, chewing the lid off the latter. 'As if I couldn't tell,' he added, looking appreciatively at Paula. 'Jesus, you're the spit of her, you are, love.'

Joey resisted the urge to tell him to take his leering looks off elsewhere, though he couldn't help feeling proud, even so. He shook the hands that were held out as introductions were made, taking in the fact – the almost unbelievable fact – that he was going to have his picture in the paper.

That could be hoicked round the neighbourhood, to impress anyone who'd listen. Even framed. That would surely change his mam's tune.

They posed for a group shot, Joey taking his lead from the others, though having to work hard to scowl – as was the look he knew they wanted, because he read the *NME* and had often imagined himself in there – because a grin couldn't help but keep re-emerging on his face. The man took their names then, taking them down in his pad in tiny writing, making sure he had them all down correctly, left to right. 'We'll get a few more, once you're on,' the photographer said. 'If you want copies, you can pop down to the office.'

'Which we won't,' Matt told Joey. 'It's, like, fifty quid a pop.' Which disappointed Joey – he'd have loved to have a copy of such a picture, and was just saying to Paula, while the men were given drinks, when he caught sight of Mo, strolling effortlessly through the crowd. It really was like he could almost walk on water. He was in a dark chalk-striped suit, his dreads in their customary ponytail, the mobile phone in his hand attracting appreciative, awed stares.

'Gentlemen,' he said, shaking the men's hands in turn, the gold ring on his pinky finger gleaming. 'Got what you need? Got a drink? Being looked after?' He then launched into a spiel about the club and what they'd planned for it, while the reporter again scribbled as much as he could down – this time using some weird kind of shorthand.

'Are you sure we can't have one of you? With the band, say?' he asked.

But Mo shook his head. 'Sorry, mate, you know the rule here. No photos. Just the talent.'

Why? Joey thought. Mo couldn't look the part more. And it wasn't like he was the shy, retiring type, was he? If ever there was an ambassador for a high-end nightclub, it was Mo. 'Up to you,' the man began. Then jerked his head to one side. 'Eh up,' he said pointing. 'Looks like something's kicking off. You might want to –'

Mo followed his gaze. 'No sweat,' he said smoothly. 'Got it covered. Gentlemen, will you excuse me?'

Though whatever was happening was happening on the other side of the club, being tall, Joey could see for himself. An altercation of some sort, between two hefty young lads, though played out soundlessly, because the music was too loud for him to hear it. But it didn't need a soundtrack, because the action was unmistakable. The beginnings of a fight – the very last thing anyone wanted.

'What's going on?' Paula said, straining to see over all the bobbing heads. But even as Joey was about to tell her, he saw a blur of black and white, followed by an arm going round a neck – one of Big Billy's ham-like upper limbs, he realised – and then what looked weirdly like the lad being levitated almost. There seemed to be no struggle – the lad almost seemed to glide across the back of the club, and, clamped to Billy's front now, to the steps back up to the entrance. The only movement was from his legs, kicking uselessly against nothing, as, at least a foot off the ground, he was transported bodily back to the foyer.

He saw Mo's unmistakable form following calmly behind them. 'Bloody hell, did you *see* that?' he said to no one in particular. 'The way he just picked him up like that? It was like he weighed nothing!'

The taller of the newspapermen had seen it all too. 'That's nothing,' he said. 'You should see him when he's riled, lad. I've seen him eject three at once, single-handed.'

'Who? Big Billy?' asked Paula.

'He's a legend,' the other man said. 'Well, if you don't get on the wrong side of him, that is.' He turned back to the other man. 'Didn't even realise he was out, did you?'

'What, from prison?' Joey asked.

The photographer laughed. 'Nah, lad. From a Swiss finishing school, obviously.'

With the fight having been stopped before it had even really started, the atmosphere in the club hadn't suffered. If anything, by the time the band took to the stage, it felt more like a party than ever. Song after song was greeted rapturously and loudly, and every time he glanced up from his kit, Joey was half-blinded by the flashes of cameras; not just in the hands of the *Argus* photographer, but coming from all over the place, as people held disposable ones aloft, creating a mini star-scape in the throbbing, sweaty darkness.

By the time they'd finished both his T-shirt and jacket were soaked in sweat; even Paula had a patch of it in the small of her back, from where she'd gyrated, like a serpent, around her mic stand.

Mo, in contrast, who'd watched from the bar throughout the set, looked cool even in his heavy three-piece suit. He lifted a hand, pointing first to Joey and then Paula, then crooked the same finger to have them go across to speak to him.

'Good job,' he said, once they'd reached him. 'Great job, in fact. Went down even better than I expected. Here –' he handed Paula a folded sheet of paper. 'You take this, since you're the driver. I have to leave now. Bit of business. And I might not be back before you've left. That's my address,' he added. 'How are you fixed tomorrow?'

Joey nodded back towards the other band members, still busy accepting plaudits and signing the flyers Mo had had printed for them. 'Meeting up for a late breakfast. But –'

'I didn't mean the whole band. I meant just the two of you.'

'Oh,' said Paula.

'Spot of lunch, I thought,' he said, smiling at her. 'Over at mine. Say around two thirty – no, call it three. Nothing poncy, don't worry. I have a girl who comes in to cook and clean for me, who does a blinding roast dinner, so …'

'Yeah, yeah, sure,' Joey said. 'I can do that. Can you, Paulz?'

Paula nodded. 'Absolutely.' Her face was sheeny with moisture.

'Good,' Mo said. 'Because I have something I want to show you.'

'Ooh, what sort of something?' Paula said, batting her ridiculously long lashes.

Mo touched his nose. 'You'll see.'

Matt picked up a soggy triangle of toast and dipped it into his egg yolk. 'So what d'you reckon it is, then,' he said. 'This "something" he wants to show you?' He was talking through the yellow mess moving around inside his mouth. He looked peeved about it, just as Joey had expected. Which was fair enough. He'd probably feel peeved himself. After all, Matt was supposed to be the leader of the band. And in truth, he wasn't sure he was comfortable with it either – he didn't want to be teacher's pet, even if Paula didn't have a problem with it – and had been ruminating on it a lot since waking up. *Was* it Paula? Was that it? That Mo fancied Paula? But then why not just ask her round? Like she'd go without him, which she wouldn't. Perhaps that's why Mo had asked him along too.

Joey couldn't shut his ears against the grim slapping sounds coming out of Matt's mouth, but he could at least turn his gaze away. He felt nauseous enough – staying on for more drinks had been a seriously bad idea – without having to look at his bandmate's masticated breakfast. 'Just you two?' Matt went on. 'Pretty odd. What's all that about?'

'I just said, didn't I?' Joey told Matt irritably. 'And I don't know. He didn't say. Here,' he said to Paula, to whom Nico had given the money (which was another thing that had obviously rankled, even though she'd apparently always done the money stuff, because she was the one with the best head for it), 'should we split this now, or what? Since we're not eating breakfast.'

'It is a bit weird,' Dan observed. 'Why didn't he invite all of us? What are you, like, his little favourites?'

'Maybe it's not about the band,' Paula pointed out, as she counted out tenners. 'Have you considered that? It might not be. Anyway, stop whining. Bit of a touch, this, eh? Can't believe we only had to work an hour for it.' She passed the cash round. 'And here's to more of the same.'

'What *is* it about, then?' Matt said again. 'If it's not about the band? What's this fucking love-in you three have going on?'

'Matt, we don't *know*, okay?' she said, patting his arm soothingly. 'We'll tell you when we *do* know. I'll call you. Anyway, you fit, Joey? We need to crack on. You still have to go home and change.'

That was another thing. Joey knew he probably smelled as rank as Matt's breakfast looked, having crashed into Paula's with her at silly o'clock, hot, damp and reeking of beer. Though clearly not enough to put her off jumping on him drunkenly, high on nothing more sinister than vodka and endorphins. It was a bright memory amid the waves of sickness he was currently bobbing on.

'We'll let you know,' he repeated. 'Honest, guys, I have no idea either. And I'm about as fit for a roast as I am to run a fucking marathon. Believe me, I'd far rather it was you lot going round there.'

Dan clapped him on the back. 'It's cool, mate. Don't worry.'

Trouble was that Joey did worry. It was creeping him out a little. Because that's how he did feel. Exactly like the unwilling teacher's pet. And even more so, once they'd driven to his place, and Paula had laid out his wardrobe to her satisfaction while he'd showered. His newest jeans, his pale-blue Fred Perry polo shirt and his best black leather jacket. His one pair of proper shoes.

'There,' she'd said, as he'd returned, with a towel round his waist. 'Get that lanky bod of yours into that lot.' She'd looked at her watch then. And back at him. 'Though on second thoughts …' she purred, advancing on him. 'Since no one's at home … It'll help relax you, babe.'

And it had. But then it was all a rush, and not for the first time, Joey envied Paula her breezy composure. She exuded confidence, and seemed genuinely in awe of no one; the sort of person for whom the concept of having a 'station' in life simply didn't exist. He tried to adopt her mindset as they both hurried to get ready, pleased that his mam and dad were out and not there to ask him why he was getting his posh togs on – and, more to the point, where he was going. He knew an interrogation was probably inevitable, whether he told them or otherwise. It was all a bit like that just lately.

Even so, despite being togged up in his best gear, Joey couldn't help but gape when, an hour later, Paula pulled the Mini up at the address Mo had given them – or, rather, the longest drive to a private house he'd ever seen.

He peered ahead, beyond the pair of ornate wrought-iron gates. 'Fuck me, Paula, he lives in a bloody mansion! Look at the size of the place! Christ, he must be loaded!'

Unsure what to do, Paula turned in and approached the imposing gates, which, as if by magic, began swinging open, like a giant jaw, without evidence of any human touch. '*Wow*,' she said, driving through them, towards the distant house. 'I think we may have underestimated our Mister Big, don't you?'

'No shit, Sherlock,' Joey answered. 'Just a bit.'

The area out front was wide and gravelled, graced by conifers and flowering plants in various urns, and, unsure where to park, Paula tucked the Mini behind a car that was already there: a big, spotless, black BMW.

Mo was already standing in the porch when they got out, and Joey again found himself staring. And then wondering what the fuck was about to happen, as Mo wasn't even dressed. He was wearing what looked like a pair of black satin pyjamas, with a matching black robe over the top. 'Perhaps that's kind of a thing in Spain,' he whispered to Paula, the word 'exotic' having sprung immediately to mind. Though that naturally brought along with it the worrying term 'exotic dancers'. Christ, had they been invited to an orgy?

But there was no time to run this possibility by Paula, as Mo had come down the short flight of steps to greet them now – every inch the perfect host – his dreadlocks, which had been neatly tied back every other time Joey had seen him, now two cascades forming a glossy waterfall over his shoulders. Could dreadlocks even *be* glossy? Evidently they could. It put him in mind of Aslan, the heroic lion from the Chronicles of Narnia series of books.

'So you found it,' Mo said, ushering them ahead of him into the house, which smelled, less exotically, of a simple roast dinner, which immediately, if illogically, put Joey's mind at rest. They surely didn't eat roast dinners at orgies. 'Marika, my girl, is all ready to go. Please –' Mo extended a hand. 'Let me take your coats.' Then, once they'd shrugged arms from jackets and handed them over, 'Come on through. I'll give you the tour after lunch.'

Joey took Paula's hand and squeezed it as they followed Mo through a cavernous galleried hallway and through double doors into a big square room on the left. He didn't think he'd ever seen such a big dining table – well, not in normal house, at any rate. But was anything about this place normal? The table, which was made of some kind of dark, highly polished wood, was set perfectly centrally, with eight matching chairs. Hung above it was a giant chandelier. Joey tried to imagine the sort of dinners that were eaten round it, and couldn't. Who came here? Who ate here? Surely not people like Big Billy? It looked like something out of one of the posh magazines his mam sometimes nicked from the doctors.

'This is a bit special, Mo,' he said as he took it all in. 'You've done proper well for yourself, mate.'

Mo came around behind them and slipped his arms round both Joey's and Paula's waists. 'I have indeed,' he said, urging them forward. 'Now, sit yourselves down while I fetch you a drink. Fancy a beer? Or a Coke, or something?'

They both opted for beer – something to make the place seem less intimidating. Joey barely dared even touch the chair arms as he sat down. 'God, this is *amazing*,' he whispered to Paula as she did likewise. 'You ever seen anywhere like this before? *Ever?*'

She shook her head. 'Never. We've definitely landed on our feet here.'

Which made Joey look to his feet, and the shoes he'd just polished. And at the cream carpet on which they were currently placed. Christ, what if he got boot polish on it? How did people relax with that kind of stress?

But Mo clearly wasn't one for putting on airs and graces. The exotically named Marika turned out to be anything but. And, strictly speaking, she was hardly a girl either. Joey would have guessed she was around his mam's age, skinny and swarthy-looking, with a broad Yorkshire accent. And she chatted away amiably as she brought in the various dishes (vegetables in separate dishes!) commenting on how much she liked Paula's hair, and asking her where she went to get it bleached.

'She's Billy's cousin,' Mo explained, once she'd left. 'I inherited her from Nico. I needed some help, she needed some work – Nico now has a more permanent arrangement – and we rub along fine. And best of all, she can cook a mean roast, eh? I've missed this – you can't get a decent roast for love nor money on the Costas. Well, if you don't want to eat with a side order of drunken British holidaymakers doing out-of-tune karaoke, that is.' He smiled at Paula. 'I like my entertainment a little classier. Anyway, tuck in.'

And it had definitely been worth foregoing the breakfast. His nausea now replaced by a raging appetite, Joey was only too happy to do as instructed, digging in gratefully while Mo regaled them with anecdotes about Spain, about the nightclub, about Nico's funny Greek ways, and, once prompted, about the lad who Big Billy had ejected so efficiently from Silks the night before.

'Oh, he's one of a kind,' Mo told them. 'Him and Nico go way back.'

'The man from the *Argus* said he's just come out of prison,' Paula said. 'Has he?'

Mo nodded. 'In and out like a swing door in a gale. Loyal – like a dog – but not the sharpest tool in the box.' He laughed. 'But then you don't employ the Billys of this world for their brains. Anyway,' he said, placing his cutlery on his empty plate. 'How about that tour I promised? Ready?'

Joey was too busy being awestruck to count them at the time, but Paula told him later that the mansion had six – six! – bedrooms, each lavishly decorated in shades of gold and cream, with sumptuous curtains, elegant lights and more expanses of cream carpet, and three – three! – enormous bathrooms upstairs, two of them what Paula described as 'en suite'.

'But I have saved the best till last,' Mo said, with his hand on another door handle – the one attached to a room at the end of the wide, galleried landing. He flashed his polar-white smile. 'Joey, look at your face, man. And look at this …' He turned the handle and swung the door open.

Joey couldn't help but gape as he looked, as instructed. 'What the fuck? Christ, Mo, that's some drum kit you've got there!'

Mo nudged them both in. '*You've* got.'

Joey turned around. '*I've* got?'

'It's for you. They're for you. I don't know the exact parlance. But I know a dude who does, and he tells me this lot is the best.'

'The best? This is epic!' Joey said, touching the rim of the hi-hat tenderly. 'I mean, Christ, this lot must have cost a fortune?'

Mo laughed. 'Relative term. But, yes, no sense in going cheap.'

'But Christ, Mo – I mean … *really?*'

'Bloody *hell*,' Paula said.

'Call it a birthday present. It's next week, right?' he tapped his nose. 'A little bird told me. Though not this one,' he added as Joey raised his eyebrows at Paula. 'Though it's not all about Joey here,' he said taking her hand. 'There's all this too. Decent amp. Decent mic stand. Wireless, see?'

'Bloody hell, Mo. Joey, look at all this stuff here!'

Joey looked, but at the same time, his mind's eye was elsewhere. What the fuck was all this about? And how did Mo know about his birthday? He barely knew him. But why wouldn't he, he reasoned then. All the band knew, after all … But … His dinner began to sit heavily in his stomach, as his mam and dad came into focus. As did the image of the top-of-the-range snare drum they'd saved so hard to buy for him – he'd forgone any sort of party so they could afford to get it for him, and had let him have it early so he could incorporate it into his kit; so he could get used to it and use it for his audition with the band.

Top of the range. Well, that was clearly a relative term, wasn't it? The name on this kit – well, it was in a completely different range – different league. Christ, what the hell would they have to say about all this? More unsettling still, how would it make them feel?

As if reading his mind, Mo turned back to him. 'I wasn't thinking of you taking it anywhere, son. I thought a dedicated room here, so you could practise; no neighbours to annoy here, of course … and plenty of space …'

Joey shook his head. 'Mo, I can't accept it. *We* can't accept it. It's too much. You barely know us … I mean, thank you. It's an incredible gesture. But it just wouldn't feel right …'

He knew Paula was looking at him as if he'd lost his marbles – that confidence, again – but he ignored it. 'I just wouldn't feel right accepting something like this,' he said again.

Mo tipped his head to one side and looked at Joey for a long moment. 'You know what, son?' he said. 'That's precisely why you *do* deserve it. And it's not just a gift anyway – think of it as an investment. Trust me, if you have the best gear, you'll play the best music. And me and Nico, we're going to fill our club then, aren't we? Win–win. And the room –' He gestured with his arms. 'This is an investment too. In all of you. The whole band. To use as and when practical. Which will surely save you many hours of lugging heavy kit around.'

'Well, I'm *all* for that,' Paula said. 'Mo, you're amazing.' Then she padded across to Mo in her stockinged feet – they'd taken their shoes off for the tour – and planted a kiss on his designer-stubbled cheek.

'My pleasure,' he said. Then he winked at Joey. 'It's okay, man. No kiss required from you.'

Chapter 8

She'd sort of known back when she'd seen Joey on the Sunday. From the minute, looking back, he'd come in through the front door. Paula had driven off – Christine wished she had come in, but she hadn't – just Joey, all tarted up and looking shifty.

She didn't ask where he'd been all day, and he didn't tell her. And at that point, she'd pondered a completely different scenario. She knew he'd been home – she hadn't snooped, it had been obvious from the wash basket. And she knew, because a cursory glance into his bedroom confirmed it, that he and Paula had been 'fooling around', for want of a better term. Which was fine. They were adults – well, in Joey's case, almost. He would be eighteen in less than a week now. And was already more than old enough to be involved in that kind of relationship, something she didn't like to dwell on (he felt still so much her baby), except when she thought about her own sorry past and how desperately she didn't want him to fuck everything up for himself, by getting some stupid girl pregnant.

He hadn't wanted tea – and she'd made a bloody enormous shepherd's pie, too – at least half of which he'd normally polish off single-handed. And when Bri asked him what he'd been up to, what kind of day he'd had, she'd known, though he'd chatted lots about the gig, and the money, and the all-too-big breakfast, there was a huge chunk unaccounted for – most of Sunday.

She said nothing to Bri, because she knew he'd go on at her. About him having a new girlfriend, and what did she *think* he'd have been up to? (Which she already knew he had.) And about backing off and giving him some bloody space and privacy. But she'd known it wasn't that. She knew her son too well. So when Monday afternoon came around – they'd both been gone before seven, him to do his round, her for an early shift at the brush factory – she couldn't hold it in any longer. Not least because she had a strong sense that he couldn't either.

She just never envisaged that, when she asked him if there was something that was worrying him, it would all go so tits up so quickly, so completely. If she had she'd have shut the fuck up.

'It's that Mo,' he'd begun, while they drank mugs of tea in the kitchen. And she'd done her best not to stiffen at the name.

'What about him?' she'd asked lightly. 'What's he done?'

So he told her – though she could see he'd still been in two minds about telling her. But, as he talked – telling her about Mo's 'mansion', and his money, and their curious Sunday lunch date – he began to open up more and more. And he was just too incredulous about the gift *not* to tell her.

'Paula thinks I'm mad, but I just don't see how I can accept it. It's too much. It's too generous. The whole thing; it's just so incredible, Mam, don't you think? I mean brilliant, yeah, but still a bit awkward. I mean, I know he's loaded, so it's not like it's his life savings or anything, but he hardly knows me – or any of us – does he? Matt – he runs the band – he's cool about it. Well, ish. So's Paula. I mean, like they were saying, that's how it happens sometimes, doesn't it, with bands, yeah? You have someone discover you. And they like, mentor you and that, and help you make it to the big time ...'

And it had been those two words on which everything had turned. That and the tendrils of dread that were coiling around her heart. What the fuck was Mo up to?

Christine wasn't sure how quite, but in the space of a scant fifteen minutes, they'd gone from the one place, where she was listening to Joey trying to fathom why Mo saw so much in him, had been so kind to him, to screaming at one another over the kitchen table.

Three words, in fact, and the way she'd accidentally said them. And the way she'd rolled her eyes so patronisingly as she'd done so. 'What big time?' she'd scoffed, and as soon as she'd said it, she wished she could grab the words back and swallow them again. Because it was Mo she was raging against. Not her Joey. Mo. Mo, who wasn't in the fucking big time, except in his notoriety as a former drug dealer. No amount of swimming in the bloody Med could wash *that* particular stain from him. Who was probably back doing it now, more to the point. And who was bit by bit moving in on *her.* boy.

But her anger had spewed out in exactly the way Brian had counselled her *mustn't* happen. And all because the one thing she *couldn't* do was tell Joey the truth about Mo. She must not. She dare not. Because, as night followed day, he would then have to learn the truth about her as well. A fear that, with Joey's latest revelations, had suddenly grown tenfold.

She'd tried to take it back twice already. She tried to take it back now. 'Joey, you have to *see through him.* See what he's up to. Him and his cronies – they're turning your head. Look, I'm not saying you're naïve –'

'I'm bloody not!' He was now bristling.

'But you've got to keep away from these kinds of people. They're shady, these bloody club people. You ask anyone. Filling your head with daft ideas about being bloody rich and famous … flashing their bloody cash around … Making out like you're some big wonderkid or something. Well, you're not. Not here. Your head's in the bloody clouds, Joey, if you can't see that. Bloody big time – God, listen to yourself!'

He'd sat back then and shot her a look of such hurt that it skewered her. 'So what am I then, Mam? Eh? Just a nothing? A stupid kid with stupid ideas?'

'*No*, Joey, but … Christ … get your bloody feet back on the ground! All this swanning around, all self-important, hanging about with knobheads and bloody dopeheads …'

'Dopeheads? Who are the fucking dopeheads? I'm in a band, Mam! We're working! Working *hard*. Doing well –'

'So *you* think. And what about when you're not? How long is all this nonsense going to last? Joey, you've *got* a job. You've got a window round. Or have you forgotten that? Something your dad –'

'Oh, Christ, not that again. I *know*. Okay? I know! And I'm grateful. How many times do I have to fucking say that? Christ, but it's not like I even asked for it! I don't want to be a fucking window cleaner all my life, okay?'

'Joey! Your dad –'

'Can have it back if it means so fucking much to him!'

'Joey – how *dare* you! Your dad –'

'My dad, my dad, my dad – what about *me*? What about what *I* want?'

'You don't *know* what you want! You're so bloody pie-eyed about your precious music career and that bloody shyster who's turned your head …' She jabbed her finger on the table. 'It's all bloody nonsense. *This* is where you belong, and the sooner you can see that the better!'

Joey stood up, banging the table, causing one of the mugs to topple over.

'Shit,' Christine said, leaping up as cold tea washed towards her.

'You're jealous. I get it now,' he said. 'You're just fucking *jealous*. You don't want me to be successful, do you? You hate it – I've seen it. You *hate* that I'm with Paula. You hate the band. You hate me doing *anything* except that fucking round, day in day out. Being good. Being *here*. Doing as I'm bloody told! Just because you and Dad have never done anything with *your* lives – that's why you *hate* it all. Admit it. That's what this is really all about, isn't it?'

And it happened without Christine even realising it was about to. Her hand shot up and outwards, almost as if she had no control over it. Then it slapped him, very hard, across the face.

'Mate, anytime! Hey, come in. You can crash as long as you want.'

Dicky's hair looked like someone had sprinkled chalk dust all over it. He'd obviously just come in from work. He was currently labouring for a firm who were putting up a new estate of houses. The kind of 'proper' work his mam would no doubt approve of, Joey thought angrily. Well, as long as it lasted, anyway. It often didn't.

'Thanks, mate,' he told Dicky, stepping into the small hall. 'And, look, I'm not planning on staying long. I just had to get away for a couple of days, you know?'

'Sure. No worries,' Dicky said. 'Want a brew? I've just put the kettle on.' He turned and led the way through to the little back kitchen, where every horizontal surface was covered in stuff, and in the sink was a teetering pile of dirty plates.

Joey's mam would have a fit. He found the thought oddly soothing. And it endorsed the decision he'd made almost as soon as he'd left the house. Not to phone Paula and go running round there.

'So what's up, mate?' Dicky asked, once he'd found teabags and a brace of mugs. The last two clean ones in the cupboard. 'Girl trouble?'

Joey shook his head. 'No, the parents. Well, Mam. God, I'm so fucking *angry*.' He touched his cheek, which still felt hot. He wondered if it was red. He still couldn't quite believe how hard she'd slapped him. It had been so hard that as he'd stormed out of the kitchen he'd felt tears spring to his eyes and it had been an effort of will not to let them flow. He'd deserved it, he knew that. But still he fumed, even so, about some of the things she'd said to him. Was that how she really saw him, deep down? Because along with his fury sat this huge, heavy lump of bewilderment. Total bewilderment. Almost a sense of betrayal.

'Well, go on, then. Spit it out, mate,' Dicky suggested cheerfully. So Joey did. And once he started talking he felt a bit better.

'Wow, a whole fucking *drum kit*?' were Dicky's first words once Joey had finally finished outlining the events of the weekend that had brought about the pathetic row today. The half-finished mug of tea was now cool in Dicky's hands. 'Respect, mate. He must think you're *well* special. Which you are –' he touched Joey's arm. 'Your mam never meant that. She thinks the sun shines out of your arse, you know she does. But, listen, mate, think about where she's coming from, yeah? Course she's jealous. And your dad. You're making your own way now, aren't you? Going places. As you've a right to. As you should do. As you're *meant* to.'

Joey managed a wan smile. 'Since when did you become Mr Philosopher? Last week?'

In reality, Dicky had always had that kind of way about him. That way of being able to see things so calmly and rationally. He'd always been the sort of kid who, if crossed, or if he'd failed at some task he had set himself, would give things ten minutes' thought, go 'Yup, fair enough' and move on. And he could see things from all sides. He was really good at that. He had calmed Joey down just by sheer force of Zen. (Or at least that was how Joey knew Dicky would put it. He'd once read some famous book about it, and ever since then, it had been all Zen this, Zen that, Zen the other. Whatever Zen was. Perhaps he should read it himself.)

Dicky grinned. 'You told that new bird of yours yet? Paula, isn't it?'

Joey shook his head. Dicky had yet to meet Paula. He'd been working long hours, and different hours to those Joey had been working, and with Joey rehearsing all the time and performing as well (actually *performing*, to an audience, the thought was still thrilling) they'd not really touched base in three weeks. He was glad he'd come. He could chill here. Give his mam a chance to chill too. The way she'd been with him these past weeks had been so bloody stressy.

'Yeah, Paula Foster,' he said. 'And no, I haven't. She doesn't need me droning on about all this, does she?' He touched his cheek again. He hadn't told Dicky about that bit, and wouldn't.

'Well, you're cool here. Long as you like. So, how about I jump in the bath then we go get something to eat? I've got fuck-all here. And you sound like you're in the money, eh? Well, soon will be, by the sound of things.' He stood up and brushed his hand over his head, causing a pale shower of dust to fall and settle. 'You just chill, mate,' he said. Then, two minutes later, 'And you fucking will, too. No bloody hot water either! Fuck. Welcome to my world ...'

Dicky's flat was in a purpose-built block just off Manchester Road, about half a mile away from where Joey lived on Canterbury Estate. It was a two-bedroom place on the first floor of the building – one of about ten that shared a long communal balcony, which looked over a big car park out front. The car park below, as well as the balconies, was a gathering point for local kids – not to mention dealers and junkies, mostly because it was reasonably hidden from prying eyes, as well as providing various vantage points for keeping an eye on any police cars that might be patrolling and – as they frequently did – taking a purposeful detour turn off the main road to sniff out any trouble.

It was also a mess, with the bins usually overflowing and tipped over, and there was more often than not a mattress or some other unwanted bit of furniture slung in the corner, or propped up against one of the handful of garages.

It felt a world away from Joey's life, but one of the few things he did know about his early childhood was that, for a time, he'd lived in a place just like this with his mum and uncle. He couldn't quite imagine it – he'd been much too young to remember any of it – but whenever he came here he felt a stirring of mild displacement; was forcibly reminded of how little he really knew about where he came from, and the mother who'd given birth to him so young. But perhaps better that he didn't know, truth be told.

Joey returned to the kitchen and rinsed the mugs out and dried them. The kitchen window looked out onto a much more pleasing view. Well, in so much that, even if it was only neglected waste ground, it was at least mostly green and looked a bit like a field. Well, it gave the impression that it was, anyway – at least at this distance. Even if he knew in reality that one day it too would be turned into cheap housing like everywhere else.

He laid out the ratty tea-towel on the hob, the way his mam usually did. This was what he needed: his own place, even a shithole like this one. And thinking the thought made his mind turn to Paula. Should he call her? She was out tonight, going to some girly do or other with Susie, her friend from the chemist's, and there was a fair chance she'd call him before she left. If his mam hadn't already called her, that was. He knew for a fact that she had the number, because she'd asked Paula for it the previous week. She'd even spoken to Paula's mam now to see about them going out.

He hoped not. He hoped she'd leave them both be.

He wandered back into the living room, where it seemed he had company. Dicky had adopted a local cat. Well, the cat, more accurately, had decided to adopt Dicky. It was a skinny black and white thing, full of attitude, always mewing. It had sauntered in now, presumably from one of the bedrooms, and was regarding him warily for a moment, before sidling across, presumably hoping for something to eat.

They'd called it Simon. 'Why Simon?' Joey had asked when Dicky had told him. It seemed such an odd name for a cat. 'Why *not* Simon?' Dicky had replied.

Joey leaned down and stroked the cat as it rubbed its flank round his shins. Then, on a whim, picked it up – it began purring immediately – and sat down with it on the low, blanket-covered sofa, where it immediately began rhythmically kneading its front claws into his jeans, and settling its hindquarters, warm and soft, into Joey's lap.

He sat back, happy to clear his mind and close his eyes for a moment, but it was impossible to still his agitated thoughts. His mam hardly ever lost it with him – not proper lost it, like she had earlier. Why would she? He'd never given her cause. He wondered if she was feeling as shitty about it as he was.

Clearly. How could she not be? And as if to endorse the fact, he was jolted from his reverie by a loud insistent bing-bonging of the doorbell. So he knew without question – Dicky was still sloshing in the bath – that it would be her, come to try and make things up. Had to be – he knew Dicky's flatmate Tom wasn't around – he spent most of his time a couple of floors up, staying with the girlfriend he'd been seeing for a year now but to whom he wasn't yet ready to throw in his lease for.

No, it didn't have to be, but he lifted the cat off his lap, put it down on the carpet, and went into the hall to answer the door anyway. It wasn't like there was any point in *not* doing so. He wasn't going to hide away like a child.

But he wasn't going home either, not for the moment. He was still too angry. So it was with some dismay that he opened the door to find not his mam, or his dad – who was still at work, wasn't he? – but his uncle Nicky, an apologetic smile on his face. He had come in just as Joey had been upstairs, packing his rucksack. He'd heard his mam crying downstairs but she hadn't tried to stop him. Was still in the kitchen with Nicky when he'd clattered down the stairs and out of the front door.

'I know, I know,' Nicky said immediately, raising his palms in apology. 'What can I do? I said I'd come and find you, so I have.'

Joey's uncle Nicky wasn't a big man. Not much taller than his mam was. But his years inside had knocked off the soft curves of his mam's features, and given him that unmistakable air of someone not to be messed with. Not because he was built like a prize-fighter and could deck anyone that challenged him, like Billy – he was still lean, despite the weeks of gorging hungrily on proper grub, to make up for lost time – but because he could handle himself. Because prison life meant you had to.

But he was all supplication with his nephew. 'So can I come in, mate?' he asked. 'Have a chat, like? If I go back without at least saying I've seen you, I'll be getting a clip round the ear.'

Joey stood aside to let him pass. 'Not a slap round the face, then?'

'I know, mate,' Nicky said as Joey closed the front door behind him. 'And I'm sure you know how she's feeling about *that*.' He walked into the lounge and turned around to face Joey, hands thrust into his jeans pockets. 'She's sorry,' he said. 'Really sorry. She really doesn't mean it, mate. You know that.'

'Just what I told him,' Dicky said, having emerged from the bathroom, a sludge-coloured towel wrapped round his waist, rubbing vigorously at his wet hair with another.

'I know she is,' Joey said. 'And so am I, and you can tell her that. But that doesn't change anything. I'm stopping here for a bit. I need some space.'

He was aware that he sounded like he was reciting lines from some crap soap opera. But then if his mam was determined to carry on as though she was in one, so be it. 'Just for a few days,' he added, then was cross with himself for even feeling the need to say that. 'Just to get away from all the earache.' He lifted a hand to his ear and motioned with thumb and fingers. 'The constant bloody going on and on at me. Like I'm a bloody kid who doesn't know anything. I'm sick of it.'

'I know, mate,' Nicky said. 'And fair enough. You're probably right to, between you and me. Your mam … well, she's just being your mam, I suppose. She gets upset about stuff. Don't worry, I'll talk to her,' he added. Like they were on the same team. Which perhaps they were. Joey had been expecting a bit more grief, and was surprised he wasn't getting it. And not getting it made him feel worse about some of the things he'd said to his mam. 'Main thing is that

93

you're okay. But listen, mate, don't leave it too long, yeah? Don't be away for your fucking birthday or we'll all bloody suffer. Give her a ring or something, at any rate.' He clapped Joey on the back. 'You're a good kid. She knows that. So does your dad. They'd do anything for you, trust me.'

'I told him that too,' Dicky said.

'Doesn't feel like it right now,' Joey said.

Nicky nodded. 'I know. But it's still true. Don't forget that, mate, will you? And they'll be there for you. *Whatever.*' He gave Joey a long look. 'And, trust me, there's not many can say that.'

And then he was gone, refusing tea, all nods and smiles and back slaps. Joey watched him drive off, leaving a plume of exhaust fumes billowing from the back of the ancient van. Carrying on like *he* was the one in the bloody soap opera.

Chapter 9

Christine hadn't expected her brother to get back so quickly and at first she felt relieved when she saw the van pulling up outside. So he'd obviously found Joey and brought him back. But as Nicky got out of the driver's seat she could see straight away that Joey wasn't with him.

She let go of the net curtain, deflated, but then almost immediately changed her mind. Perhaps it was just as well that he hadn't brought him home. She wasn't completely sure she wouldn't cave in and spit it all out.

She went into the hall and opened the door for Nicky. 'Well?' she asked him as he came loping up the path.

He shrugged as he passed her and went into the kitchen, where he slung his keys down on the worktop and picked the kettle up to gauge the weight.

'What do *you* think?' he asked mildly. 'He's pissed off with you because he can't get his head round why you're so angry with him. And how could he, when he hasn't got a clue what's going on? Oh, and he says he's sorry.'

'Sorry for what?'

'For whatever it was he said to you. Christ, I didn't ask him for a word-by-word bloody run-through.'

'So what have you told him?' she asked him anxiously. She wouldn't put it past Nicky to let something slip. 'You've not even been gone half an hour.'

'Nothing,' he said, once he'd filled the kettle and put it back on its stand. 'Which is precisely why there wasn't much I *could* say, was there? I just told him you're stressed. That you're worried he's going to throw the window round in –'

'Oh, for fuck's sake –'

'Well, *aren't* you?'

'Course I am. But I never said that.'

'You didn't need to. He thinks you and Bri think he's a fucking idiot who can't see beyond the end of his nose and has a head full of stupid dreams. And no, he didn't say that,' he added. 'Because *he* didn't need to either. That's the line you've been spinning him because it's the only one you've got. And he's much too bright a kid to buy it.'

Christine felt her hackles rising, despite herself. Her brother had only been back in their lives a matter of weeks, and he'd already nailed it. She hated that. 'Nicky, I'm not saying he doesn't have a chance,' she said. 'Just that he's got to be realistic. To know that the odds against him actually *making* it are just –'

He shook his head. 'No, you're *not* saying that, sis. Okay,' he added then, correcting himself, 'say you *are* saying that. Well, you're wrong. The thing is that Joey *does* have a chance – you of all people should know that. You know how good he is, and if you bit the fucking bullet and went and watched him in action, you'd *see* that for yourself.'

Christine winced. Here we go, she thought. Now I get the big-brother lecture. 'Course I'd bloody see it,' she snapped. 'I don't need *you* to tell me that, for Christ's sake. But this is the real world, Nick. As you, of *all people*, should know. How many bloody kids like Joey have the same crazy ideas? This whole pie-in-the-sky idea that they're going to *be* someone? Be lording it around the place, driving bloody Ferraris? You know as well as I do that most of them end up scratching a living – that's if they can make one at all. I just don't want him chasing some stupid dream because that bastard's turned his head – given him all these ridiculous ideas that he's going to be some bloody rock star, and plying him with –'

'Chris, that's not what I meant and you know it. Joey's not that stupid – or that naïve, for that matter. And what's so bad about him just playing at weekends? What's wrong with that? What's wrong with giving him a bit of bloody encouragement? Christ knows, you're a bloody fool if you think pushing a bloody window cart round the street's going to make him happy – because it won't, however much you and Bri keep banging on about him not getting ideas above his station. Yes, he'll do it. He's a good kid and he's a worker. But perhaps he *should* be aiming higher and you – we – should be supporting him. Believe me, if you'd spent the amount of time I have banged up in a fucking cell, thinking about all the things I could have been doing, maybe you'd appreciate that.'

They locked gazes. And it was Christine who lowered her eyes first, torn between slapping her brother (and she knew she wouldn't regret it this time, either) – for playing *that* bloody card; that bloody ace he always held – and drumming her fists against his chest and sobbing at the unfairness of it all.

'Look, I'm sorry, right,' he said, before she could do either. 'But you know as well as I do that if the name "Mo" wasn't in the picture, you'd be as excited for him as he is, window round or no fucking window round. You'd be round the bloody neighbourhood like a dose of clap, telling everyone who'd listen. Bottom line is that this is *all* about Mo.' He reached for her Benson & Hedges and pulled one from the packet. 'May I? And look, don't go off on one, but I was thinking about all this on the way back, and has it ever occurred to you that maybe all this is a *good* thing?'

Christine stared. 'I can't believe you even said that.'

Nicky shook his head as he lit the ciggie. 'No, no – hear me out on this, sis. I mean, is it such a terrible thing that Mo is actually *contributing* something to his life? And I don't mean that bloody drum kit – I mean actually giving him a bit of a leg-up.'

'Oh, yeah, right. And there's a bloody pig flying by!'

'But what if it *is* that? What if that *is* all there is to it? That he's taken a shine to him – and why wouldn't he? Joey's sharp and he's talented. And I've heard nothing that makes me think it's anything more than that.'

'Oh, yeah, right.'

'Chris, don't pull that face. If there was, you know I'd be the first to tell you. And what about trusting Joey a bit more, for that matter? He's not *that* wet behind the ears. He wouldn't get involved in anything dodgy. Christ, he's had enough opportunities to – and he hasn't gone off the rails yet, has he? He's so squeaky clean he could wash those fucking windows with his bare arse, and you know it. And besides,' he added before Christine could respond, 'this is about him, not about you. Why should he be denied the chance to get to know his dad just because of what happened to you nearly twenty years ago?'

Christine bunched her hands into fists. How dare her brother call Mo that. 'Because he's a monster!' she said. She knew her voice was getting shrill now. 'Because he has no right – no *fucking* right! – to be doing this! Christ, if Joey knew how he'd abandoned him –'

'Oh, and you're going to tell Joey that now, are you?'

'I bloody should. The more I think about it …'

'Like you think that would help him?'

'It would at least mean the scales fell from his fucking eyes!'

Nicky nodded. Almost to himself. 'Yeah,' he said. 'Yeah, it would definitely do that. And what then? How would that help him? What d'you think that would do to him?'

He was tapping his temple. 'Oh, for Christ's sake, Nick,' she said, the frustration and anger boiling in her. 'You think you're so bloody clever. But you're not. I'm his *mam*, okay? And Mo has no fucking right –'

'It's not *about* rights. It's about what's best for Joey!'

'Yeah, right,' she said again. 'So what's best for Joey is to be in the pocket of a fucking drug dealer, is it? One who couldn't give a shit about him till he pops up and adopts him as a fucking project. The big I am. Father of the fucking century!' She took a breath, overwhelmed by the enormity of it all. 'While we just sit back and watch it happen. That's it, is it? Yeah, that's a brilliant plan, that is.' She reached for her cigarettes and pulled one out with fumbling fingers. 'Over my dead body. God, I wish *he'd* just die.'

'Yeah, well he's not going to, and you keep on the way you are, that's exactly what will happen. You've got to keep *your* head, Chris. Let it take its course. Chances are Joey will reach that conclusion himself anyway. But maybe he won't. That's the thing here. You made the choice not to tell him a long time ago –'

'Yeah, like you *would* have, in my shoes?'

Nicky paused, seeming to think.

'Yeah, you know what? I think I would have. I mean, look at us. Look at how it was for us, not knowing who *our* dads were. Look how fucking messed up *we* were. We *are*.' He looked hard at her. 'It's not *about* you,' he said again, more softly. 'You don't get a say in this – it's done. And anything you say now will just make it worse. You've got to let it run its course.'

His relentless reasoning was becoming like vinegar in a cut. 'You just don't get it, do you? He's up to something. To get back at me –'

'Why the hell would he want to do that?' Nicky said. 'He's probably not given you a thought in twenty fucking years!'

'Eighteen, actually,' she pointed out. 'No, make that seventeen – when he fucking denied he was even his father! Nick, you're not seeing it. This *is* as much about me as it is Joey. I just *know* it is. He's worked it out and he's just bloody playing me. Just because he can. Me *and* Bri. Just for the fun of it. Just like a fucking dog pisses up a wall to mark its territory.'

'For *what?*' Nicky asked. 'You really think he cares that much about some girl he got up the duff twenty years back?'

The kettle had boiled and began belching steam between them. 'The only thing Mo cares about is Mo,' she said. 'Mo and money. And power,' she added bitterly. 'He'll be doing it just because he *can* do it. For sport.' She crushed out the cigarette Nicky had just lit for her. 'And he holds all the cards, doesn't he?' She felt chilled. Hounded by dread. Like she was being dragged behind a runaway horse. She looked at her brother. 'And how soon before *he* tells him who he is?'

Christine was woken by the sound of rain slapping against the bedroom windows. The quarter light was open and the sound seemed to fill the room. Heavy rain, which seemed as if it was being chucked at the glass almost horizontally by the bursts of squally wind. She thought immediately of her washing. Had she left any out? No. And then about Joey, who wasn't tucked up in his bed.

It wasn't yet fully light, and Brian was snoring beside her, his sleep apparently dreamless and untroubled. As it would be, because she'd decided not to tell him about the words she'd had with Joey. She didn't have the stomach to go through it all again. She never lied to him, and having done so had left a bad taste in her mouth, but with Nicky already out again when Brian had come home from work, it had just seemed so much easier not to mention it. Kinder to leave it. Brian was tired after a long shift at work and didn't need it. And knowing him he'd probably go haring off round there himself. So she'd kept things light, popped to the chippy, and they'd sat down and eaten, and she'd told him Joey was staying over at Paula's. The lie – the white lie – had tripped all too easily off her tongue.

She stared up at the ceiling now, gripped by a powerful urge to wake him and tell him. And she would have, had it not entered her brain with such conviction – the notion, half-formed as she'd drifted off finally in the small hours – that, sooner or later, Mo *would* tell Joey. She knew it. She knew him. And in a way neither Brian nor Nicky did. She knew, as a woman, exactly the kind of man he was. That was the thing everyone else seemed to forget. She knew him well enough to know how his twisted mind worked. He was like an elephant – people crossed him and he never forgot. Or missed an opportunity to get even. Particularly when it came to women, whom he treated with contempt.

No, there was only one way she could be sure Mo wouldn't bring her world crashing down. If she bit the bullet – that was the stupid term Nicky had used, hadn't he? It felt appropriate. If she took a trip to his sodding club and spoke to him herself.

Chapter 10

Be the man your father never was. Mo had never forgotten being told that. By his mum's younger sister – his dead mum's younger sister. A woman whose memory burned much more brightly than his mum's did, because she'd died when he was not much more than three.

He remembered where he'd been, too, when he'd been told that. Not long out of prison, not long settled in Spain – as far as he could get to escape the ferrety attentions of DI fucking Daley. A place where he could rebuild his empire undisturbed. At the Tikki Bar in Puerto Banús, more specifically; a piece of the Caribbean on the posh part of the Costa, that he'd set up with his partner and friend, Brown Benny. Like Mo, Benny had done time – in his case, in London – having been caught with a car boot full of fake twenty-pound notes.

The call had come via the girl Mo employed to mind his villa, and who'd given his aunt the number, as being the place she could most likely track him down.

He remembered being in two minds about whether to take the call, too. As a rule, Mo didn't need to take calls he didn't want to. The name Marcia hadn't immediately registered either. When Benny's lad had come across and said there was a call for him from a Marcia, he'd first off assumed it was some bird he might have messed around with, or just messed around. No doubt with some tedious teary female rant.

'She said it's about family,' the boy had persisted, and Mo had hesitated. The lad was well trained in interrogating unexpected callers. If he thought Mo should take it, then maybe he should.

'It's Shah,' she had said, without preamble, once he'd answered. She'd only ever been known as that – just between the two of them, always Shah. He'd no memory of it himself but she'd told him when he was older. That, back during those first terrible months after his mum died, he'd wail for her apparently – 'Marcia! *Marcia*! Mar*shah*!' And his dad, mad with grief, would go running to fetch her. And she'd come. For a while, at least. Till it all got too shitty. Till she met a 'decent' man and moved far, far away – somewhere in London, they'd gone. And even she – saint that she'd been through it all – couldn't, wouldn't, separate him from his dad. And so left him to his fate. Which became even shittier. Because his dad had lost a wife and been left with a son, when – and he never tired of telling Mo this – it should have been the other way a-fucking-round.

He barely saw her after that. Couple of times a year, no more. And each time she did she'd have this look in her eye. Something like regret, but never quite enough. When he'd run away, he'd gone there, but he was too big, too angry. Even she couldn't deal with him then.

'Your father's dead,' Shah said briskly. 'Thought you might want to know.'

'You thought wrong.'

That's what he'd said. And he'd meant it. The scars – emotional and physical – were too deep. The memory of endless evenings cowering in his filthy box bedroom while his father, blind drunk, but with ears like a fucking elephant, played cards with his dole money and more often than not lost. It made little difference. Win or lose, he'd still strap him.

Mo still meant it now. That would never change, ever. But he'd never forgotten what she'd said to him, either, ten minutes into what had turned out to be an epic conversation, mostly detailing the reasons why he needed to sort his life out. Stop dealing in gear. Stop going to prison. Stop treating the world like it owes you a bloody living. Try making one – an honest one. Make your mum proud, you hear me? You've learned your lesson now. Grow up. Be the man your father never was.

Well, he was always going to be *that*. Hardly fucking hard, was it? He leaned forward on his chair and blew cigar ash off the papers he was sorting. Silks had had a good week. A great week, in fact. A week certainly good enough to make his unlikely extravagance vis-à-vis the lad Joey feel justified.

Be the man your father never was. I'm doing that, Shah, he thought, as he spiked a pile of receipts. And, of course, the takings from the club were only half the story.

'Boss?' Mo looked up. Big Billy had popped his head round the door. He was sound, Billy – the sort of hired hand who knew where his bread was buttered. He was really Nico's lad (if 'lad' was strictly the word, which it wasn't) but now they were partners, and they were both paying his wages, Billy seemed to have no difficulty adopting Mo as a boss too. Which tickled Mo. Though at the same time, he knew how things worked. If he ever crossed Nico – highly unlikely, but never say never – there'd be no 'boss' about it. And Billy's particular brand of talent was well known.

Mo raised his eyebrows in enquiry as he stubbed his cigar out.

'There's someone here wants to see you. A bird.'

'Name of?'

'Christine,' said a woman's voice, this time, pretty shrill. Then the sound of a slight scuffle outside.

Billy's head popped back out of sight then the door fully opened. 'Hey,' he started. 'You can't just – *hey*!'

And in she bowled.

How long had it been now? Mo wondered. Then he mentally corrected himself. Sixteen years, give or take. And she'd changed. So much so that it gave him pause – Jesus, she looked *so* like her mother. He held her gaze. She looked like she had inherited her mother's attitude as well.

He raised a hand. 'You're alright, Billy,' he said. 'Go on. I've got this.' Then, once Billy had shuffled out and pulled the door shut after him, to Christine, 'Well, well, girl. Long time no see.'

He gestured to the chair she was currently standing behind. Slim rather than skinny. Still pert. Good hair. A T-shirt and jeans on. He let his gaze linger. No trace of the raddled addict he'd last clapped eyes on years back. Mo had no time for drunks or crackheads. He'd had no time for her.

He wasn't sure if he did now, guessing what she'd come to chew his ear about. He wondered if her own ears might have been burning lately, too.

She sat on the chair, pulling it forward by digging her heels into the carpet. 'What's your game?' she said. 'What d'you think you're playing at, Mo?'

He leaned back in his own chair, conscious of his bulk and how slight she looked in comparison now she was seated. He watched her eyes taking stock, her gaze darting round the office, lingering here and there, looking for trouble.

'I don't play games, girl. You know that,' he said mildly.

She made a sound, a sort of snort. Pushing her lips out in a kind of pout. 'Yeah, right,' she said. Then seemed to want to correct her expression. Like she hadn't yet decided – now she was in here – quite how to play him. If that were even possible, which it wasn't. She should know that.

'Yes, right,' he repeated. Then tented his fingers and waited.

'Mo, what do you think you're *up* to?' she said, leaning her body forwards. 'What's your game? A fucking *drum* kit?'

He enjoyed seeing her agitated. Shades of the fiery mother he'd so often sparred with. To think blow-job fucking Brian was shagging her. It beggared belief.

He spread his hands. 'I like the boy. He's got something. He's –'

'So what are you? Father bloody Christmas? Mo –' She leaned closer. 'Why are you doing this? What do you want from him?'

'Nothing.' It was the truth. And he was happy to admit it. It irritated him that she couldn't seem to see that for herself. He knew Joey didn't need anything from him anyway. That was his charm. Bottom line, Joey didn't *need* anything from anyone. Wanted stuff, sure – what kid didn't at his age? But didn't *need* anything. Because he was in a good place in his head. Because he hadn't had a fuck-up of a life, bottom line. Fair play to Brian. Though that beggared belief too. How did so much shit end up coming up roses?

'I like the boy,' he said again. 'I told you. He's a good kid. You should be proud.'

His words seem to electrify her. 'Christ, you think we're *not*? He's our boy, Mo. *Ours*. You can't just turn up and start trying to turn his head like this. You can't just come waltzing in and messing with his head the way you're doing. You can't –'

'Tell him who I am?'

'*No*! You even *think* about it and –'

'I hadn't been.'

'Yeah, *right*,' she said again. 'I know you. Don't you forget that. I don't know what's going through that twisted fucking mind of yours, but if you so much as put the slightest idea in his head, then –'

'What?' He shook his head. 'Babe, you know, you've not thought this through. Why would I want him to know who I am when we're getting on so well?' He leaned in. He could smell her. Some cheap body spray. Not unpleasant. Something had shifted between them. He wasn't sure what. 'He's a nice kid,' he said again. 'And a looker. Good genes.'

He raised his brows, but only slightly, the reference clear enough.

Her eyes glittered. 'Just back off, okay? Just back off him. Leave him alone. You've no right –'

'It's not about rights. Joey's an adult. I'd say it's up to him what he does, wouldn't you? And right now I'm in a position to help him.' He smiled. 'And I'd like to. If he'll let me.'

She exhaled hard. Then drew a breath in. '*Why*, Mo? Why are you *doing* this? All these bloody years and you come back and – are you trying to get him off me? Get back at me? Is that it?'

'I'm not trying to get anything,' he said. 'I just wanted to do right by him. Well, as far as I can do. Which doesn't take me far, I know. Whatever. It's what it is. Call it a whim.'

'A fucking *whim*? This is his *life*, you scheming bastard! A life you have no right to meddle in. You had your chance, you walked away. You didn't fucking want to *know*!'

It was in that moment that Mo properly saw her. Saw the piece of scraggy arse she'd once been and how soon, having bedded her, he'd come to despise her. He'd not spent a single moment thinking about it since, much less regretting it. But now he saw it all so well. He'd been a piece of shit too.

He almost owed her. But not her. He owed the kid, just the kid.

'And I hold my hands up to that,' he said softly, sensing the power he had over her. It suddenly hit him that perhaps she had more to lose in this than he did.

She seemed to shrink a little. Had she just had the very same thought?

'Just don't, Mo,' she whispered. 'Just don't.'

'Is that a threat?'

'And don't fucking speak like you're in a bloody gangster film,' she spat at him. 'Just don't tell him. Back off, Mo. I mean it.'

'I had no intention, babe. I just told you,' he said.

And in that instant, he realised he didn't mean it at all. She'd forgotten. No one told him what to do.

Chapter 11

Joey climbed down the ladder he had only just climbed up. 'Bloody typical,' he huffed as he finally reached the ground. Heavy raindrops were already soaking into his T-shirt, and he knew there was little point in carrying on.

Not that he hadn't had due warning. In what had seemed like no time – no more than half an hour, tops – the sky had turned from brilliant blue to grey and then to charcoal, as a mass of hefty storm clouds had rumbled across the horizon, effectively putting paid to his plans – not to mention his earnings – for the day. How could the weather change so bloody quickly?

He could hear his dad's voice in his ear then, because he'd heard it so often. *That's what it's like in this job, son. So you'd better get used to it.*

But had he? He went round the ladder and rapped on the door of number 26, and waited for the lad inside to shuffle out.

'Tell your mam I'll be back later in the week to finish off the front,' he told the boy. 'No point doing it in this, is there? I'd just be taking her money off her for fuck-all.'

The lad was mixed-race, like he was, around fourteen or so. He held up his hand to reveal a fiver and grinned before stuffing it decisively into his inside parka pocket. 'Nice one,' he said, giving Joey a satisfied smile. 'Gives me a couple of days to earn this back then, doesn't it?'

Joey laughed. 'That's my bloody wages, that is, you little toerag. Well,' he added, as he began to collapse his ladder. 'On your own head be it. If she kills you, she kills you.'

He was just about to add that he at least admired the boy's sense of enterprise, when he felt a buzzing starting up in his jeans pocket. Managing not to jump – the bloody pager surprised him every single time – he puffed out his chest as he produced it. 'You'll have to excuse me a minute, mate,' he said, noting the kid's look of awe. 'I've got to be off now. Got to get hold of my business manager.'

'Fucking hell,' the lad said. 'Didn't realise window men even had *business* managers.' He hoicked a thumb up and jabbed it over his shoulder. 'You can use our phone if you want. Mam's out shopping but I know the pin code.' Joey smiled. Impressed by the pager, the lad was clearly keen to impress as well. 'Always uses my birthday, she does, the dozy cow.'

Joey pondered for all of five seconds. The lad's mam wouldn't mind – she was one of his regulars. And if Mo was trying to contact him this early in the day, it was odds-on that it would be something important.

He followed the boy into the stuffy interior, then stood and watched as he broke his mother's code to use the phone.

'Cheers, kid. You'll go far,' he said, as he took the receiver and punched out the numbers, turning his back slightly so the lad couldn't see them. Not that he was paranoid, exactly, but neither was he careless, and Mo had told him it was confidential.

'Where are you, lad?' Mo asked as soon as the line connected.

'At work. Well, I was,' he said. 'Fucking rain's put paid to that now.'

'Good,' said Mo. 'Good.'

'Well, I'm not sure about that, Mo. It's –'

'So you're free?'

'Well, I suppose so.'

'And your Paula's not with you?'

'Nah, she's at work, she's –'

'Good. I'll send Billy round to you then.'

'Billy?'

'Big Billy. To bring you over to mine.'

Joey was struggling to keep up. 'What, to the club?'

'No, to the house.'

'But I've got my cart and that,' Joey pointed out. 'I'll have to take that home first –'

'Twenty minutes then? Let me see. At The Bull car park? Yes, that'll work. He'll see you there.'

'But –' Joey began.

'Nothing to worry about, son,' Mo said. 'I just need a word.'

The line clicked to end the call before he could answer.

* * *

Joey had been home two days. Paula had made him. So he could wake up at home on his birthday, which she'd insisted was important. He smiled at the memory of his first birthday present, too, because Paula had stayed over as well. And he'd been glad that his mam and dad had had a bit to drink that evening, because she wasn't that good at keeping quiet about giving him his present, either; she'd been giggling and larking about like a bloody schoolgirl. Who knew sex could be so funny? But it was. And he'd jammed a pillow down the back of the headboard for good measure.

She'd bought him a beautiful pair of drumsticks with his name engraved on them, and a posh brand of aftershave, and a denim shirt. And Nicky had slipped him a surprising twenty quid – which Joey knew he couldn't afford – and had been all wet-eyed and soppy and embarrassing about it too. He didn't quite get his uncle Nicky now he was properly getting to know him – half the time he was this ex-con hard man, who nobody would dare mess with, and the other half as emotional as fuck.

His mam had even baked him a birthday cake. Chocolate, three layers, the full eighteen candles. 'Got up early specially,' she'd told him, 'while you were both *fast asleep* in bed.' Which had made him and Paula blush to their hair roots.

And bit by bit they'd arrived at a strained kind of truce. Nothing said. Well, bar his mam saying sorry for slapping him and him apologising for what he'd said. Least said soonest mended. Done and dusted. Forgotten. And it was okay. Not quite normal, but okay.

Still, given where he was going now, he didn't want to face her – or his dad or uncle, for that matter – so, just in case they were in (he wasn't sure what shifts they were working, he could never keep track) he took the cart round the back way, where it was unlikely they'd see him, and wheeled it behind the shed before walking down to The Bull.

Big Billy was already there, revving up Mo's black BMW, one pudgy pink arm – it was almost like a leg of lamb, Joey thought – hanging from the open window. Seeing Joey, he raised it in greeting.

'What's the emergency then?' Joey asked as he slid into the embrace of the smooth leather passenger seat.

Billy shrugged. 'Fucked if I know, lad,' he said. 'I'm like the three wise monkeys' dumb cousin, me – hear fuck-all, see fuck-all and say fuck-all.' He laughed loudly at his own joke as he pulled out of the car park. 'I'm just the hired muscle, mate. No good asking me owt.'

So Joey didn't. He was happy enough to listen to the radio anyway, and just enjoy the sensation of being driven around Bradford by a hired driver, in a top-of-the-range Beema. Though, were it his, *he'd* be the one behind the wheel. And it wouldn't be a BMW, it would be a Jaguar. Though he couldn't help wondering about his unexpected summons. And to the house rather than the club. Alone. Why?

It was no more than fifteen minutes before Billy pulled up at the gates to Mo's mansion, which looked no less imposing than when he'd been there before. More, even, on account of him not feeling quite prepared. He wished he'd nipped inside and changed into a different pair of jeans – his were still slightly damp, and a small mark on the thigh that he'd only just noticed made him feel slightly anxious and scruffy. He can take me as he finds me, he told himself sternly as he climbed out, echoing another of his dad's endless sermons.

'You can walk up from here,' Billy said, 'while I fuck off and play with the car for a bit. I'll see you when I see you.' He then must have pressed something – or Mo had, from inside the house – because the gates began parting to admit him.

Just like the previous time Joey had come here, Mo was already standing on the doorstep, only this time he was dressed in normal clothes. Well, normal for Mo – which was a world away from normal for Joey. A dark grey suit – had he come from, or was he heading to, a meeting? – and a brilliant white shirt to match his teeth.

His dreads were tied back, and a pair of shades was stuck into them.

He pulled them out and donned them as Joey began taking off his trainers; placing his left foot behind his right so he could wriggle the first foot out. 'Don't worry about that, son,' Mo told him, touching his arm. 'Just wipe them. This isn't Buckingham Palace – just my home.'

It seemed an odd thing to say. But then this felt like an odd encounter. Joey didn't know why, exactly, but it felt so even so. He wiped his feet on the coir doormat, then followed Mo over the threshold, where he wiped his feet on the inside doormat as well.

This time, he followed Mo into the vast chrome and granite fitted kitchen – which, even more than last time, looked like somewhere no one actually did any cooking. Had Mo's 'girl', Marika, just been? But then he reflected that Mo probably didn't spend much time here. Living alone, in this vast place, must be a very different business than in the overcrowded terrace he shared with his mam and dad, and now Nicky. He wondered if Mo ever felt lonely.

He felt glad, then, that Paula had persuaded him to go home. As his dad had said gently to him only yesterday, he'd punished his mam enough.

'Take a seat, boy,' Mo said, pointing to a black leather bar stool – one of four that were arranged around a free-standing breakfast bar. 'It's called an Island,' Paula had whispered to him the last time. 'You want some coffee?' Mo asked him, nodding in the direction of a complicated machine that stood hissing on the adjacent worktop.

Joey climbed up onto the nearest stool, careful not to place his hands on the pristine and fingerprint-free granite.

Joey had already smelled the coffee, and he nodded a yes. Wake up and smell the coffee, he thought to himself. Well, he was certainly doing that right now. He drank in the aroma. Proper coffee, too. He couldn't wait to tell Paula. And with the thought came a memory that he held very dear. Of Paula saying, when she'd stayed over, the night he'd gone back, that when they got their own place, the first thing they would do would be to buy a proper percolator. How did that happen? How'd you get from going out a couple of times to planning to live together in so short a time? It was as unexpected as it was exhilarating, but it was infinitely more exhilarating. Was that how it worked? That when you knew, you just knew?

After some ceremony – elegant cups in matching saucers, a fancy cream jug, tiny teaspoons – Mo finally handed Joey his coffee and sat down opposite him.

'This is the life,' Joey said, because the occasion seemed to call for it. 'I tell you what, if me and my Paula ever make it big, we're going to have a place just like this too.' He felt himself redden under Mo's benign scrutiny. '"If" being very much the operative word,' he added quickly.

Mo, who'd taken a delicate first sip, set down his cup and shook his head. 'Don't use the word "if", boy,' he said. 'That's just setting yourself up to fail. Use the word "when", always. Say "when" you make it big. And even if that isn't what you're doing right now – yet – always *intend* on making it big. Always.'

Joey grinned. 'Is that what you brought me here for, Mo? A pep talk?' Then cursed himself for his boldness because it seemed to displease Mo, who stood up abruptly, and went to the window, where he stared silently out across the vast expanse of garden. Or at least that was what it looked like; he could be staring into space. He had his hands in his trouser pockets and Joey could see the tense way in which he was holding himself.

Joey picked up his own cup – the handles were so small it was a job getting his finger into the hole – and wondered if Mo was about to let him go. Or tell him things at the club weren't working out. Something bad, anyway. The little speech – and the way Mo had said it – had felt altogether like the sort of thing you'd say when you were about to let someone down.

'What is it, Mo? Did we do something wrong?' Joey asked finally, the sound of silence getting altogether too loud. 'Are things still alright down at the club?'

He braced, waiting to hear that everything had gone tits up before he'd even got started. He hadn't forgotten how many clubs had been set up and closed down before this one. Oh, how his mum would bloody crow.

Mo shook his head and turned around, then crossed one ankle over the other, leaning back against the run of kitchen units. His shoes were as brightly polished as the worktops. Did he look like things were going tits up? No.

He sighed. 'There's no easy way to say this, boy, okay? So I'm just gonna say it.'

'Say *what*?' Joey asked him. 'You're fucking scaring me now, Mo.'

Mo's teeth flashed white as he returned from his vigil at the window. He sat down again. 'You're my boy, Joey,' he said. Then nothing more.

Again came that sense that Mo was setting him up for a disappointment. 'Yeah, I know *that*,' Joey said. 'Course I do. I know you have my back.'

'No, Joey,' Mo said. 'I mean that I'm your *father*.'

* * *

When he recounted it later, to Paula, as he obviously would, Joey knew he would struggle to find words to describe it – that 'what the fuck?' moment when he thought Mo was kidding, then the thump in his chest and, as the blood flowed in his temples, a sensation of falling – of almost spinning out – when, no more than half a second later (it was almost instantaneous), he knew without question that Mo was not kidding at all.

And perhaps he *had* disappeared somewhere, even as he was rooted to the spot.

'Joey.' Mo's voice was sharp. '*Joey*, are you hearing what I'm saying? I'm your father. You're my son.'

Joey grabbed the slab of granite now, making claw marks instead of fingerprints, entirely clueless as to how he should process what he was being told. What exactly did you do with that kind of information anyway? What did it mean? What did it change? He pulled Mo back into focus, seeing him anew. Seeing him as a man he barely knew. And was his father. It changed *every* fucking thing.

'Look, boy,' Mo said, reaching out a manicured hand towards him but not touching him. 'I'm not out to make trouble. I'm not out to make a cunt out of you, okay? I just wanted you to know. So you know. So you see where I'm coming from. Fuck, boy, I knew the very minute I first clocked you. Someone told me you were Christine's and it was, like, whap!' He clicked his fingers. 'I'd have known even if they hadn't. I'd have worked it out.'

Joey felt a sudden welling of emotion that he couldn't put a name to. Just everything, he decided, just the whole fucking *bigness* of it all. He searched Mo's face – not for meaning; Mo's meaning couldn't have been plainer – but for points of physical similarity; for landmarks he could recognise in the handsome, leonine face. Features that could be singled out and ticked off and counted. The same jawline, the same eyes, the same fucking smile, even. Why the fuck had he not noticed any of this before?

Oh, you are so your mother's son! People said that to him often. Had done so all his life – *oh, you're the spit of your mam, Joey! Such a Parker!* And all this despite the one glaring bloody fact that no Parker alive had ever had brown skin and a head of wayward curls. Despite? Or because of? That point hit him hard now. Just how hard everyone worked to try and help him forget the stark reality that he wasn't just a Parker – he was something else too.

He was Mo's. He shared half of his genes.

'You need some time,' Mo said, clearly interpreting his racing thoughts. 'I get that, and I'm sorry to just lay it all on you like this. It's a lot to swallow. But it's a fact, and you needed to know the truth.'

Truth. Joey found himself jolted into a completely different mindset. Truth. And its opposite – lies. The lie he'd lived with all his life, more specifically.

The questions teeming in his mind became more and more urgent. 'Why?' Joey asked Mo, the polite coffee break now forgotten. 'Why now? Why not fucking years ago?' He paused, but not for long. 'Why not back when I was a kid and didn't know why my dad didn't want me? Had *disowned* me. Why my mam wouldn't tell me. Why I had a step-dad but –' Another thought hit him hard. 'Does my dad even *know* about this?'

Mo nodded. 'Yes, he does. He's always known, Joey. And listen' – he raised his hands, the gold of his rings glinting – 'I have no intention – none, okay – of trying to step in and mug Brian off. He's always been your dad, and from what I've seen so far, it seems like he's made a great job of it, too. No matter about our past.' *What* past? Joey filed the thought away. 'I have respect for him for that. Big respect,' Mo continued. 'And, you know, you and me are both men now; we don't need to have *that* kind of relationship. Just a kinship. If that's what you want, of course. You might not. And in answer to your question, I never thought I'd see you again, and that's the truth of it. And I can't make up for all those years. Fuck me – I'd never attempt to even *try*. I just hoped – and I still hope – that once we became friends, we might stay that way, you know? Which is why I had to tell you the truth. Friends don't lie to each other, do they? I didn't want to deceive you for any longer than I had to.'

Joey felt a flash of anger, trying to understand what he was hearing. So this man – this man who'd *made* him – who had walked away from him and not looked back – and then, his whole lifetime later – *Christ* – had turned up, realised what he'd been looking at and had calmly thought it all through? The job. *Christ* – the fucking *drum kit*. He thought back to how much he'd preened and simpered about it. What he'd said to his mam and dad. How fucking arrogant he'd been. And he felt unclean. Manipulated. But most of all unclean.

'So you thought you'd *buy* me first?' The words came out unbidden. Words he didn't think he had the balls to say. He registered somewhere that his new status had actually *given* him those balls. 'Give me a job, sort out our kit, lay on a fucking rehearsal room. *Then* spring it on me?' He pushed away his coffee cup, pushed back the bar stool, and stood up. 'Mo, you can't buy me. You're right, I've been brought up better than that.'

Mo shook his head. '*Buy* you? No, boy. Never that. I have no interest in buying you. Why would I?' The hands were raised again. 'What exactly would I be buying?'

He let the question lie and Joey realised he couldn't answer it – well, not if he had any sense of his own utter insignificance in this successful man's life. Which he did.

'I *liked* you,' Mo went on. 'Simple as. I liked you and I saw something in you. I wanted to help you get set up.' He smiled an awkward smile. 'Who knows; maybe I'd have done all that even if it wasn't for all this.' He slipped off his own bar stool and came around the island. 'Listen, let's get you a drink, eh? A proper drink. You look like you could use one.' He put a hand on Joey's shoulder and patted it lightly. 'And so could I.'

Joey had thought he would go then. Just leave the house, walk away, try to get his head round everything. The kitchen – the vast kitchen – felt increasingly claustrophobic. But he had too many questions tethering him there; rooting him to the spot. So he was still there – staring out across the perfect lawn, just as Mo had done earlier – when a deeply engraved glass was pressed into his hand, containing some kind of amber liquid.

'Here,' Mo said. 'Get that down you. Take a moment.'

Joey took a glug. It tasted sharp and burned his throat. Whisky, he presumed. 'So how did I come about?' he said eventually, having taken a second sip.

Mo seemed to have been anticipating the question. He stood alongside Joey, gazing out again on the country garden vista. He obviously had someone in to do that for him too, Joey realised. To make the garden look like it was out of some fancy *Country Life* magazine. In the middle of fucking *Bradford*.

'Me and your mum,' Mo said, not turning to look at Joey. 'Well, it was complicated. Not a healthy relationship. Not by any means. And once we were done … well, we were done. It was simple as that, Joey.' He turned to look at him. Joey met his earnest gaze reluctantly. 'I didn't walk away from you. I never even knew she was pregnant until after she'd fucked me off, I swear. And then … well, let's just say she made it clear I should stay out of her life, and yours too.' A long pause. Mo drained his own glass. 'Things were crazy back then,' he said. 'Things were different.'

Different. Well, yeah, they would be, wouldn't they? Joey started remembering snippets of conversations he'd retained over the years. The silences whenever he asked about his past. The whispers after he left the room. The way Nicky often looked at him. Fucking hell, chances were his uncle *Nicky* knew as well. But then, why wouldn't he?

His sister had had a baby – and what had his mam been when she'd had him? Sixteen? Seventeen? He tried to imagine Mo with her. And then tried hard not to instead. She'd been so *young*. And how old was Mo? Older. So much older. Fuck. No wonder his mam and dad had lost their minds knowing he was back in Bradford. Specially his mam.

He turned to face Mo. 'But why all the secrecy? I mean, it wasn't like it was ever going to be any big fucking secret that I wasn't Dad's, was it? I mean, *look* at me. Why wasn't I told? Why wasn't I told that my real dad had fucked off out of my life, like every other kid like me always is?'

He glared at Mo, feeling that same power again in asking the question. In seeing Mo having to conjure up some excuse for himself. As if he could. As if he ever could. Fuck, so-called adults – and it wasn't the first time he'd thought it – were so fucking *un*-adult sometimes. 'Why,' he asked again, 'why all the secrecy?'

But Mo lowered his gaze and only shook his head sadly. 'You'll have to ask your mother about all that, I'm afraid, boy. It wasn't my decision, it was hers. It wasn't my life, it was hers and *yours*. And I had to respect that. Look,' he said, putting his glass down and placing his hands on Joey's shoulders. 'I can be whatever you want me to be, I swear on that. I'll be happy just to see you from time to time – at the club, here, wherever – and support you if you need it. No strings. Beyond that, it's up to you. Your life. Your pace. Nothing needs to change – you know, with the band and the club and that. I just wanted you to know. How you feel

about it, how you act on it, what you want to do about it
– well, that's for you to work out, son.'

Joey looked into Mo's eyes, remembering how he'd been
when he'd approached him. Was that how it had been for
him too? That when you knew, you just knew?

Son. It sent a shiver through Joey.

Chapter 12

Paula had been surprised and a little embarrassed to get the phone call at work, and even more so to find out it had been Joey. Mr Hunter, her boss, didn't approve of staff getting phone calls at work, something she'd established not long after starting work there, when her mam had telephoned her twice in one morning, with various pharmaceutical shopping lists.

'I mean, it's jolly nice,' Mr Hunter said (he often used the word 'jolly'), 'that your mother's giving us her business but, as a rule, it would be better if she told you before you got here. Because I have to keep the line free for emergencies.'

In all the time she'd worked there, Paula hadn't witnessed a single emergency call coming in – such emergencies as there were tended to involve kids with bleeding knees and lips, dragged in by their fractious mothers, or addicts in a stew about getting their methadone dispensed – but Mr Hunter was a nice bloke (a jolly bloke, she'd joked to Joey) and as he bent over backwards to accommodate Paula's musical engagements, she really didn't want to piss him off.

'Fancies you,' Joey had decided. 'End of.'

But Mr Hunter (who Paula was fairly sure *did* fancy her, given the way he looked at her, though not in a way that creeped her out) hadn't seemed displeased when he'd related Joey's message. Which was that he'd be coming to meet her there as soon as she was finished. 'Very polite young man,' Mr Hunter had remarked. 'And I'm sure he wouldn't have called you at work if it wasn't important,' he finished, before Paula had had a chance to apologise.

Now, an hour later, while carefully folding up her whites, she wondered what the important thing was. She popped her name badge in the little plastic pot she and her workmate Susie used for the purpose, and hoped it wasn't an impromptu rehearsal. She already had a date tonight – with a long hot bath and a pedicure, and a read of one of her mam's magazines.

Still, it would be nice to see him. Seeing Joey, though she was loath to admit it, still gave her butterflies. She smiled to herself. And who knew? Perhaps it wasn't a rehearsal he had in mind. Though their options were limited because she'd walked to work this morning; parking was a pain, and when the weather was dry she enjoyed the fresh air and exercise as well.

Not wishing to be scrutinised by Mr Hunter, who was now doing his after-work 'pottering', she said goodnight to Susie and went out to wait in the street. She wondered what Joey had been up to today – after the fine start it had rained in biblical amounts, drying up too late, she reasoned, for him to set out again. Perhaps that was it. Perhaps he was simply at a loose end, and thought he'd come down to meet her just because.

She saw him coming down Little Horton Lane long before he saw her – mostly because he never lifted his head once. She began walking up to meet him, waiting for him to meet her eye so she could wave, but she was almost up to him before he lifted his gaze and saw her.

But, if preoccupied, he still looked pleased to see her. He bent to kiss her and thought better of it, instead wrapping her tightly in his arms. 'God, you smell nice,' he said into her hair.

'Then your nose must need testing,' she said, lifting her head to smile at him. 'I've had half a bottle of cough syrup spilt over me this afternoon. This old lady – one of the regulars, she –' And then she stopped, seeing his expression. 'Babe, what's the matter? What's up?'

Joey had been looking past her and now he looked back. 'You didn't bring your car in today, then?'

'No, I didn't.'

'Can we walk to yours and get it then? I need to get away.'

'What?' Paula said, wondering what on earth he could possibly mean. Back to Dicky's again? What kind of 'away' could he mean?

'Not *away* away,' he corrected, letting his arms fall and taking her hand instead. 'I just need to get my head straight before speaking to Mam and Dad.'

'About what?' Paula asked.

Joey sighed and shook his head. 'I don't even know where to fucking start, babe.'

'At the beginning?' she suggested. 'But, no. No, that's fine. Let's do that. Get the car and go for a drive somewhere or something. Maybe go for some food …'

'That'll be good,' Joey said, tugging on her hand. 'Yeah, let's do that. Come on.'

Joey's stride was long and Paula had to keep adding little skips to keep up with him. 'This thing you've got to get your head straight about,' she said, once they'd covered the length of Southfield Lane without him speaking again. 'Is it a good thing or a bad thing? Can you at least tell me that much?'

He slowed his stride slightly – he could obviously tell she was a bit breathless. And seemed to consider the question before answering. 'It's not good, babe, but it's not bad. Fuck, I don't even know *what* to think.'

'Joey, *tell* me, for God's sake. You're stressing me out here!'

He stopped on the pavement then. 'It's Mo. I've been round his place this afternoon.'

'What, his house?'

'Yes, his house. Paulz, you won't believe this. He says he's my fucking *father*!'

That was the curious thing. Paula believed it absolutely. Yes, she was shocked at first – course she was – but no sooner had she expressed that than she realised it all fitted perfectly. Just from the way her own mam had been

– which she'd not seen at the time – when she'd told her and her dad about the drum kit and the rest, and how Mo had set everything up for the band to rehearse there. She'd seen the look that had passed between her parents; such a strange look, which at the time she'd barely noted. She'd more or less dismissed it as the usual parent thing of being suspicious of those kinds of gifts. You get nowt for nowt in this world, love, remember that. She'd been told stuff like that all her life. But revisiting it now, as they walked the last half-mile before home, she realised that the look had been subtly different. That her mam and dad's eyes had met, and something had passed between them. Like they already knew what the other was thinking. That they knew something about Mo that she didn't.

'I mean, what the fuck am I supposed to think?' Joey was saying, as they reached her house and the car. 'What am I supposed to *do*?'

Her dad's car wasn't there but it was odds-on at least a couple of her siblings would be inside, her mam probably making them their tea. Her car keys were in her bag though, because her door key was with them, so, hoping no one saw them, she quickly unlocked it, and fired it up as soon as Joey had folded himself into the passenger seat. She reminded him to do up his seatbelt.

'I mean, why the fuck did my mam and dad never tell me all this?' he said, once they were driving off down the road.

'Because they thought he'd buggered off and was never coming back?' she suggested. 'Maybe your mam thought it would be easier for you that way? Maybe she thought that was better than missing what you couldn't have?'

'God, I've been such an *idiot*,' he said, as Paula drove. 'This is what it's all been about, isn't it? All the shit she's been giving me lately hasn't been about me at all, has it? It's been about *her*; like her worst nightmare has happened, hasn't it?' He turned in his seat to face Paula. 'But that's what's been doing my head in. Why the hell didn't she just *tell* me who he was? I mean, she must have thought he might tell me, mustn't she? So why didn't *she* do it? Soon as she knew?'

'Maybe because she was sure he wouldn't,' Paula said. 'Maybe she thought that was the last thing he'd do – you know, given that he'd left you so young.'

'Fuck,' he said. 'I just can't *deal* with this.'

They drove on in silence for a bit, before she flicked down the indicator. 'Shall we park up here? Get some fish and chips or something?'

'Yeah, yeah,' Joey said distractedly. 'Yeah, fine. Let's eat something. God, and I was, like, just getting my head round it. You know, with Mam and Dad. Now I don't know what to do, I really don't. Actually, drive on to the one on Park Avenue, babe. I like that one better.'

They did so, then parked up and headed for the chippy, which had been open long enough by now that the inevitable queue had disappeared. And, given that the sun was still warm, opted not to sit in there, but to take it across to the bench beside the bus stop where they could sit in the shade of the huge oak tree behind it.

Paula felt a strange mixture of mild excitement (it *was* exciting, the thought of someone like Mo being Joey's father) and, at the same time, a kind of deflation. All the flattery, the regular gig at Silks, the praise, the lavish rehearsal room, had none of that been quite sincere? She'd always thought it a bit unlikely that he'd bestow so much attention on their modest little tribute band – it had always seemed a bit suspect, truth be told, though she'd been happy to ignore that. And never look a gift horse in the mouth, and all that. So had it all been about Joey? And, if so, what was that all about? What did Mo expect from him in return?

'So what did he say to you?' she asked, while Joey worked rhythmically through the pile of steaming chips. 'You know, about why he told you. What's his plan?' She nudged him. 'Apart from showering you with gifts and compliments, that is.'

Joey held a chip between greasy fingers just short of his mouth. 'There *is* no plan,' he said. 'Well, so he says. Says he just wanted me to know and, like, be friends, kind of thing. That he was happy to help me out – if I wanted him to, anyway. You know, with the music and that. With the band.'

'Which your mam's going to *love*. And your dad. Christ, he's got to be *well* unhappy about all this, isn't he?'

'Why? He's got no reason to be. He's my dad, end of story. Though, Christ, Paula, why didn't they just sit me down and tell me the bloody *truth*? That's what's really got to me – that all this time I've been talking about Mo, and they never thought it would be a good idea to tell me?

Instead they give me all this grief – warn me off him, treat me like I'm a fucking baby – making *me* feel bad, when they've known all along! And just leave *him* to tell me. I mean, why? Why would they fucking *do* that?'

Paula placed her hand on Joey's forearm and leaned against him. 'Calm down, alright? I'm sure they will have had their reasons. Which you're not going to hear unless you sit down with them and *ask* them. And you know what? You've got one answer at least, haven't you? You've always wanted to know who your dad – well, your *biological* dad – was, and now you do. And now it's all out in the open – well, it could turn out to be a real plus in your life, couldn't it? I mean, whatever the differences between him and your mam – well, they're history, aren't they? And your dad doesn't seem the sort of bloke to go off on one about stuff like that. And I'm guessing he didn't even know your mam when, well, you know … And, hey' – she tugged a lock of his hair – 'even better is that you already know him and like him. That's a big plus, isn't it?'

Joey didn't seem so sure. 'Yeah, but it's all different now, isn't it? I looked up to him because I thought he was cool and successful – someone to aspire to be like. Whereas now … Well, whatever he says about it being down to my mam, he still buggered off, didn't he? He didn't *have* to do that, did he?'

Privately, Paula wondered if, actually, he might have. Might have had a short-notice stay at Her Majesty's pleasure – same as Joey's Uncle Nicky. She knew enough about enough to know that Mo and Nico, and their entourage

– not to mention the world they routinely inhabited – weren't exactly shining examples of honest, law-abiding folk. Which didn't worry her unduly – her mam was a Hudson, wasn't she? – but might well explain his disappearance. Not to mention Joey's mam wanting him out of her life. And presumably out of it again now.

But there was no point in speculating. 'You don't know,' Paula told Joey. 'So it seems to me that you need to do as Mo says. *Ask* your mam. See what *she* says about it. What else *can* you do?'

'See, love?' Joey's dad said when he appeared in the living room an hour later. 'Told you he'd be home soon, didn't I?'

Joey's mam's expression made him wonder if he should say anything after all – at least for the moment anyway. She was on the sofa, same as his dad was, both in their usual positions – him at the fire end so he could 'warm up his bones', and her at the other, with her feet in his lap. The electric heater wasn't going – it was too warm for that. But they sat in the same places month in, month out.

Nicky's bedding was becoming a familiar presence, too – thrown every morning in a colourful heap behind the armchair. Home, Joey thought. *His* home. His parents. His family. The only parents – the only family – he'd ever known. The new knowledge he now had about his place in the jigsaw was beginning to feel increasingly unreal.

They were both smoking, and his dad picked up his packet of B&H. 'Want a smoke, son?' he offered, proffering the pack. 'An' there's some stew on the stove if you're hungry.'

Stew in August. His mam and dad's plates and cutlery were on the coffee table, so they'd obviously already eaten. He thought of Mo's elegant dining table. The sheer scale of the room.

'I've already eaten with Paula,' he told them as he took the packet and lighter. His mam glanced past him. 'Is she here, love?' She started getting up.

Joey shook his head. 'No, not tonight. She just dropped me off.'

'Aw,' his mam said. 'It would have been nice to see her. I'm meeting up with her mum later in the week,' she added lightly. And mentioned it for no particular reason, as far as Joey could fathom, except – another thing struck him. They went way back, his mam and Paula's. How far back? Since before him. He'd always known that much. Did she know about Mo as well?

His dad still had half an eye on the telly. He watched the news avidly – especially anything political, and right now they were going on about Northern Ireland – again – and some ceasefire that might be on the cards.

Joey lit a cigarette and inhaled deeply, feeling justified in doing so. He'd been trying to give up – Paula hated him smoking – but right now he knew it would help calm him down. Northern Ireland washed over him – as did his dad's intermittent political rants – but right now he felt a flare of anger against the box in the corner. Back in the real world – his *real* life – a bloody bomb had gone off too. What did his dad – who surely knew – think about *that?*

He went and sat in the armchair. There was no point in going upstairs to dwell on everything. After all, what purpose would it serve apart from winding him up even further? He could see his mum looking at him anxiously.

She knows, he thought. *She knows he's told me.* He met and held her gaze.

'Mam,' he said. 'Dad, I need to talk to you.'

Brian picked up the remote and lowered the volume to a whisper. Why the fuck didn't he just turn it off? 'What's up, son?' he asked, his face suddenly full of concern.

Joey took a breath, and stabbed out the only half-finished cigarette. Where the fuck did you start a conversation like this?

'I know who Mo is,' he said simply. And was about to say more, but the expression on his parents' faces made it clear he didn't need to.

There was a moment of near silence; only the telly continued twittering. And before either spoke, his dad surprised Joey by shunting up the sofa and putting his arm around Christine. He then watched as her face contorted into sobs. It was so far removed from the reaction that he thought he was going to get that for a long moment he didn't know what to do. He didn't think he'd ever seen his mam looking so desolate and it gave him a massive whump of an emotional jolt.

'Mam, why didn't you *tell* me?' he said finally. 'Why did you let this happen? All these years of hiding it from me. *Why?*'

He knew he sounded like a whining child and when Christine stood up, as she abruptly did, it only heightened the sensation. He stood up too, as did Brian. They formed a tense triangle.

'I don't want to talk about it, Joey,' his mam said. 'No, no, I don't mean that. I just can't, Joey.' Her voice was small. 'Not right now. I just *can't.*'

'But *why?*' Joey persisted, feeling his emotions shift again. No way was he letting her just excuse herself like that. 'Mam, I don't understand,' he added. 'And I'm not some kid, you know. I'm a grown man. And I deserve an explanation.'

His dad's warning look made Joey realise how aggressive his tone sounded and though he'd not even shouted at her, Christine had paled. She looked wobbly, even – like she might faint. His dad obviously saw it too, because he grabbed her round the waist. 'Son,' he said, 'you need to leave it for now, mate. Seriously.' Then he turned Christine round and led her out of the room and up the stairs. She was sobbing pretty wretchedly by now, which was doing Joey's head in. What the fuck was going on? What the fuck were they hiding? Could she really be in such a state about something so simple as having had a kid when she wasn't married? Those days were over, weren't they? Or was it because Mo was black? Had there still been some shame in that back then?

Joe didn't think so. And his mam had never seemed ashamed of him. Quite the opposite – she'd have punched anyone who called him names – she used to say that to him often. And bang on and on and on about him being as good as anyone, and to never let anyone ever tell him different. It says everything you need to know about *them*. She'd say that to him all the time. So what, then? Why was it all upsetting her so much?

Joey knew his mam and uncle had never known who their dads were – and he actually believed them when they said they'd never cared. But he *did* care. Only now did it really strike him quite how much. And it wasn't like Mo was some old loser – some useless deadbeat – after all. Did his mam hate him so much that she couldn't see past that? See that Joey had a right to make his own mind up about it?

But it seemed clear he wasn't going to get any answers tonight. They'd been gone ten minutes and his dad didn't seem in any kind of hurry to come back down. Like how *he* felt didn't matter much at all. He shrugged on the jacket he'd only just taken off and left the house again, shutting the door quietly behind him.

'Why the hell are you having a go at me? What have I done, exactly?'

Paula's tone was as defiant as her hands-on-hips stance. And Josie – as she often did these days – heard her own voice, her mam's voice, her *gran's* voice, in her daughter, God help her. She was famed (and she didn't mind) for having one of the loudest gobs on Canterbury Estate and it occurred to her that Paula might soon dethrone her. And as if to ram the point home, Paula hadn't even finished. 'I'm only telling you what Joey told *me*, okay? *Okay?*'

Josie sympathised, but at the same time she knew that taking a firm line was important. Before her daughter went off half-cocked on the whole Mo appreciation thing. It was a delicate job, when it came to youngsters, trying to impart words from the wise and persuading them to listen. Come over too heavy-handed and they tended to go the other way by default. 'And I'm telling *you*, madam,' Josie snapped, 'that you should leave well alone! What's past is past, and you should tell Joey that too. Why's he raking all that shit up? It'll come to no good, trust me. I told you that you lot should never have left The bleeding Sun. You were alright there.'

'All *what* shit?' Paula persisted. 'And we're perfectly alright now, thank you very much. We're making good money and we're enjoying it. Nothing's changed, except for the better. We just now know that Mo's Joey's dad. Simple as that. And it's not like Joey went hunting him down, was it? He found us, remember? He found *us*.'

'Oh, I'll bet he fucking did,' Josie said.

'There you go again,' Paula railed. 'What d'you mean by *that*? Mam, you can't just go off on one about all this and not explain *why*. What's so bad about Mo? If you know something, tell me!'

Josie put a finger to her lips. 'Will you pipe down, young lady, for Christ's sake? You'll have the kids piling in. And if your dad bloody finds out –'

'What?' Paula said. 'What if he does? Mam, you need to tell me because Joey already knows there's some big secret – and he's going to find out anyway.'

Josie wagged the same finger. The sense of inevitability was beginning to weigh heavy. Because Paula was probably right. And *then* where would Christine be? 'Look,' she said, 'it's not for me to say, okay? That's all I can tell you right now. So you just stay right out of it – *right* out of it – till I've had a chance to speak to Christine myself.' She shook her head. 'God, I've always known this was all going to come back and bite her in the arse. Well, now it has, and she's going to need me.' She raised her hand to stop her daughter's next 'What?' coming out. 'That's all I'm saying so don't bleeding pester me about it anymore, Paula. I mean it.'

Paula threw up her own hands. 'Okay, okay!' She looked exasperated with her mother – a look Josie noted she did so well these days. Her baby girl was all grown-up. It was frightening. '*Okay*!' Paula said again, as she stomped off to her bedroom.

But that was just it. When it came out – as it so surely would – things would not by any means be okay, would they?

She set her mouth in a grim line. Damage limitation was probably the best they could hope for.

Chapter 13

Christine lit up her third cigarette in ten minutes. And as she paced the living room, she tried not to allow her mind to become overloaded. *Push it to the back, Chrissy*, she told herself as she drew in the smoke, refusing to focus on anything other than waiting for Josie to arrive.

She hadn't heard Joey come in last night, and felt terrible about letting him go. She didn't even know where he'd gone. And neither did Brian. To that bastard Mo's? Just the thought of it filled her with dread. That and another thought – different, but related. Was there going to be a time when she'd have to stomach them having an actual relationship? She didn't think she could bear it – just the thought of them being buddies together made her feel physically sick. It was only the much bigger thing that lay before her that shut the line of imagining down; so much could happen – so much bad stuff – that if she thought about it too much, she realised she was crazy to even try and see beyond it, no matter how reassuring Brian kept trying to be.

She wouldn't be seeing her son yet today, either. What she *had* heard was his alarm, which had gone off just after five, and then the sound of familiar movements in his bedroom. To think that a few short weeks ago, her biggest

142

anxiety was how she was going to cope with the loss when and if he moved in with Paula. Which had seemed likely – still did – but the business of her missing him paled into significance in comparison to what might happen once he dredged up some answers and found out who his mother *really* was.

That was the horror of it – that he rightly would have so many questions. And barely any of them could she answer honestly. And if he looked at her while he asked them, in the same way he had last night, she wasn't sure she'd be able to keep it together.

She stubbed out the cigarette and looked out of the window for Josie, feeling horribly guilty to have to ask Brian to tell the boss she was sick, but knowing, had she gone in, that she wasn't fit to function. She'd forgotten just how bad she could feel about herself. Quite how shitty. It had been a long time.

'Fucking teacher,' Josie huffed, when she finally burst through the front door. 'Called me *literally* as I was about to walk out of the front door.'

'An emergency?' Christine asked, feeling guilty about that too – that she'd imposed herself on one of Josie's invariably busy days. But her friend shook her head. 'That little git of mine, Louise. Been up to her tricks again. I'm going to have to straighten her *right* out. Only got caught with a bottle of fucking vodka in her school bag. The little twat. Eddie'll kill her when he finds out.' She threw her bag down on the coffee table and jerked her head back towards the hall. 'Where's your Joey? Is he up there?'

Christine flopped down onto the sofa and started saying no, but 'He's gone to work' simply refused to come out of her mouth, Instead she just burst into tears. 'Oh, Josie, I'm proper fucked, mate,' she sobbed, finally letting it out now. 'What the fuck am I gonna do? He's doing his round, but he's bound to be back lunchtime. I feel like running away. Honest. What the fuck am I going to do?'

Josie sat down beside her and patted her lightly on the knee. No fuss, no cooing, no 'there there' kind of stuff. And Christine was glad of it, because it wiped out the years. They might have been sitting there eighteen years back, having a very similar conversation. That was the thing with Josie. She wasn't that much older, but she'd always been like a second mum. Something that right now Christine keenly felt the lack of.

'You could try just telling him the truth,' Josie suggested as she picked up Christine's pack of cigarettes and helped herself to one.

Christine stared at her. 'Oh yeah, right,' she said miserably. 'Course I bleeding can. Um, by the way, Joey, your fucking dad just happened to be shagging your gran when I slept with him and got myself up the duff. Oh, and then,' she said, taking another from the pack Josie was holding out, 'I became a fucking junkie as well. Oh, and while we're on that, that's why you were dragged off to foster care.'

She held the cigarette in shaking fingers, while Josie held out the lighter. 'Trust me, I'd rehearsed all that a million times in my head. Not to mention the bit about Bri being an ex-junkie. Not to mention the whole of the fucking rest.'

'Well, not like fucking *that*! God, *obviously*!' Josie said. 'But yeah, as it happens, I think a version of that might help. Christ, it's out there now, Chrissie. I mean *proper* out there. To be honest it's a fucking miracle he doesn't know the half of it already. It's not like it's ever been a state secret!' She stood up then. 'Come on, you. Come into the kitchen. I need a cuppa, and you need to pull yourself together.'

Christine obediently followed her old friend into the kitchen, already feeling, if not better, at least calmer. Just a bit. 'I went to see him,' she said quietly, while Josie picked up the kettle. 'Mo, I mean. I went to see him.'

Josie span around, almost dropping the kettle. 'You *what*? You have to be kidding me. Are you right in your fucking head, Chrissy? Why on earth would you *do* that? Red rag to a bloody bull!'

'I went to warn him off. I couldn't not. I just had to do *something*.'

'And?' Josie said, jamming the kettle spout under the tap.

'And a fat lot of good it did me. He even seemed to enjoy it.'

'So what did he say?'

'He said he liked Joey, that he wanted to help him. It was bloody horrible. The way he looked at me. Like I was a piece of shit, basically, and he was –'

'Bradford's answer to God all fucking mighty, no doubt. Dear father, who art in heaven … Shit, Chrissie, what possessed you? You'll have just made him worse. Christ, I thought you *knew* what he's like.'

'He's got an ulterior motive, I know he has.'

Josie flung her hands up in the air. 'Tell me something I don't know! He's got a long memory and all, and you're not going to be on his Christmas card list, are you? One word from you and he was always going to do what he fucking wanted. Half a dozen and he did – Christ, mate, what did you think was going to happen? That he'd bow down and apologise? That he'd drop to his knees and beg forgiveness?' She sighed heavily. 'I'll bet he relished every frigging minute.'

Christine started crying again. The tears just seemed to fall out of her eyes. 'He did – I know he did. He fucking loved it all right. I don't know what I was thinking. I was just so *scared*. I still am. I mean, what if all the other stuff comes out?' She let out a big shuddering sob. 'What will my baby think of me then, eh? His mother the slag. His mother the junkie. His mother the … his mother the *murderer*.'

Josie turned to the cupboard and set about making two mugs of tea. 'Babe, get a grip, okay? There's no reason for him to know that. Hardly anybody knows that. Thank God! And those that do – ah. Mate, can I open these digestives?'

Like Josie could even eat! Christine ripped some kitchen roll from the holder and slapped it against her hot face, trying to breathe deep and slow to quell her rising hysteria.

'Come on,' Josie ordered. 'Let's go sit back down.' Then

herded her back into the living room. 'Only a handful of people,' she said again. 'And one of them is dead, so …'

'But the *rumours*,' Christine said. 'You heard them. We all did. What if Mo heard them too? Shit, Mo was even in the same nick as Nicky for a bit.'

'Oh, like Nicky's *bound* to have told him. You're losing the plot, you are. Christ, if you're beginning to worry your own brother was tittle-tattling, you have a screw loose. Why the fuck would he *ever* do that when he went inside for you?'

'But what if –'

'If me auntie had balls, she'd be me fucking uncle!' Josie snapped. 'If *nothing*. You know as well as I do that your Nicky would never have opened his trap, ever. Look at all those years he did, just to protect you. Do you think he'd have given up all that just to accidentally blurt it out? Would he fuck as like!'

Christine knew everything Josie was telling her was true. And felt more guilt for even entertaining the possibility that her brother – so loyal, so good, so bloody heroic – would breathe a single word while there was breath in his body. But knowing that – knowing deep down that it was all so unlikely – didn't ease her anguish much. What Joey could know and might soon know was the full sorry story of his own shabby mother. How much it would hurt him to know the truth about the circumstances of his birth.

She said so.

'You underestimate your son,' Josie told her. 'I've been getting to know him better now. The man – not the kid.

And if you think he'd love you less, you need your head screwing back on. Mate, you're no murderer. It was an accident. It was the fucking drugs that killed Malley. That and the shit you got told about him being a nonce. That wasn't you. That's *not* you. Stop killing yourself over it. Joey wouldn't. Joey won't. I'd stake my own bloody life on that.'

Christine dabbed at her eyes. Perhaps Josie was right. Perhaps he wouldn't. But that wasn't the same as forgiving her, was it? She could already picture the look in his eye, the disappointment, the shame. He might still love her – she loved her own mam – but would he forgive her? She looked into her own heart. Had she? 'Okay,' she said, 'so, say you're right. Say Mo never gets to know all that shit. But why's he done this? That's what frightens me. What's he scheming at? What does he want?'

Josie dunked her biscuit, hung it to drip, then put half of it in her mouth.

'Look, Chrissie,' she said, once she'd swallowed it. 'You won't want to hear this, but I've been thinking, and I really don't think this about you. To tell the truth I don't think there *is* anything else to it. I reckon Mo fucked someone over or something, out in Spain – or wherever he's been hiding out. Who knows? Then had to come back to Bradford, and start up again and all that. And then, bam! Just bumped into the kids one night, just like they said he did. And someone told him who Joey was, and – bam again – he realised. And he *did* like him. Who wouldn't? Simple as that. And if that's the case, what the hell can you do about it? If Joey wants to know him then there's nothing you can do to stop him. You'll just have to suck it up. Come clean and take the flak, if there even is any – God, there's probably half a dozen women within spitting distance of us who've had a kid in exactly the same circumstances as you. Just take it one day at a time. That's all you can do. It's insane to worry over something that hasn't even happened yet.'

'But that's another thing,' Christine said. 'Who the fuck spends years away in prison, then abroad, and can just come back, and walk into a fucking mansion on Oak Lane? Not to mention set up in that sodding great club. Just like that? Come on, we both know where the money must be coming from. He's still up to no good, isn't he? *Must* be. And my Joey –' She had to swallow. She was welling up again. 'My son mixed up in a bloody drugs empire!'

Josie finished a second biscuit. Then she shrugged. 'Well, they say a leopard doesn't change its spots,' she said, 'and yes, you're right. Mo is probably bang at it, just like he always was. But hey, that could actually be *good* for you. If he's handling dodgy money or running Bradford's drugs again, then he's bound to get caught at some point, isn't he? Then, voila – problem solved. Daddy dearest is back behind bars, where he belongs.'

Christine found herself smiling for the first time in what felt like for ever. 'I never thought of that,' she said, because she genuinely hadn't. 'I mean, I could never be a grass, *ever* – but it's only a matter of time, isn't it?'

'You know I'm right,' Josie said, grinning. 'I always am, aren't I? But in the meantime, you need to sell him some plausible story. Keep it brief. It was a fling. He was too old and too fucking hairy. Whatever. But something simple – and let Joey lead the way. You don't know what Mo's told him, after all, do you?' She laughed then. 'Christ, for all you know, he's given him all kinds of nonsense. You and him. Him Romeo and you fucking Juliet!'

And Christine laughed again.

It was only once Josie had gone and the house was again silent that she remembered the one Shakespeare play they'd done in school. *No*, she thought miserably, *it's more like I'm Lady bloody Macbeth.*

Chapter 14

Mo grabbed a bottle of rum from the bureau in his office and set it down on his desk. Two polished crystal glasses were already there.

'You want a large one, brother?' he asked Nico as he pulled out the stopper. 'I think we deserve this, don't you? To us and a successful first month.'

It was late, a quiet week night, and they were done for the evening. Beyond the office familiar sounds floated through. Sounds of the world – well, one of the worlds – Mo felt most at home in. Yes, the house on Oak Lane was now home, but a sense of home was a concept that Mo had never fully felt. Home was this – this environment – wherever it happened to be. From back in the day, when his 'office' was his spot in the dingy alcove in The Perseverance on Lumb Lane, to the outside bench at Arthur's Bar, where he'd mostly run his pre-prison empire, to the bar he had run with Brown Benny out in Spain. He felt alive in such places. He felt alive here. At home here. In the pulsating darkness, where hedonism reigned, he felt strong and centred, in the eye of a perfect storm. The sweet smell of sweat, the sour smell of spilled drinks. Even the growl of the vacuum cleaner being dragged across the acres of carpet. The clanks and bangs of crates being taken back to the cellar. The low hubbub of voices, occasionally punctuated by a laugh or a 'Bye!'. The bumps and knocks of the night's band taking the last of their gear out. The final clang as the last man standing – usually the head barman – shut the heavy doors. It was becoming a living thing, the club now. And that was food for his soul.

But it was the sound of notes being counted that pleased Mo the most. The month had in fact exceeded both their expectations. Either they'd seriously underestimated or Bradford was on the up. There'd been nothing like this kind of money being splashed around here before. Not by punters; the bread and butter that made the drug-dealing jam possible.

Nico finished counting the bundle of twenties he had in front of him and slipped a paper wrapper round its middle. Then took the tumbler Mo passed to him. 'Indeed. To us,' he said, smiling as they clinked glasses. 'And also to family?' he added, raising one ink-black eyebrow.

In some ways, Mo and Nico were almost like brothers. Having bonded in prison, such a long time ago, their connection, since they'd hooked up again on Mo's return, had fast become a close working relationship. No, not one that would ever quite tip over into full-on friendship, because Mo didn't believe in having friends of any stripe – you came in on your own, you went out on your own. You were on your own, ultimately. That had always been – and probably still was – his way. The line he'd drawn might be invisible, but it was there even so.

Still, as a business partner, Nico was as close as a partner could be. Down to expediency, yes – Nico was formidable, strong, unforgiving and ruthless, and conveniently he also shared Mo's ambitious vision, both above and below the police radar. But it was also because Mo respected where Nico drew his own personal lines. He might be far from his kids – they lived in Athens with their mother for the most part – but he was a committed, emotional, almost over-protective father. And his teenage children, boy and girl, both adored him. That he would kill for them, and easily, was without question.

But they were far away. Safe. They existed in a separate universe. Nico smiled. 'Yes, to family, I think,' he said again. 'I am pleased for you, Macario. The boy is very special.' Then he chuckled. 'Mo, the father. It takes a little bit of getting used to.'

Mo laughed as well. 'Tell me about it.' Though in truth he was well aware that he was almost certainly a father several times over. Yet he had no interest – not a flicker – in the products of the other wild oats he'd sown. He knew he probably had offspring – grown-up offspring – all over Bradford. But they weren't even on his radar. The girls involved had had choices. They'd made them. Up to them. But Joey … was it because he reminded him so much of his young self? Was it age? Was he at that age now where men feared mortality? How could that be? He felt as strong and alive and vital as he'd ever felt. Just circumstance, perhaps, then – the chance meeting, the connection. The knowl-edge that his line wasn't just carrying on, but getting stronger. And better – that sense of 'betterness' was key. Joey was a good lad. Intelligent. Not street-smart but canny … Mo downed the rum. Fatherhood, he mused, must evoke some powerful shit, because he'd never felt as keenly as he felt at this moment that Joey was the thing that would make Marcia proud. Fleetingly, he imagined how they might one day meet.

'You know,' Mo said, surprising himself at being so candid, 'I never really knew what people meant when they talked about their own flesh and blood. He just makes me want to do better – know what I mean?'

Nico placed his glass down on the desk – nudging bundles of cash out of the way as if so many bits of scrap paper – and poured them both another inch of the toffee-coloured rum. 'You mean give up our life of crime?' He laughed at the absurdity. There was a kilo of heroin in the safe currently, set to net them a cool eighteen grand, and which one of their main dealers, Darren, would be round to collect and cut before the birds were up tomorrow morning. 'Because, my ebony friend, I'm afraid I would need another partner. I can't have you going all soft on me now.'

Nico was smooth but never soft. Only for his family. No one else. 'Don't be daft,' Mo said. 'It's exactly that – *this*. *All* our enterprises – that make the timing with the boy so good. I can afford to make up for all the years I spent fucking around with women and drugs, can't I? I can set him up properly. Teach him the trade.'

Nico caught his eye. 'You thinking of bringing him in?'

'In some capacity, yes.'

'Well, you know I'd have no objection to that. Though *he* might. He has his own plans, I think. And I'm not sure they involve dealing drugs, *o filos mou*.'

Mo had been thinking about exactly that. Even assuming Joey was interested, which, as Nico had said, wasn't a given, he wasn't even sure in what capacity he could best use him. As a musician, yes, but an hour's set a week was hardly anything to write home about. Though it was his passion, and passions needed very careful handling. He was just glad that the lad had been back to see him since he'd delivered his bombshell – hadn't blanked him. 'We're cool,' he'd told Mo, the next day. No, it had been the day after, hadn't it? 'It's fine,' Joey had said gravely. 'We're cool.'

And they had been. And that had been good enough. More than good enough for now. Downing the second rum, he stood up and picked up his car keys. 'I'm heading home for some shut-eye,' he said. 'You okay locking up tonight?'

'Shut-eye?' Nico asked him. 'It's not even one yet.' Then he winked. 'Oh, to be free and single. Yes, go on, friend. And have one for me, yes?'

'Just the one? You're getting old, my friend,' he said, reaching for his coat.

In truth, Mo wasn't looking for that kind of action. A bath, a small rum and the loving embrace of his high-end Egyptian cotton sheets were all he needed, even if he was happy to let Nico think otherwise; that he'd be off down Lumb Lane looking for a fuck. But once in the car, which he parked in front of the International curry shop just at the end of the street (and taken care of, by Sinbad, for a modest nightly fee) he sat awhile, thinking, while the engine of the BMW purred, the dustbins and bin bags – which had by now been dragged to the edges of the pavement – all made prettier within the halo of the headlamps.

Then, on a whim, he took the mobile from the passenger seat and paged Joey. He sat back, then, not expecting to get a call from him at this hour, but willing the phone to ring even so.

In the event though, it took less than a minute.

He put the phone to his ear. 'Mo,' Joey whispered. He sounded out of breath. 'Wassup?'

'You free at any point tomorrow, boy?' Mo asked.

'Well, I'm supposed to be working. Forecast's good, but, well, yeah. Yeah. Of course, Mo. Maybe lunchtime or something?'

Mo's ears, always keen, detected that Joey wasn't alone. 'You and Paula too, if she'd like,' he said. 'Maybe a bit after lunch, though.'

'Course. Though she's working.' A low mumble. 'But maybe.'

'Whatever,' Mo said lightly, a picture quickly forming. 'Call me again tomorrow morning, yeah? Cool.'

Then he hung up, the image of them in bed together bright in his mind's eye. The memory of young flesh – of unblemished female flesh – trembling and bucking at his touch. Memories of Christine, damn her, invading his thoughts. Did he hate her? Yes, probably. So it annoyed him intensely that she'd managed to stir him. Perhaps he'd head down to Lumb Lane after all.

He put the car into gear and swung out into the road. Any hole was a goal, after all, he thought grimly. Well, as long as the hole's owner wasn't a smackhead.

Joey turned the corner into his road and his heart sank. His dad's car was parked up outside the house, which meant he was home from his shift early. Joey wasn't sure why but for a moment he thought he'd rethink his plans; he didn't really want to face his dad right now.

Not that they hadn't reached a manageable understanding, because they had. If he was anything, Joey's dad was a relentlessly pragmatic man. If he felt anxious about the appearance of Joey's real dad in his life, he was at least trying hard not to show it.

No, it was his mam who was giving Joey the most difficulty currently. She wasn't ranting and raving, which had been something of a shock – she wasn't usually slow in letting him know how she was feeling – but she was definitely different. Not quite herself in ways that Joey couldn't quite get a handle on. Distracted – yes, that was the word.

She'd been waiting for him the day after they'd had their big blow-up (though not in any way the sort of blow-up Joey had been expecting), waiting by the back door for him when he'd returned from his window-cleaning round and had wheeled his cart round to its usual place by the shed. She'd had her arms crossed over her chest and smiled tightly as he'd come up the back-garden path. 'We'd better get this done, then,' she said, moving aside to let him pass. He could see from her eyes that she'd been crying.

And then it had all been a bit weird. She'd sat him down in the living room – no sign of his uncle Nicky, who was obviously off doing whatever odd job he'd managed to get that day – and, wiping her nose on a tissue that she'd plucked from the sleeve of her cardigan, said, 'So, what's he told you then?' in a slightly chippy voice.

'What I told you,' Joey had said. 'That you and he –' God, he really didn't like seeing his mum in that way – 'you know, had a fling or something, and that he was too old for you, and that … and that the whole thing was done with before you even knew you were pregnant with me.'

She'd nodded. 'That's about it,' she'd said, placing her hands on her knees. 'So,' she'd added, 'what else do you want to know?'

Joey's wanted to rail at her then. To say '*Everything*!'. Have her tell him something else. Give him some inkling as to why she'd never told him. Because that was the real thing. The big thing. Why the hell *hadn't* she told him who his father was? How would it have hurt him? Which was what he'd asked her next.

She'd sat and thought – or at least given the impression she was thinking. 'Because what would have been the point, love?' she said eventually. 'He was long gone out of my life – and I mean *long* gone, believe me. And I was with your dad, and we were happy –' She smiled thinly, as if they hadn't been, not quite. 'And, well, how would it have helped you to know? You were just a little lad. You already *had* a dad. Why give you all that extra shit to deal with? Trust me, I've seen how it goes for some kids – all that yearning for something they can't have – that's the thing. Putting thoughts in your head about why he'd buggered off and left you –'

'But he *didn't*, Mam. He told me you were the one who told *him* to bugger off. Did you?'

She nodded, her lips a thin line. Another pause, as if she was struggling to know how to answer. 'Yes. Yes, I did. Love' – she grasped his hands – 'look, these things – well, they're hard. I didn't want to be with Mo and he didn't want to be with me. It would have been the *worst* thing – it really would. It was better to … there was no *point* in him being in your life. He was …'

'*What?*'

'He was … Christ, don't be naïve, Joey. He was never going to be a father to you. Not then. And your dad *was*. Yes, maybe I should have told you. But I didn't, and it's done. We were long over before you were even born. So what would have been the point? I didn't want him in my life and you didn't need him in yours. And what's happening now …'

'Is that my head's royally fucked, Mam! What am I supposed to do? How am I supposed to play it?'

'Joey, I can't answer that, can I? What does *he* want?' Her eyes glittered. Please don't let her start blubbing. He couldn't handle it.

'Nothing,' he said. 'He just wanted me to know, Mam. He wants to help me – not play daddy. He even said so. Just be a mate, like.' He sighed. 'Like that's not a bit fucking weird in itself.'

His mam's shoulders dropped. She sniffed again. 'Well, what can I say? None of that's up to me, Joey.'

'Yeah, but you're not happy about it, are you? And that's messing my head up as well. Mam, I need to know you're okay with it.' He slipped his hands from between hers and enveloped them in his own. 'I know it's a shock – Christ, it's a bloody shock for me as well. But you know, tell me he's a bastard – tell me he's a piece of shit and I should have nothing to do with him – and then fine. Then I won't. But from what I can see, all he's done is be straight with me. Wants to help me. Make up for shit and that. I like him, Mam –' Again, that wince. 'But –'

'I'm not going to tell you that, Joey,' she said. 'You … you know … you do whatever *you* want. Get to know him. Whatever. It's just –' Her eyes brimmed. 'You're my baby, that's all. Mine and dad's … And it's …'

'It's what?' Joey said, as she freed her own hands and dabbed her eyes with the scrap of tissue.

'It's just *hard*.'

And that had been that, pretty much. And a week on, Joey wasn't sure what to make of it. It was like fine, he's your dad, do what you want to. It's cool. And in that way that always happened when there was something big and did your head in – they'd just carried on as per, skirting round it, as if on tiptoe. Like it was there but not there. And loads of pats on his back from his dad. Like it was Joey's thing to deal with – you crack on, son, your call – and they weren't getting involved.

Weird. He carried on walking now, down the road, and as he drew nearer, he could see his dad's head bobbing up and down behind the fence. Then the sound of the lawnmower starting up – what lawn? It was nearing the end of hot, mostly dry, August – and what grass there was was all brown and flat and parched.

And he'd have to have a conversation that he didn't want to have. Why you back? Have you finished? Where you off to? All that kind of shit. And acting like that he'd got this friend that they didn't approve of – like he was thirteen or something – and his dad's tight-lipped nod when he told him – to see Mo. That look of disapproval and disappointment.

Perhaps his mam had been right. He was half coming round to the idea that perhaps her choice *had* been the right one. Dicky's mam – how many times had he seen her in action? Whenever Dicky would come home from seeing his dad – who was shacked up with the woman he'd left his mam for, but he was *still* Dicky's dad, wasn't he? – you didn't want to be around her. She could create an atmosphere so toxic that it would choke you; she could shout and bawl for Britain. 'Having another of her S and B sessions,' Dicky'd say, seeking sanctuary round at Joey's. He'd remembered Dicky once saying that it was like *he* was the one who'd left his mam, he always felt that guilty.

That was what weighed heaviest – that having time for Mo felt so much like a betrayal.

His dad saw him, and took his hand off the handle of the lawnmower. His hair, lifted by the breeze, exposed his balding temples. A thought flew into Joey's mind, unbidden. His dad must be, what, ten years younger than Mo? He banished it again, feeling terrible.

'You're home early, son,' his dad said. Completely textbook.

And if, at that moment, Paula's car hadn't come down the road, perhaps, out of guilt, he'd have had the conversation he was expecting. As it was, he took a view not to burden himself with it. 'Worked like a demon. Got a date,' he said, gesturing to where Paula was pulling in to pick him up.

Which wasn't exactly the truth. He realised that.

But at least it wasn't exactly a lie.

Chapter 15

Mo had asked Marika to knock up a lasagne. She could clean and she could cook and that suited him fine. She wasn't his type – she was olive-skinned and skinny with sharp features – and not wanting to bed her made things so much more straightforward.

Good food round his table. That was always going to be the way. Instinct had told him that in order to keep Joey sweet, he'd have to tread carefully around Paula. And that meant chatting her up a bit, getting her on side – and, most importantly, offering her something she thought she wanted too.

Mo had already realised that the girl was definitely a chip off the old Hudson block; more front than Blackpool, a tendency to chippiness, and shared too many of her own mother's traits for his liking. But she was Joey's girl and that meant she had to be given a bit of respect. He could live with that. He liked her. The respect wasn't forced.

He was already standing in the doorway to greet them, having buzzed the car through, and he waved as the ridiculous little Mini rolled up.

'You must be a fucking contortionist, boy, to get in and out of that,' he joked as Joey eased – or more unfolded – himself out of the car.

'It's not that bad,' Paula chirped up from across the car's roof. 'And it serves me alright. Not all of us have a daddy that can afford brand new BMWs.'

Mo wondered if her tone was anything to do with his small-hours interruption to whatever the pair of them had been up to last night. Remembering his own small-hours entertainment, he took it in good spirit, but filed it away anyway, as was his habit. 'Well, that's me told,' he said, laughing and holding up his hands in mock surrender. 'Just a joke, sweetheart. No harm intended. Anyway, come on in, I've got a lovely bit of scran all ready for us. I hope you're both hungry.'

Joey grinned and told him he could eat a scabby horse with relish. Mo smiled indulgently. He really did have it all, did the kid. Good looks, a lovely nature and a cracking sense of humour. He certainly had the makings of someone Mo could use in the business: though not as one of the heavies he regularly required. Yes, Joey could no doubt handle himself, but Mo – for whom violence was an every-day fact – found himself uncharacteristically appalled at the thought of his flesh and blood getting scarred or carved up. Not at his age. Not at any age, ideally, even if a central part of a man being blooded involved getting bloodied, in Mo's book.

No, he had something in mind, down the line, that was a little less fraught with danger. There were plenty of roles in his main business – as opposed to Silks nightclub – that a bright kid like Joey could excel in. But it would require gentle persuasion and an extended bedding-in period first. Joey needed the scales falling from his eyes a little before that could happen. That and an introduction to the many benefits being part of Mo's empire could bring.

'I'll get straight to the point,' Mo said once they were all settled round the dining table, tucking into the food Marika had provided in her usual chatty fashion. He looked directly at Paula as he placed a forkful of salad in his mouth. 'I brought the two of you here both for pleasure and business. To offer you an exciting opportunity, if you're interested.'

He watched Paula's facial expression subtly rearranging itself; from the excitement that had been her immediate and natural response to a look that was trying to convey that she was distinctly *un*interested. Mo enjoyed it – this cat-and-mouse game between him and his son's girlfriend. It amused him, and even more so as he saw her then redden, clearly now aware of his amused scrutiny. She automatically reached for her shirt collar and fiddled with it as if checking the button, then dabbed the sides of her mouth with the crisp cotton napkin she'd had on her lap.

'If it's more nights performing, we'd certainly be interested,' she said, before Joey, who had a mouthful of food, could answer. Now she looked at Joey. 'And I'm sure the rest of the band would appreciate it too.'

'Well, there's that,' Mo said, smiling. 'It seems that the punters love your spots, so yes, if you'd like both Friday and

Saturday nights on an ongoing basis, that's fine by me. It was one of the other things I was going to suggest to you all. And I will do that – don't want Matt – it *is* Matt, isn't it? – to feel sidelined. No, this was something extra. Something I had in mind to go alongside it.'

'We're listening,' Joey said. 'And this food is spot on, by the way. Top class.'

'I take no credit,' Mo said smoothly. 'No culinary skills whatsoever. I'm more of an ideas man – and my idea is to see if you'd be interested in becoming the club's entertainment managers. Both of you.' He smiled at Paula. 'Not fulltime initially. But certainly, if things continue as well as they've been doing, with the potential to be so.'

'But doing what?' Joey asked. 'I don't think I've ever managed anything.'

Mo saw Paula glance at Joey. A 'Shhh, don't do yourself down, you numpty!' look, if ever he saw one. 'There's always got to be a first time,' he pointed out. 'And you manage a business, don't you?'

'A window round,' Joey said.

'Still your own business,' Mo qualified. 'And it isn't anything that complicated. Just booking bands and DJs and so on – that sort of thing. Keeping some accounts.'

'I'm good with figures,' Paula piped up.

'Well, there you go,' said Mo. 'Perfect. And there are other things you probably know more about than I do. Specially having been out of the country for so long. You'll be much more aware of what's current. I've also looked into hiring the room out during the day for practice sessions and so on, so I'll need someone to sort out the schedules. And, if you're interested, down the line there's the day-to-day running of the place, too – the bar and the cellar, the ordering, the hiring and firing …'

He put down his fork, taking simple pleasure in the awe on both their faces. 'So?' he said. 'Spill. What do you think?'

Now Joey spoke first. 'I love it, I really do. And, God, yes, it's an incredible opportunity. But what about our jobs? It's not just my round – Paula works almost every day at the chemist's, doesn't she?'

'It's just a window round, lad,' Mo said. 'You're not tied to it for life. Nor should you be. And this is a guaranteed income. A good one at that.'

'And *my* job?' Paula asked, slightly snappily. 'And Mo, I know to you it's just a window round, but Joey's spent a lot of years and hard work building up that round. You can't expect him to just let it go just like that.'

Ah, so that was how it was going to be, then. Him and her, both staking their claims on Joey. It amused him. He sat back in his seat. 'No pressure. No rush,' he said. 'I'm just putting it to you both. You'll obviously need to think things through. And for a start, love' – he watched her eyes narrow – 'I wouldn't expect you to give up your job at the chemist's. From what Joey tells me, you really love it there. So perhaps think about reducing your hours? Entirely up to you. And as for your round, Joey, maybe you could bring in a young lad to train up? Maybe take a bit of the load off?' He turned his gaze to Paula. 'Give him the opportunity to explore other careers for a bit?'

'Well, yeah, in theory,' Paula said. 'And I'm sure Joey *could* get some help in, couldn't you, babe? But how would that all work with you, Mo? What hours would you need us to be doing? Because we clearly couldn't both be there at the same time, could we?'

Progress, Mo thought. She was warming to the idea. He spread his hands. 'That's entirely up to you two, to work out between yourselves. As long as the work gets done, I don't care how or when you do it. You'll have a set of keys each – how you organise your hours will be up to you. Be there when you can, or if you're needed, get the jobs done, and that's it. You'll be the managers – so I'd expect you to do the managing. Just a question of keeping Nico and me in the loop. Anyway' – he leaned forwards again – 'how does two hundred quid a week each sound?'

'Each?' Joey almost spluttered the word. '*Each*? Fucking hell, Mo, that's a lot of dosh! Is the club really doing that well?'

He blushed then, presumably realising his relative ignorance about such matters. Mo could see him reassessing just what 'that well' might mean. All good. If he could do one thing for the boy it was to open his eyes to the potential beyond the world of his low-achieving parents and their obvious notions (obvious because it was the same rut proles like them always fell into) that you were born into a social stratum and you stayed there.

'What do you think?' Mo said, grinning – not least at the irony of the situation; because the club definitely wasn't the place where the real money lay. 'And, yes, each. I'm a busy, busy man, and to have people I can trust take all that hassle away from me is definitely worth a few hundred quid a week, believe me. So, do we have a deal, or do you want to go away and think about it?'

He noted the look that passed between the two youngsters. So it wasn't starry-eyed Paula that was going to need convincing – it was Joey.

Paula nodded. 'Can we let you know in a couple of days?'

Mo smiled, already knowing he had his answer.

Chapter 16

With a late set the previous night and it being a Sunday morning, Paula would normally have enjoyed the luxury of a lie-in – well, at least to the extent her younger siblings would allow. More and more she kept thinking about getting a place with Joey. They'd only discussed it round the edges – more if and when than when – but she knew it was what they both wanted. And with this new work – though she wasn't silly enough to think nothing came for nothing – perhaps they'd have sufficient funds to do so.

She was too old to be at home now. She felt it increasingly. Partly because of the hours she worked, which would always cause friction, but also because she knew her mam and dad weren't happy. Yes, they had plenty of time for Joey, but they were constantly banging on at her about the nature of the industry she was going into, and about what might happen if she gave up her steady job. Like the world would bloody end if she did.

She rolled over irritably. She wasn't due in the club till two – to attend an impromptu meeting Mo and Nico had called – and then, despite being knackered, back again tonight, too, to watch a potential new DJ's first set. Another reason she badly needed her sleep. But there was some sort of racket going on downstairs that was too loud to ignore. And, bit by bit, amid the white noise of her brothers shouting and bawling, came a sound she thought she recognised – was that her mam she could hear, crying?

She threw off her duvet, and was just blearily donning her dressing gown to go and investigate, when the bedroom door opened – no knock, she noted crossly – to reveal her mam standing in the doorway. 'God, love – I can't believe it!' So her mam *had* been crying.

'What?'

'Princess Diana – she's dead!'

'*What?*' Paula said again, because she couldn't believe it either.

'Dead in a car crash,' her mother qualified. 'In a tunnel, in Paris. Chased by the fucking paparazzi. I can't take it in. Christ, can you? She's actually *dead*.'

Paula crossed the room and put her arms round her mam. Tough as old boots, she was, in all things. She had steel wires running through her veins. Except in this. Her Diana love was – had been – as enduring as it had been soppy; one of the few things that could make her dad's eyes roll.

'Those poor babies!' Josie sniffled. 'To lose their mam like that … I can't believe it. It's like a nightmare. God, and who's going to tell them?'

Paula hugged her mum tightly. Her love for Diana was only matched in intensity by her adoration of William and Harry – whose fortunes she'd followed from the moment they'd both been born. ('I'm a mam,' she'd always said whenever Paula and her sister ribbed her about it. 'Just you wait till you're mams. You'll see.') And since the break-up of the royal marriage, she'd become even more passionate, declaring Charles to be a monster, Camilla a prize witch, and the situation of the princes – the progress of whom she followed with the zeal of a religious manic – to be akin to child abuse, as, pushed and pulled between the warring factions, they couldn't possibly know which way to turn, an abomination visited on them by a cruel world that had no respect for family, or the institution of marriage.

'And now they're orphans,' she said, as Paula accompanied her back downstairs. Her siblings, she noted, had scattered.

'Hardly,' said Paula's dad, who was still staring grimly at the telly. 'They've still got a father, remember.'

'And that bitch for a step-mother!' Josie snapped back.

'She's not that, Mam,' Paula felt it her duty to point out. She felt a bit sorry for Camilla Parker Bowles, truth be known. It was hardly her fault the Palace made Charles marry Diana, after all. But she never revealed that to her mother, and definitely wouldn't be doing so now. 'Anyway, now I'm up, who's for a brew?'

Her dad shook his head. 'I'm just off, love. Promised I'd go and fix Hare Lip Lenny's car for him.' And with a look on his face that made it abundantly clear that, though he might have offered to do so – even promised, as he'd said – he almost certainly hadn't promised to do so today.

She tied the belt on her dressing gown and headed off to the kitchen. Perhaps, after a suitable period comforting her distraught mother (or, rather, gawping at the telly with her while she railed at the Royal Family, the 'gutter press' and the Fayeds), she would remember that she too had something very important she had to rush off to do.

They had been two weeks into their new part-time role of entertainment managers and, so far, though tiring, it had been working out largely okay. Matt and the rest of the band had accepted the offer of the new regular Friday slot and though it meant less time for rehearsing, they all decided it didn't matter – yes, they'd go on adding new songs to their sets, which meant learning them, obviously, but to play for decent money two nights a week was too good a gift to turn down.

Joey, similarly, had thrown everything at making it work. So positive had he been that he'd even taken on a young lad – a pimply boy called Daniel, fresh out of school, and distinctly wet behind the ears, but who seemed keen to learn, and also happy enough to trail around with Joey, getting to know the routines and all the regulars, in the hope of taking on part of the round in the short term, and, in the longer term – well, as Joey'd said, who knew? By this time next year, who knew where they'd be? And though Paula's first love was still singing, and her cherished dream of being a pop star, she shared the same feeling as Joey – that, however it had come about, and however much their parents worried for them, this was an opportunity they should grab with both hands.

Taking her own advice, she'd made excuses and made her escape as soon as she was able – she'd called Joey while her mam was in the shower and arranged to collect him earlier than planned; he'd been as eager to get away from it all as she was.

It wasn't quite two yet, and having left their families to their appalled vigil by their respective televisions, they had breakfasted at the Tuck Inn, and were now sitting in her car, which Paula had parked up in the registry office car park on Manningham Lane. Silks was still a few minutes' walk away from there, but it was a safer place to leave the car unattended.

'So what d'you reckon this is about?' Joey asked her, as she touched up her lipstick in the rear-view mirror. He sounded nervous – *was* nervous – and she loved him for it. She'd always known she would find herself a good man like her dad. She had no time for oafs and thugs or hard nuts.

'You tell me,' Paula said. 'It was you who spoke to him, wasn't it? A new initiative – wasn't that what he said to you?'

'Yeah, but what?' Joey said. 'You think they're pleased with us so far? The new initiative might be bringing someone else in, mightn't it?'

She squeezed his thigh. 'You still don't get it, do you? He loves you. He *rates* you. Whatever it is, it's definitely not going to be that. Anyway, we've done well, haven't we? The new DJ's going down a storm. I'm sure tonight's will be good too. And we've already got the room booked out for three rehearsal sessions a week. I'd say we've already done bloody well.'

'I know, but –'

'But nothing. You're such a bloody worrier, Joey Parker. Come on, look at us,' she said, as she twisted down the lipstick and popped it back in her handbag. 'Attending important business meetings on a Sunday afternoon. We're on our way, kiddo, so take that anxious look off your pretty face.'

Which he did, and when they'd gone inside, Paula had no way expected that it was an expression that was soon to be transferred to hers. But less than twenty minutes into the meeting – round a table by the dancefloor, their voices echoing as they went through a bunch of logistical and bookings stuff – it seemed that was exactly what was happening.

Mo was in expansive mood, after another successful Saturday evening, and full of praise, as she'd predicted, at their various efforts. But there was also an edge to him; she realised that she was beginning to know how to read him, and what she read now was something intended just for her – a strong sense that he knew that they were about to propose something that he wasn't sure she was going to like.

And he was right.

'So let me get this straight,' she said, through gritted teeth, after Nico (not Mo, she noted) had outlined their new idea, sitting there, all smiles, in his smartly tailored suit. 'You want to turn Silks into a strip club.'

She saw irritation flash across Nico's craggy face. 'No, not a strip club,' he said slowly, 'just a place that offers that particular form of entertainment on one night a week only. It's a money-spinner. As they say in America, a "no-brainer".' He had an expression on his face that suggested she must lack one. Patronising in the extreme.

She ignored it and looked at Mo. 'But pole dancers? I mean, here? I mean, pole dancing and stripping ...'

'The club needs to be brought into the twenty-first century, sweetheart,' he said, spreading his palms. 'We're talking classy. Decent girls. Not the sort of birds the scratty pubs always put on. Trust me,' he added. 'Nico's right. It was a licence to print money back in the day, and, done right, since we'll be the only upmarket joint doing it, it could be so again.'

Paula wanted to point out that there wasn't anything remotely classy about strippers and pole dancers; and that, point of fact, it wasn't the twenty-first century yet, either. Not to mention that, to her mind, the twenty-first century should be an altogether less shabby, demeaning place for women, where they weren't exploited and objectified and ogled at. But she didn't. Instead, lost for words to express the depth of her revulsion, she looked pointedly at Joey. 'How about you?' she asked him. 'You're okay with this, are you, babe?'

Both Mo and Nico looked at Joey too, heads swivelling in unison. She could almost see him shrink under their scrutiny. 'I don't know,' he said. 'I mean, look, babe, I ...'

'I what?' she asked, stunned; her gaze drilling into him. Joey? Her Joey? Going along with all this?

'I think ...' he looked stricken now. 'I mean, you know what I think. It's just that ... well ...'

'Well what?' she snapped.

'Babe, I just think we should … well … at least hear Nico out. I mean –'

'Exactly,' Mo agreed, before Paula could answer. 'Let's not throw our toys out of the pram, yeah? We're talking decent birds, Paula. Girls who like what they do, and aren't fazed by what people think. Trust me,' he said again, 'they make a good living too. We're talking top-drawer. Girls with attitude.' He looked pointedly at her. 'I know what you're saying,' he went on. Though – point of fact – she hadn't said anything. She was too busy still gaping at Joey. 'But there are plenty of girls who feel differently about it than you clearly do. Who don't feel exploited. Who aren't all feminist about it. Who'd be proud to be given the chance to audition for a spot here.'

Paula had been about to point out that being 'all feminist' was what every bloody woman *should* be – not least because they clearly couldn't trust a bloody man to stand up for them. But the word 'audition' stopped her in her tracks.

She plastered a grim smile on her face. 'Oh, and there's to be auditions, is there? And who will be doing that? Me and Joey? Or would you just be needing Joey?' She looked pointedly at Mo now.

He shrugged. She could see he was not only impervious to being wound up – he was even amused by her. *Amused*! She could also see Nico grinning out of the corner of her eye. *God*. They were actually *enjoying* this.

'We'd value your participation too,' Nico said, clearly speaking for both of them. 'If you'd deign to offer it. Always

good – always sensible – to have another woman's input.'
Then, before Paula could protest that she was in no way
qualified to assess the potential of a stripper, 'Always help-
ful, I've found, to have another female in the mix anyway.
Sets minds at rest, creates camaraderie, makes the girls feel
more secure.'

Like he was managing a bloody cattery or something.
And him with a fucking teenage daughter, too! 'I'm sure it
does,' she said, trying to keep from screeching that very
thing at him. What kind of idiot would she have to be not
to realise that, actually, there were men everywhere who'd
be queuing for such nights round the block? But *her* be a
part of it? *Joey* be a part of it? 'But for Silks, I mean, *really*?'
she said. 'Is that the sort of thing we want to be known for?'
Or, more accurately, she thought miserably, the sort of place
she wanted to perform in? It would mean everything else
the club did was tinged with seediness. It was the very last
thing she envisioned for herself. She wanted no part of it.

Mo clapped Joey on the shoulder, as if he already knew
he had him on side. Christ, *did* he? 'This is business,' he
said to her. 'And doing strip-nights is *good* business. And
good business,' he went on, 'is all about providing what the
punters want, no?' He looked at Joey. 'What say you, my
man? Isn't that the truth?'

Joey hesitated for no more than a second, but it was
enough that he'd hesitated at all. Enough for Paula to
know that she didn't want to hear more. She pushed her
chair back and stood up. She felt suddenly, ragingly, tear-
fully furious, and unable to trust herself not to lose it.

'Look, whatever,' she said, over Joey's 'Come on, calm down, babe'. 'Whatever you feel you want to do, up to you. It's just not something I think I want to get involved in, and if –'

'Fine,' Mo said, standing also. 'We've got this.' His hand was on Joey's shoulder again. Why the fuck didn't Joey *say* something? 'You get off and rest. We're done here. No worries, okay? We'll see you later.'

Rest. Patronising sod.

Without looking at Joey, she left the bar, and the club. Joey didn't follow.

Her mam was half-cut by the time Paula got home. Still on the sofa in her dressing gown, still staring at the TV, which seemed to be showing nothing but endless recycled news bulletins. Her dad was back too, and judging by the empty lager cans – Christ, it wasn't even four yet – had obviously decided that if you couldn't beat 'em join 'em. Like it was a bloody bank holiday or something. And putting paid to her hope that her dad would drop her back at the club later; she took the car at night sometimes, but never happily. She didn't like leaving the Mini there at any time, but especially late at night. Classy as it was – and she was beginning to revisit that opinion, wholesale – Silks was still in the town centre, and a dodgy part of it too. But she'd now have to either take it or get a cab, which made her all the crosser.

Too strung-out to talk, she only wondered aloud where her siblings had gone. 'Lou's taken the boys to the pictures,' her mam explained, sniffing. And them back in school in the morning, too, Paula thought. What the hell?

'Well, I'm off for a sleep,' she said. 'I've got to be back at the club for eight.' And so apparently all-engrossing was the horror being played out in Paris that her mum didn't even come back with her customary response of 'that bloody club', and on the very day that Paula might have been inclined to agree with her.

Instead she took herself up to bed and lay down on it fully clothed, where sleep claimed her from the headache that was pounding in her temples, and the tears – Joey hadn't come after her; he'd just let her *go* – that were threatening to spill. Her last thought as she drifted off was that, even though it meant letting the DJ down, she'd a good mind not to turn up at all.

Chapter 17

The club was in full swing by the time Paula returned, negotiating the steps carefully as she headed down them.

'Now there's a sight for sore eyes,' chortled a suited and booted, if only just, Big Billy, who was stationed, as ever now, by the door. She gave him a tight smile; one that was really no smile at all. But she had at least taken a grim pleasure in getting herself ready this evening. For reasons she couldn't fully articulate, but that had seemed compelling anyway, she had pulled all the stops out tonight. A small rebellion, she decided. Making a statement, that was it. About class, and what it meant. Fucking strippers. To even use the words together upset her feminist principles. What was the term when two things couldn't exist side by side? Whatever it was, it was that. You simply couldn't be classy and be a stripper at the same time.

She touched her hair. Her sister Lou had been granted special privileges. Instead of the way she usually styled it to get into character as Debbie Harry, tonight she'd scooped it up and pinned it and had Lou curl the ends she'd teased from it. She'd also chosen to wear a maxi – hardly *Blondie* attire either; a metallic bronze number she'd picked up in

181

the market back in the spring but never worn – halter-necked, with a thigh-high, but not too high, front split. *They want classy, I'll fucking show them*, had been her thinking as she'd donned it, though as she teetered round to the back of the bar she could see its limitations – she was having to take care not to catch it in her heels or let it trail in the already beery floor.

'Babe!' Joey called, rushing to greet her from the side of the stage. Whether by accident or design, he'd obviously stayed on at the club, and she felt a pang of guilt that she'd left him down there with no lift home. He was in the same jeans and T-shirt as he'd been wearing earlier and, she noted with dismay, also seemed a bit pissed. Had Mo been plying him with his bloody rum to talk him round?

'God, you look fantastic,' Joey said, the afternoon's debacle clearly forgotten. Or purposefully ignored, she thought, as he kissed her too firmly on the lips. 'Come on, let's get you a drink,' he said, sliding a hand over her buttock then, as if noting how stiff she had gone at his touch, up nearer to her waist.

'You look like you've had a bit of a head start on me,' she pointed out as she linked his arm rather than have him putting sweaty hands on her dress.

'Aw, babe,' he drawled as they made their way to the bar, 'you're not still mad with me, are you?'

'What do you think?' she said. 'Joey, why didn't you say something? I know it's Mo and that bloody Nico – God, he's so fucking *oily* – but you can't be serious. Pole dancers? Strippers? In here?'

She waved an arm to indicate to the largely young, fresh-faced and decent-looking people all around them, thinking of the sort of clientele – older, hornier, dirtier, so much bloody scuzzier – that would be here instead, if they went ahead with it. The idea still appalled her.

'Babe, what could I say? It's their club. Their decision.'

'And you're fine with that, are you?'

'No, not fine. Not exactly *fine*. But if it's only one night a week … And it's not like you have to get involved in it, is it?' He gave her a wry smile. 'Trust me, you made your feelings on that point pretty clear.'

The thought of Joey sitting and discussing her with Mo and Nico appalled her further. 'And so I bloody should,' she said, as he ordered a vodka and Coke for her. Ordered *for* her. Suppose she'd wanted something else? She stared ahead as the barman poured it. Joey didn't try to break the silence. She wondered what he was thinking. What had been said. 'Peace offering?' he said eventually, as it was set down on the bar.

Something snapped in her. 'No, maybe I don't have to get involved in it, but I'm guessing from your expression that you will be. Will you? Or did you get a sudden attack of conscience and tell them where they could stuff their idea as well?'

For a second, she almost thought he was going to tell her what she hoped for. That while he understood the position – it was their club, as he'd said – no way did he want to be involved in it either. After all, as Mo's son, he could do that, could he not? Mo thought the sun shone out of his bloody arse, after all.

But she was destined for disappointment. 'Listen, babe,' Joey said, 'I know the idea gets to you, but, trust me, none of them will be a patch on you. Nowhere even *close*.'

She almost threw her drink over him then – her mam's speciality in her youth. 'Christ, is that what you think, Joey? *Christ*. That I'm *jealous*?'

Though, in truth, though her feelings were mostly born out of politics – about the exploitation of women that just went on and on and on – there was another truth buried in there that he'd unwittingly hit upon; the idea of him ogling bloody pole dancers and strippers, assessing them – taking notes even? Probably. Why the hell couldn't he see how it must make her feel?

She had no stomach for talking politics now – she was much too worried he'd disappoint her even further. 'How would you like it, Joey?' she asked instead, 'if my bright idea for the club was to hire a male stripper? Hmm? And I volunteered to personally interview all the candidates?'

His expression darkened. 'Oh, for God's sake, babe, come *on*,' he said. 'As if I'd even look twice at them. Look, all we have to – all *I* – have to do in the process is sort a day, place some ads and sort the music during the auditions. Mo and Nico will be the ones choosing who to hire, obviously.'

Paula was gobsmacked. How was that so obvious? That wasn't what Nico had said at all. And how could Joey be so blasé about it? It wasn't so much the fact of the bloody thing – it was that he'd be there, eyeing up the talent, no matter how much he said he wouldn't, without giving a second thought to the idea that it would really piss her off. Both as a female *and* as a girlfriend. She wished he wasn't so bloody drunk. Would he be telling her this so calmly if he was sober and had actually gone away and thought about it a bit?

He was better than this, that was for sure. Or was he? He was Mo's son, after all. Her temper suddenly got the better of her. 'I tell you what, Joey,' she said, 'you know, I don't think I'm going to stay. You can check out the DJ on your own. I'm too fucking fuming with you right now.'

'Christ, Paula,' he said. 'What's *wrong* with you? Why are you going off on one like this? You're carrying on like I've committed some terrible bloody crime. What d'you want me to say? That's what they're doing. Just the same as a million other bloody nightclubs do as well. Just as this bloody nightclub has been doing since, like, for ever – whatever name it's had painted over the door.'

'So that makes it right?'

'No, that just makes it *life*.' He sighed heavily. And she knew then that his words weren't his own. That Mo and Nico had fed them to him. She could hear them bloody saying them. But just as she opened her mouth to tell him they could do it *all* without her, he shook his head, raised his hands, glared at her.

'Fine,' he said. 'Fine, Paula. You stay right there on your high horse.' Then he stomped off across the dance floor, weaving in and out of people, till he was lost to sight, bar his hair, which was briefly haloed in the chandelier above the main door, before melting away into the darkness of the night.

She stood for a moment, stunned. Had he really walked out on her? And if so, what was she supposed to do now? Follow him? Undecided, and also embarrassed now, she downed the vodka and Coke, avoiding the barman's eye – God, he must have heard every word. Then, because she couldn't think how to play it, and still half-expecting Joey to return, she ordered another, and downed that as well.

It was through the fog of vodka (they'd both been doubles, and drunk on an empty stomach) that she stood in that same spot by the bar, giving off 'don't come near me' vibes, and watched the first half hour of the young DJ's set. But when it became clear, shortly after ordering a third (and fending off chit-chat from various staff members) that if she didn't go to the loo soon she might well have an accident, she made her own unsteady way out to the toilets. It was only a short hop then to taking herself outside, and, her responsibility discharged (the DJ would probably do, she decided), to going right outside and trying to flag down a cab to get her home. And back to the bloody wake of the 'People's Princess'. She'd also snagged her dress now. *The glamorous life, eh?* she thought as she clumsily unsnagged it. It certainly didn't feel like that tonight. She looked daggers at Big Billy as she left.

She stood on the pavement for a full fifteen minutes, and was just contemplating the awfulness of having to schlep it round to the nearest minicab office when she heard a voice behind her. 'Come on. Come inside, honey,' it said. A male voice. Not Joey's but one she also knew well. She turned around to find Mo standing beside her. Where the hell had he come from?

He had his car keys in his hand. Was he arriving or leaving? He put his hand on her back. 'Sorry, I would have come out sooner. Glad I didn't miss you. You've no chance of a cab this early, and you really don't want to be hanging around out here. Not looking like that.' His gaze travelled the length of her body, but for some reason it didn't make her feel uncomfortable. It should have, after his performance earlier today. But he suddenly seemed too much the dad-figure, checking if she was decent.

If anything, Paula hated that he was being so kind to her. She was that close to tears and she knew it wouldn't take much to tip her over the edge. The very last thing she needed was someone being nice to her. Still, there was no sign of a taxi, so what else should she do? He was right. It was too early for the cabs to be cruising round here. Perhaps he would at least run her home.

But not quite yet, apparently. 'Let's get inside, get a drink down you, eh? Pete told me' – Irish Pete, she assumed, who'd have been monitoring the CCTV, watching her – 'that you and that young hothead of mine have had some words.'

Now the tears came, though she managed to stem the tide sufficiently that, going back in ahead of her, Mo thankfully didn't see them.

'Here you go, darling,' he said, once they were both in his office, turning back to face her after having poured her a tumbler of drink. 'Don't worry, girl,' he said, 'it's only brandy. I know you don't have a taste for the strong stuff.'

Like brandy wasn't strong? She took a gulp anyway. It tracked down her gullet in a warm welcome stream.

'There, better now?' Mo said, clearing some papers off the nearest chair. 'Get the weight off your feet and calm down, eh?' He perched on the edge of the desk while she arranged her split for modesty. 'I know it must be hard for you – you're only young – but this kind of life is what it is, Paula. And I'll tell you something else for nothing – Joey thinks the world of you.'

She felt a flash of anger resurface. So they *had* been discussing her. But another sip of brandy helped melt it away. 'I know that,' she said, her head swimming slightly, suddenly feeling childish and silly under his paternal gaze. It didn't help that Mo, against the desk, towered over her. 'But how could he just leap straight in – go along with it all so easily – without even thinking about how I would feel? Any girl would be mad about that, wouldn't she?'

Mo smiled at her, chuckled, then shook his head – and his dreads. 'Oh, Paula, you don't realise how beautiful you are, do you? As if Joey – as if any man, come to that – would prefer to look at some tart when he has someone like you on his arm.' He moved from the desk and went across to the small stack of chairs in the corner. Lifted one up and set it down in front of hers. 'In his *bed*. It's just a bit of titillation for the less fortunate, babe. You know that. A bit

188

of titillation for the punters that is very, very lucrative. We're just supplying a service, that's all. Just like any other business.'

'But it's so degrading –' she began.

'Sweetheart, no one *makes* them do it,' he said. 'Their choice entirely.'

'But it's *exploitation*,' she persisted.

Mo laughed. 'Oh, Paula, surely you can't be so naïve? Those girls – those poor exploited girls you're talking about – will be queuing down the street and round the block for a chance to perform here. Those girls *love* their work, believe me. I know what I'm talking about. They love the dancing, the attention, the cold, hard, cash. I tell you what, girl,' he leaned forward again and touched a finger to her cheek, 'with a body like yours, and the front you've got to go with it … well, let's just say I've seen how you work the audience, remember.' He touched her cheek again, and this time let it meander to her chin. Which he lifted. 'Well, let's just say that if you ever thought to try it – pole dancing, that is; I don't see you as a stripper – you could earn yourself an absolute fortune.'

Paula knew Mo was flirting, and though it registered with her somewhere, she made no move to bat his hand away. Mostly because the stronger sense was one of being desired by him, and finding that curious – and not minding it half as much as she'd expected. Because she could see Joey in him? Perhaps. Or was it just the drinking muddling her mind? Unsettled, she lifted her glass instead, which made him move his hand anyway.

Mo studied her face for a long moment, their knees almost touching. Then he chuckled again. 'You're hard work, you are, girl,' he said finally. 'You know that? A proper handful, God help the poor boy.'

But just at the point when she thought he was about to try and kiss her – which she was braced for deflecting; she knew she could handle it – he stood up abruptly and cleared his throat. 'Now, let's get you that cab,' he said, reaching for the office phone. 'Let's get you home so you two lovebirds can kiss and make up again.'

Paula watched him over the rim of her glass. *Kiss.* Said low and slow. It was almost like he was imagining them doing so himself.

Chapter 18

Paula glanced up at the small staff-room wall clock, willing the hands to move faster towards two. She'd come in early, but with Mr Hunter having been so accommodating about her reducing her hours, she didn't think it fair to push it by asking to leave early as well.

Her friend Susie, still on lunch, begged to differ. 'Just go,' she said. 'It'll be well past two by the time he gets back. And if you don't leave now, you're going to miss your bus. *And* your chance to progress the cause for women everywhere. It's almost your civic duty to get down there and state your case. And I'm sure that, old fart that he is, Mr Hunter would agree.'

So she'd left work, feeling better that she'd shared it all with Susie, because her attitude towards strippers and pole dancers was unequivocal – as it would be, given that Susie's former fiancé had been caught in flagrante with a bloody lap dancer. So it at least put the lie to Paula's early-hours concern that it might be her, and not the men, who was out of step with the real world; that she was being prissy and old-fashioned; that some girls *did* feel empowered by that kind of work. No, her resolution – that she would *not* back down on this – had been the right one.

She knew digging her heels in again might mean she would have a fight on her hands – God, Mo could even sack her if he felt like it – but she felt strangely calm as she hopped off the first bus at the interchange and ran into the baker's to pick up a pasty.

She didn't suppose she'd be eating again till teatime at least and, having foregone breakfast in favour of arguing (though not that unpleasantly) with Joey, needed something to soften the sharp edges of the hangover that were still hammering gently at her temples. In a day full of mistakes – that dress; what had she been thinking? And sitting there snivelling with bloody Mo – staying up with her mam till the small hours, drinking lager, had to rate as the worst. Even if the hangover, which had woken her too early, and still fuming, had at least helped to crystallise her thinking. Whatever impression she'd given to Mo the previous evening, she was now doubly resolute. She mustn't budge on this. Not an inch.

And Joey, whose call she'd refused to take when she got home, had clearly had second thoughts too. Not about the strippers exactly; as he'd said when she'd deigned to call him back on her break this morning, Mo and Nico could and would do exactly as they pleased. But about his *own* stance. If Paula didn't want any part in it, then so be it. He'd tell Mo he didn't want any part in it either. He was a prize idiot (his term), and she was worth way too much to him.

She ate the pasty on the second bus and made the club just on time, where inside the bar, Joey, Mo and Nico were sitting around one of the tables chatting, and thankfully drinking coffee rather than alcohol. The mood seemed light, which was a relief – they all greeted her amiably enough – but she still took a deep breath before walking over to join them.

'Afternoon,' she said cheerfully as she pulled a chair across from an adjacent table. 'Did you decide to do all the bookkeeping for me?'

Mo slid the pile of green-backed books towards her. 'Not at all,' he said, smiling. 'Just been looking at some totals. Don't worry – we've left the donkey work for you.'

She pulled them towards her. The bookkeeping didn't feel like donkey work to Paula. She'd felt proud to be entrusted with it, not least *because* of the trust – she was now privy to the amount of money the club was making, which was pretty impressive. She enjoyed the work for its own sake as well. Numbers had always been her strong point, and she derived great satisfaction from poring over all the receipts, wages and till rolls and transferring the information into neat, unblemished columns in the gold embossed Sage accounts books. She did a professional job, and she knew that was important. Mo had told her more than once that her accounts needed to be 100 per cent accurate, as they were going to be looked at by the taxman and their accountant.

She reached for the other paperwork and the plastic packets that held all the invoices. 'Business is good, then?' she asked, scooping all the various bits up. In truth, though the figures all seemed very impressive, she still didn't have a full picture of just what it might cost to run a huge place like Silks. The size of the figures were, for the most part, pretty mind-boggling.

'Oh, indeed,' Nico agreed, winking at Mo as he spoke. '*Very* good.'

A few papers fluttered to the floor as she tried to make a pile of them. 'Well, in that case, maybe I can put in a requisition for a desk,' she said, wondering quite when the elephant in the room was going to come up.

'We can do better than that,' Nico said. 'As of next week you shall even have an office. Billy's working on fitting it out as we speak. On which note –' He stood. 'I need to speak to my wife. She is a very expensive woman, and I need to indulge her, so she'll be very pleased to know just *how* good.'

'Even *without* the strippers,' Mo said, once Nico was safely out of earshot.

'Mo, look,' Paula began, but he held a hand up to silence her.

'There's no need to worry your pretty little head about that further.' He glanced at Joey. 'Assuming I'm allowed to use a phrase like that?'

'For God's sake, of course you are,' Paula began. 'Mo, it's just that –'

'It's fine, babe,' Joey told her. 'Me and Mo have had a chat about everything, and –'

'And the subject is now closed,' Mo said firmly. 'Well, at least for the moment. It was just one of many ideas we've been throwing around. But as we're doing so well already

– well, we don't even really need it, do we? And the last thing I want to do is cause trouble between the two of you, for the sake of a few grand, so, as I say, consider it forgotten.'

'Really?' said Paula. Could it really be that easy? Joey obviously had more influence over Mo than he'd thought. More than *she'd* thought. While Joey and Mo knuckled down to sorting out the stocktaking and the following week's brewery order, she took her bookkeeping to another table feeling much lighter of heart, even if somewhat bemused.

Paula's buoyant mood wasn't destined to last, though. The bookkeeping done, and after a much more fond farewell to Joey (who was off to see his friend Dicky for a lads' night in), she headed home with a quieter evening in prospect. Susie had invited her over, so she could hear the outcome, but Paula had declined. After last night, her needs were of a less sociable variety – tea, a long hot bath and a welcome early night. But as soon as she entered the house, she knew it probably wasn't going to happen. She could see that straight away, by the expression on her mother's face – not to mention the way her arms were folded across her chest and the fact that she was tapping one slippered foot. If Paula had had a hangover, her mother would almost certainly have had a worse one.

'So you're finally home then,' her mam said. 'I need a word with you, young lady.'

'What d'you mean "finally"?' she countered, irritably noting the 'young lady'. 'I've been at work all day, haven't I? And I'm knackered. Can't it wait?'

'No, it can't,' her mam said. 'And come into the kitchen please, where your brothers can't hear us. They're trouble enough, and I don't want them knowing their big sister still doesn't have the sense she was born with.'

Paula gaped at her mam. Where had all this come from? Then at her father, who was sitting on the sofa, pretending to read the paper. Seeing it, she wondered if the write-up on Silks was finally in, plus the much-anticipated photo, having been 'spiked' or so they'd told them, due to a factory fire. Was that what this was about? The bloody photo? But what could she possibly have to object to about that? She felt glad she'd had the good sense not to mention the stripper idea the night before.

She followed her mam into the kitchen. She wanted a cup of tea anyway. 'What are you on about?' she said as her mam shut the door. 'Christ, I'm a grown woman, you know – not a child.'

'Then it's high time you started acting like one then, isn't it?'

'What?'

'Don't play the innocent, Paula. *God*, I can't believe you're so taken up with that cunt of a bloke that you can't see beyond the end of your fucking nose.'

Paula gaped again, bewildered. What the hell was all this about? Joey? No, it couldn't be. 'Mo?' she said. 'You mean Mo, I presume?'

'Who the fuck else would I mean? Of course Mo. Or Rasta Mo, to use his full name, formerly of this fucking parish.'

'It's Macario Brown, *actually*,' she corrected. What was her mam *on*? 'And what exactly is it that I'm supposed to be seeing anyway?'

'Don't take that tone with me,' her mother said. 'And take that look off your face, too. If you don't know what you're getting into, then you're even stupider than you look.'

'What then, Mam?' she said, sitting down on the battered stool her mam usually sat on to peel veg straight into the rubbish bin. 'Thanks for the compliment, but what exactly *am* I "getting into"?'

'You tell me.' Her mam folded her arms across her chest again.

'Tell you what?'

'Paula, are you seriously telling me you don't know what goes on there?'

'What *does* go on there?'

'Trouble, that's what. Criminal trouble. Pimps and drugs. And don't look so surprised. Christ, even your little sister seems to know more about that bloody place than you do.'

'Lou?'

'Yes, Lou. Did you happen to know, for instance, that it's now the number one place to go to these days to buy your street drugs? Did you know that every pimp in bleeding Bradford goes down there to tout his wares?' Her mother shook her head. 'And that's probably just the tip of the fucking iceberg.'

'Lou? How on earth would *Lou* know about stuff like that?'

'Because that dozy friend Chloe of hers knows all about it. Because her brother's a bloody dope dealer, that's why. Paula, don't be dense. You can't be blind to the reputation that place is getting!'

Paula was tempted to suggest her mam take her rants elsewhere. Like to wherever her sister was, for instance. 'That's ludicrous,' she said instead. 'That's just gossip and you know it. Malicious gossip. Probably spread by competitors. I work there, remember? I do the books, run the entertainment. It's all bullshit. I've not seen a single thing that would make me even remotely suspicious. And no, before you say it, I didn't come down in the last shower of rain. Anyway, I need a bath. I'm –'

'It's the God's honest *truth*, Paula,' her mother said. 'And it's not just from Lou. Your dad keeps his ear to the ground and he's heard stuff too. You might have been born yesterday, but your father and I weren't, and we've decided –'

'Decided what?'

'That you're to have nothing more to do with it. You're to tell him you're leaving, as of now, this very minute. That you're having nothing more to do with the place – or him, for that matter, and –'

'*What*? But that's ridiculous!'

'No, it's not. And I'm telling you that's what's happening.'

'And I'm telling you it's not. Jesus, Mam – I'm twenty! You can't just decide between you what I can or can't do.'

'Yes we can, and we are,' she said. 'I won't have you down there, Paula. It's bad enough that Joey's so bloody embroiled in it all, but that's not our problem. *You* are, and –'

'Hang on, hang on, hang *on*,' said Paula, getting up from the stool. 'You really think I'm going to just throw everything in on the basis of some nonsense my gobshite of a little sister has been spouting at you and whatever gossip you got from your cronies down the post office?'

'Don't you dare call your sister that!'

'Well, she is! And I'm *twenty*, in case you'd already forgotten – an adult. An adult who'll make my *own* decisions, thank you very much. Christ, you think I wouldn't *know* if there was dodgy stuff going on? It's me that does the bloody books! And anyway – Christ, Mam – why the hell are you starting on *me*?'

'I'm not starting on you. I'm just telling you. It's not up for discussion. You're to hand in your notice, and you're having nothing more to do with it. They're a bad lot, the lot of them. You have no fucking idea, Paula … God, you're so bloody *naïve*!'

'And you're fucking pre-menstrual, clearly,' Paula couldn't stop herself from saying. Which did it – blew the fuse that had obviously been sparking; she was just quick enough to avoid her mother's tiny but efficient fist.

'I'm *telling* you!' her mam yelled as Paula ducked it a second time.

'No, I'm telling *you*. You can't tell me what to do.'

'Oh yes I can – all the while you're under our roof, you'll do as you're told!'

'*Fine*, then,' she said. 'Then I'll get out from under it. I'm not staying here to listen to this crap. I'm off to sleep at Susie's, where I can get a bit of fucking *peace*.'

Grabbing her handbag, Paula stormed out of the house, slamming the door behind her. She fumbled in the bag for her car keys as she marched down the path. What the hell was *that* all about? Had her mother completely lost it?

Her head was reeling. She rummaged some more, but her car keys weren't in her bag. Fuck, she thought, of course, because they were sitting in her fucking bedroom, because she'd – *damn it* – decided to go in on the bus today.

Which left her two choices. To walk to Susie's (or maybe to Joey's, but she dismissed that idea immediately – he was over at his mate Dicky's and she didn't even have the number) or to sneak back into the house again and get them. And while she was at it, some spare undies and a blouse for the morning. Hopefully without her psycho mother hearing her.

Chapter 19

Happily, her mam and dad were now both in the kitchen, both speaking loudly, and presumably – no, almost definitely – discussing her. Good, she thought. Let them. Let her mam keep droning on. Christ, how badly she needed a place of her own, where she didn't have her every move dissected and could make her own decisions. And what was particularly galling was that the gloss had somewhat come off the place anyway; strippers and pole dancers – perhaps her mam had got wind of some of that. Though who from, she hadn't the slightest idea. But it was still galling. Who the hell did she think she was, telling her what to do?

She slipped her shoes off, and made her tentative way up the stairs, placing her feet on the treads with care and precision, just as she'd done countless times after a too-late night out, opting for listening to a lecture in the morning, once the temperature had cooled, over one of her mam's legendary rants at the time.

She made the landing without incident, and tiptoed to her room, moving silently in the dark to grab all the bits she needed; the knickers, a clean work blouse, the bag with her keys in. And, after groping around for a good bit in her wardrobe, the half bottle of vodka that had been sitting there for ages. Hopefully Susie would have some Coke to go with it.

She headed back across the landing then, but stopped by the stairs. Her parents' voices were now louder. Were they properly arguing? She tiptoed down a little way. Yes, they were, and that wasn't at all right. Yes, her mam could mouth off loud enough to have the neighbours banging on the walls, but not her dad, ever. That wasn't his style. He normally just sat and waited for her to calm down. And, in this case, had clearly been happy enough to let her mam do their dirty work. What the hell was going on to have him raise his voice to her? She took another few steps down and rested her head against the banister, so she could hear the muffled voices more clearly.

'I'm fucking telling you, Josie, you've gone too far,' her dad was saying. 'Why do you have to go off at her like a bull at a fucking gate? You've just got her back up now, like I told you you would. And she's going to start noseying around now, asking all sorts of questions, and all kinds of shit will kick off over it. You just don't know when to keep it shut, do you? You know what we agreed. Yet off you go, like a bloody banshee, as per.'

She? They meant her? Paula strained to hear better. 'So bleeding what?' her mam snapped, as if responding to her request. 'Let the fucking truth come out. He deserves it!'

What truth? And who? What were the pair of them on about? She glanced back up to the landing, half-expecting Sam and Tommy to have their noses poking out from round their own bedroom door, but there was no sign of either, which meant they must be keeping their heads down. They had the survival instinct and nose for danger of experienced assassins, and had presumably scarpered upstairs when her mum had started on at her. And no Lou, either – but perhaps she'd already legged it round to her mate's. That's what she'd have probably done at her age, hearing her dad kick off like this.

'That's not up to you, me, or anyone else, for that matter!' Her dad was properly shouting now. 'And if you had any fucking sense you'd stay out of it. *Well* out of it. You know what you'll do, Josie, don't you? You'll just bring it to our fucking door. *Our* door. Ours and our kids'. And I'm not having it. Just stay out of it, you hear me?'

But bring *what*? That was the burning question. What on earth was her dad on about? 'You moron!' her mam yelled. 'It's *already* at our fucking door!'

'No, it's not,' her dad said. 'But it soon bloody will be if you keep on like this. Just keep out of it, okay? If you don't hold your tongue you know full well what's going to happen. Sooner or later the *whole* truth is going to come out – just you wait – and then the shit is *really* going to hit the fan.'

'So what?' Paula's mum's voice was getting shriller by the minute. 'You don't get it, do you? I don't *care*! Perhaps it *should* all come out. Perhaps it should never have been buried in the first place. I know she's my friend, but there are limits – and we've reached them. Gone way past them, like a bloody racehorse. This is *our* daughter we're talking about, and I'm not having it, Eddie. It's all very well, all this pussyfooting around trying to protect poor innocent fucking Joey, but how long are we supposed to just sit here and say nothing? Till he moves in on Paula? Till he rapes her as *well*?'

Rape? Paula gasped, trying to take it all in. He? She'd said 'he' – did she mean *Joey*? It made no sense at all. Couldn't be. That was just too ridiculous. So what the hell *were* they on about? She heard some sort of scuffle then – though it didn't sound violent. Her dad was never violent. Wasn't capable of violence. It was probably just the sound of a chair being scraped across the lino, as if someone – one or other of them – was standing up.

But the door didn't open and her dad spoke again then. 'Pipe down, Jose,' he hissed. 'The kids'll hear you. Enough now.'

More than enough, Paula thought, her mind reeling with questions. Worried now that she might be discovered at any moment, she padded down the rest of the stairs, slipped her shoes back on and left.

Josie snatched up her cigarettes and lit one. Enough? Like doing nothing would make it all go away? Why couldn't Eddie see that? It was all just getting worse.

She watched him light one too. He was shaking his head. 'Come on, Jose, you're being hysterical. It wasn't exactly rape, was it? Christ, you really think that's his style? And as I remember it, she would have chopped off her own bloody right arm to get back with him once Joey was born. Amazing how short everyone's bloody memory is! Particularly hers.'

'I can't believe you're defending him.'

'I am *not* bloody defending him. I'm just pointing out that it wasn't as simple as you're saying. And it's not *our* business to dredge it all up again.'

'I bet a judge would call it rape. She was sixteen, remember. Frigging *sixteen* years old. She was ripe for the fucking taking, and he took her. And while he was supposed to be with her fucking mother – how sick is *that*? He's an animal. And I know for a fact he worked one over on her, too – spent weeks, bloody months even, telling her how fucking gorgeous she was, and how things were so bad between him and her mam. She was sixteen, Eddie – not much older than our Lou – Christ, we of all people know how easily led girls are at that age. And she wanted an out – and that makes all the difference. Her brother off his head in the land of fucking smack, and her mam – well, God rest her soul, but she was shitty to Chrissy too – not to mention her nan and granddad, and –'

'But it isn't our *business*. You wade in like you always do and see where it bloody gets us.'

'I don't *want* to wade in – I want to wade bloody *out*!'

'So why the hell are we even arguing? So do I!'

'So she has to leave there. End of.'

'Which she won't – not now you've laid the bloody law down to her. She'll do the exact bloody opposite, like she always does.'

'Which is why she needs to know the truth. *All* of it.'

'Not from us. We're not involved in this. *She's* not involved.'

'God, Eddie – stop being such a divvy. It's fucking Rasta Mo we're talking about. The biggest drug dealer in Bradford, and now he's into putting girls out on the batter, as well. And our daughter works for the prick. How is she not involved? What if the place gets raided, eh? What if that happens? And our Paula's *working* there. Fuck, she does all his fucking books and you can bet your life they won't be kosher. Of course she's involved! She could end up in bloody prison!'

Eddie was silent for a few minutes, rubbing his hands through his hair. 'Well, in that case, it's Christine you have to speak to, isn't it? Tell her it's up to her to sort it. Tell her to tell that lad of hers a few home truths, and hope he's got the sense to walk away as well. But please, Jose, don't go screaming accusations about rape, okay? That will bring all kinds of shit to our door, as you bloody already know. Your Vinnie, for instance. He'd love to have a pop at him. And he would, too, he'd have a pop at fucking anyone these days. And he's out again soon, isn't he? Trust me, you'll just cause World War fucking Three.'

'Yes, but would she though? *All* of it? I can't see it, can you? Her head's way too far down in the bloody sand.'

'It doesn't need to be all of it,' Eddie said. 'Just enough so the pair of them see him for what he really is, before it's too late.'

Josie stubbed out the cigarette and nodded grimly. If it wasn't too bloody late already. She had a terrible premonition that it might be.

Chapter 20

Susie lived on her own, on Little Horton Lane, in a cottage she rented just near the Brown Cow. It was handy for work and also handy for Paula to nip in for a coffee if they were on different shifts. Or outside, in Susie's little suntrap of a back yard. Paula had great respect for her friend, not least because of her independence. She was only a couple of years older than Paula, but had been long engaged – almost married – till her fiancé was unfaithful, and where she could so easily have headed back home to her parents with her tail between her legs, she'd chosen to remain there and go it alone, even though, financially, Paula knew it was a struggle. Her mam's words about her own naïvety still rankled. It was a word that really rankled, full stop.

It was getting dark when she pulled up in the pub car park and locked the car – where had the time gone? How could it be so late already? – but there was a light burning a welcome over the front door.

'Changed your mind?' Susie said as she opened it. 'What a lovely surprise. Come on in, mate. I have wine. Not much in the way of food, like, but wine I can do. You okay?' She scrutinised Paula more closely under the light in the hallway. 'You're not okay, are you? What's up?'

'I wouldn't know where to start,' Paula said as she followed her friend into the shabby but cosy sitting room, breathing in the familiar scent of cheap floral air freshener. 'Pour me a large one of whatever you've got while I get my head straight and I'll tell you. I'm not sure I've got my head round it yet myself.' She flopped down onto the little two-seater sofa while Susie went to get glasses and a bottle from her galley kitchen.

'You look like you've seen a ghost,' Susie observed when she returned with their wine, and threw a family pack of crisps down on the sofa. 'Have you?' she said, sitting down in the single armchair.

'It's not so much what I've seen as what I've heard,' Paula told her. 'Christ. If I've heard right – and I keep thinking it over and over – Mo – as in Joey's *father* – must have raped Joey's mum. It has to be. It all fits. That's what all this has been about. God, Susie. It all fits. That's how Joey came to be. Because Mo bloody raped her!'

Susie sat agog then, while Paula recounted the ridiculous argument her mam had given her about handing her notice in at Silks, then what she'd overheard being said by her mam and dad about Joey. And as she spoke, Paula's mind teemed with questions and realisations. That was so obviously why Joey's mam had never told him where he'd come from – not because of who his father was, but *how* he'd been conceived. It was sickening.

And everything else, in the here and now, started to make sense as well. The idea of the strippers and the pole dancers; God, was she seeing *that* in a different light. Mo, who had sat and calmly broached the idea, had done so because that was how much women meant to him. Christ, much as she hated the idea, her mam had been right – hard though it was to swallow, she had no choice but to do so. Just how naïve *had* she been?

'Fucking hell, Paula,' Suzie said, when she'd finished. 'What a bastard! God, and her so young, as well – how old did you say she'd been? Sixteen?' She shook her head. 'That's disgusting. And d'you think your mam knew? Is that it? That she's known all about it all along?'

'I'm sure of it,' said Paula. 'That's what she's been hiding from me, isn't it? That's why they've all been so weird about everything. God, I just don't know what to do.'

'Have another glass of wine,' Susie said, standing up, holding out her hand for Paula's glass. 'You look like you need one.' Paula handed it over.

'You should tell his mam. That you know, like,' Susie called from the kitchen. 'I think that's what I'd do. Perhaps she'll know what's best to do. Maybe it's better that he doesn't know, after all,' she said as she returned with more wine. 'Or perhaps she's the one who should tell him, don't you think? You really want something like that coming from you? I'm not sure that's the best way, is it?'

Paula took her wine and sipped it. It tasted sour. Or perhaps it was just the bitter taste in her mouth. 'No,' she said, shaking her head after giving it some thought. 'God, I know what you're saying. I don't want it to be me telling him either, but I can't speak to Christine about it. I know what'll happen if I do. She'll swear me to secrecy and beg me not to tell, won't she? Then *I'm* tied up in the whole fucking conspiracy as well, aren't I? Carrying around the same lie. And there's no way I could do that to Joey.'

'Tell *your* mam, then? That you know? That you heard what she said. See what she thinks you should do about it.'

But Paula shook her head again. 'No, I've got to tell Joey. Just the idea of telling anyone, and him *not* knowing … I can't do that. A secret that big? And, Christ – can you imagine it? It would mean everyone knew about it – my parents, his parents, Mo himself, *me* – no, no. I couldn't.' She placed her wine down on the little side table by the sofa. 'Sorry, Susie. I have to go. I have to find Joey and tell him.' She picked up her bag and put her hand in to find her keys again.

'Not *now*,' Susie said. 'Surely? Anyway, you can't drive. You've had a drink. And what's the rush? Stay over. Leave it to the morning. It's senseless going haring off when you're all agitated and upset. Sleep on it first, at least.'

Paula considered. One glass of wine. No more than a sip or two of the second. And would she sleep? Like, in a million years? No, she wouldn't. And she *needed* to see him – it was almost like a bodily need to see him. She'd felt that so strongly. She stood up. 'I'm fine,' she said. 'I'm still under the limit. I can't just sit here and fret … and I can't face my mum. I need to talk to him. I'm sorry …'

'Stop saying sorry,' Susie chided her, standing up as well. 'I'm fine. Long as you're sure. Sure you wouldn't rather try and get him on the phone, have him come here or something?'

Paula hugged her friend. Her friend who she didn't want involved. Not in this kind of mess. No, she felt resolute.

'At least take the crisps,' Susie said, picking them up and pressing them into Paula's hands. 'Eat them on the way or something. Paula, you haven't *eaten* …'

'No, you keep them,' Paula said, hugging her a second time, thinking even as she said it how ridiculous it was to be having such a conversation at such a time. Then a thought hit her. 'Actually, could I use your phone after all? I will call his mam. I need to get hold of Dicky Turner's number.'

'Under the thumb, mate. You can't see it, but that's what you are …' Dicky's mate – some bloke from the flat down the hall – was pressing down his own thumb on the arm of the sofa. 'The slippery, slippery slope, mate – that's what it is.'

'Fuck off, Carl,' Dicky told him. 'You're just fucking jealous because you don't have a Debbie Harry lookalike to get your paws on. Seriously, mate,' he said to Joey. 'You get off downstairs and meet her. It's cool. I don't think I'd want to be sitting here on a bloody PlayStation if I were you either.'

'Sorry, mate,' Joey said. 'You know how it goes. Birds, eh?' he added, more for effect than anything. Right now, he was feeling anything *but* cool.

But how could she have known about it? They'd only bloody discussed it this afternoon. But that shouldn't necessarily reassure him. Because that was when he'd discovered that, actually, it had been going on a while now. He'd been oblivious, of course, because what the hell did he know about such things? The punters were the punters and he was just in the band. That and half in charge of the entertainment. Well, what he thought was the entertainment – turned out that what Nico had said had already been true – there *were* other entertainments on offer at Silks, and probably had been since day one.

But why would he have twigged that some of the women who went there were anything other than girls on nights out, or blokes' wives and girlfriends? How was he supposed to know that bloody half of them were doing business?

Because that, it turned out, was exactly what they did do. Mostly organised by Nico – though Mo too, no doubt. With the club taking a cut – 'a very healthy one', according to Nico – to facilitate (and that had been the exact term he'd used) the smooth running of their lucrative little sideline; in the privacy of the booths, hundred quid for a bottle of wine, extra for dances, and so on, and so on. 'It's the best way to do it,' Nico had explained to him. 'It ensures the safety of the girls, with Billy on hand to keep everything nice and friendly, and as it's not on the streets it's not even technically prostitution. All above board and legal – well, 'ish, my boy, 'ish.' And he'd then clapped him soundly on the back and almost sent him flying. 'It is simply what it is, eh?' he'd chortled.

About none of which Joey was exactly happy. Far from, in fact. Even more infuriating was the knowledge that it had been going on around him – and Paula – and he'd been too dense – too bloody innocent – to even realise.

He pulled on his jacket and downed the last of his can. His third, but he figured he was still way off pissed. And he was still in two minds about what to do about Paula. If deciding what to do about it was even still an option, that was. No, she hadn't sounded angry, but she hadn't exactly sounded jolly either. She must have found something out about it. Must have. Why else would she be so keen to track him down?

Accepting Dicky's mate's jeers with good grace (Dicky was right, Carl probably was jealous – Joey had him pinned straight away as the sort of lad who spent way too much time sitting in his pants, killing aliens), Joey headed down the outside staircase to the car park. She'd said she'd only be ten minutes or so, and by the time he emerged, the lights of the Mini were already swinging in an arc round the entrance.

He waited for her to pull up, then opened the passenger door and climbed in. 'Well, this is nice,' he said, trying to gauge her mood from her expression. But it was too dark once he'd clunked the door shut for him to see it.

'I'm sorry,' she said, yanking on the gearstick and executing a messy three-point turn. 'I don't know what the fuck I'm doing, to be honest. I just had to – look, we need to go for a drive or something, okay?'

'Not off a cliff, I hope,' he joked, hanging on as she yanked the car round back onto the road in pretty much the same fashion. But she didn't laugh.

Fuck, Joey thought, putting his belt on. I'm for it.

They drove for twenty minutes or so, not exactly in silence, but not exactly in conversation either. He'd asked her if she was okay, and she'd told him that she was, but that she had something she needed to talk to him about and she couldn't do it while she was driving. Why not, he'd asked her anxiously, fearing the worst. Because I just can't, she'd said.

I just *can't*, she'd said again, half a minute after that, too, so he'd put some music on, and, apart from asking her where they were going (and her telling him she didn't know) he didn't try to ask her anything else.

By the time they got to where they were going – if, indeed, they'd actively been trying to go anywhere – he'd narrowed it down to two possibilities. Either she'd found out something about the prostitutes – though increasingly he began to doubt that – or she was simply preparing to tell him she wanted to finish with him. He was shocked by the knot that clenched in his stomach when he thought that. But then that didn't feel quite right either. Why the fuck drive him off somewhere to tell him something like that? What *after* that? Just drive off and leave him by the side of the bloody road?

'This is, like, seriously fucking with my head, babe,' he said, when she finally flipped the indicator and parked the car up on the edge of a big industrial estate off the M606. He peered out. He could see cars thundering by in the distance. 'What the hell are we doing *here?*' Not that he was completely sure where 'here' even was. The other side of Rooley Lane, by the look of it, opposite the big motel that had just been built there.

Paula twisted in her seat, so she could see him, though the light was still gloomy. What little illumination there was came from a security light that was a good dozen feet away. It bathed both of them in a pale, ghostly glow. 'We couldn't go to mine, and we couldn't go to yours,' she said. 'And we couldn't go to the club –' Uh oh. Perhaps it was going to be about the girls after all. 'And I didn't want to go anywhere where there were people around.'

'We need our own place, don't we, babe?' he said. The words just popped out of his mouth.

And then she burst into tears.

'For fuck's sake, Paula,' he said alarmed, an idea suddenly coming to him. 'Christ, you're pregnant – is that it? Babe, it's *fine* –' But that just made her cry all the more. He put an arm around her and hugged her tight to him. 'Babe, what's wrong? What the hell are you so upset about?'

'I'm upset for *you*,' she said. 'Oh, fuck, Joey! I don't know if I can even tell you. But I can't *not*. I have to. Oh God, I so wish I didn't, but I *have* to.' She lifted her head then and kissed him, making his face wet because hers was. 'You know how much I love you, right?' she said finally.

'Christ,' he said. Was she dying or something? 'Now you're really beginning to scare me.'

'Don't be frightened,' she said, smoothing his damp hair. 'It's not something to be scared of. It's about your mam. Your mam and Mo.'

'Fuck, Paula – *what*, for Chrissakes?'

And then she told him.

You know how much I love you, right? That was the first thing that hit him. That, and a nauseous churning in his stomach as he tried to process – and couldn't – the image that had come to him, of the first ugly moments of his life on the earth. The image of his mam being pinned down and raped. Fucking raped. Did she scream? Did she fight? Did she beg him to stop? He was so big. So fucking strong. And that was then, too. When he'd been younger. How could she ever have stopped him? His little mam. He thought he might be sick.

Paula was twittering on at him, but he couldn't even hear what she was saying. There was so much going on inside his head that the outside couldn't penetrate. He opened the car door and got out. It had started raining heavily.

Paula clambered out as well, came rushing round, tried to put her arms round him. *You know how much I love you, right.* Like it was almost to reassure him. Almost knowing – *Christ*, he thought, *she really gets it, doesn't she?* – that he'd feel like he was feeling. That he'd feel so *unclean*. He let her hold him, well, hold onto him, resting his chin on the top of her head, a nest of soft hair. Breathing deeply, the way you did when you thought you might vomit. He stayed like that a long time, till the nausea passed.

'Look, I've been thinking,' Paula said at last. She'd been happy to just stand and breathe with him. They were beginning to get wet. 'About your mam not wanting to tell you and being so upset about everything. It all makes sense now, doesn't it?'

'He told me it was a fling,' Joey said, staring out beyond her, to the expanse of motorway. 'A fucking fling. Like, what, he flung her on the floor? Flung her clothes aside? Flung himself on top of her ...' His pulse thumped. 'A fucking *fling*.' He felt shot through with electricity, as if two exposed wires had met, in the rain – and suddenly fizzed into terrible life, like in Frankenstein's Monster. On the one hand, he was beyond appalled, on the other he was beyond astonished. 'How could he even *do* that?' he asked Paula, having pushed her away a little in order to look at her. 'How could he even stand there and look me in the eye, and say all that sick shit to me, knowing what he'd done? How could *any* human do that? That's sick. Seriously sick.'

'I know,' Paula agreed. 'Well, more accurately, I don't know. No wonder your mam wanted the whole horrible business buried. It would have been the last thing she'd have ever wanted you to know, wouldn't it? You have to forgive her for that, Joey. You really do. Don't be angry with her.'

Joey started at the thought. He was about as far away from being angry with his mam at this moment as it was possible to be.

'God, it must have been the absolute worst time in her entire life,' Paula was going on. 'Can you imagine? I can hardly begin to. God, no wonder she wanted to protect you from him. From having anything to do with him. He's a monster, babe. God, she must have spent your whole life praying she'd never clap eyes on him again. God, when you came home and told her you'd met him ... Can you imagine how she must have felt?'

He was only half-listening, his mind too busy going about its own business. What the fuck had his mam and dad being doing since? Knowing what they knew – his dad must have known as well, *had* to. If Paula's mam and dad knew, his dad had to as well, surely?

'Why the fuck didn't she *tell* me?' he said, bile rising in his gullet again. 'Christ, me telling them all about him buying me that shit, raving on about him like a bloody idiot, telling them *they* were the bloody idiots – *why*? Why not just say, look, son, you're being a wanker. The guy's a fucking rapist, okay? What possible reason could they have for *not* telling me?'

Paula gripped him again, bunching his jacket labels between her pale hands. 'Because they didn't want to start trouble? Because they were frightened to start something up? That's why my mam's been going off on one, isn't it? Because they're frightened of him, all of them. Mo's a powerful man, Joey. Christ, we both know *that* much.'

His fucking house, his fucking car, his carpets. His bloody band room. His bloody star-fields of granite. His fucking coffee percolator. It was like he was in a cartoon and someone had waved a wand and 'poof!' – all of it vanished. It felt too huge to process. He felt like a contestant in one of those game shows his mam watched; arrived with nothing, and on the brink of winning something pretty awesome, then failing – some tiny error or miscalculation – and 'poof!' again. The prize being denied him. *But it's no loss, because they came on the show with nothing, didn't they?* That was his mam all over. Tutting at their disappointment. Talking at the telly. *Why are people so bloody greedy? They don't know they're born.* He almost laughed at the irony.

But a deeper rage burned. What kind of bloke would he be if he just let the cunt get away with it? What kind of man was his dad, that *he* hadn't done anything?

Paula seemed to be crying. 'You're frightening me, Joey. Say something. Listen, babe, I've been thinking. Why don't we just fuck off out of here? Just drive off somewhere. I mean, move somewhere else. Just get some stuff together, pack up and leave. Set up somewhere else. Go to Leeds, maybe. Or London. Or wherever. Just – fuck it, Joey – just run away.' She jiggled her hands, pulling him back to her. 'We want to make a life together, don't we? Well, let's just *go*. That stuff is all in the past. I know it's bad, but we can't change it. The only thing we *can* change is now. You can't do anything about the past, babe.'

He looked down at her, all damp and soft and beautiful. Trust Paula to try and see a silver lining in a bag of shit. He wished he could too.

He kissed her cold mouth, decided. 'Yeah,' he said. 'You're right. I can't change what happened. But I'm not running away. Because I can certainly do something about the fucking future.'

And then he shook her off. And ran away.

Chapter 21

'What the fuck?' Paula screamed at him. 'JOEY!'

She started running too then, but she soon slowed to a stop again, gasping for breath. It was hopeless. She didn't stand an earthly of catching him.

She sprinted back to the car and jumped back in. She *could* catch him. She *must* catch him. But within minutes it became clear that she could drive all she liked. There were just too many ways he could have gone, too many side roads and alleys. And her stuck on the bloody main road. Not only that, her petrol needle was in the red already. She'd be lucky if she had enough fuel to make it to Joey's, let alone chase him round the town.

Christ, she thought, banging her fist on the steering wheel in exasperation. She'd been such an *idiot*. What the hell else had she expected?

It was almost eleven by the time Paula pulled up on Joey's street. Parking the car a few doors up, so if he was already home, he wouldn't see her coming, she set off on foot towards his house. She didn't for a single moment think he was going to be there, but by a process of elimination, she had at least arrived at a plan, and it helped to calm her. Though a part of her cursed Christine for leaving her no choice. For making her be the one who had to tell Joey the truth, for having now to find more words, as well.

What the fuck have I got myself involved with? she asked herself as she knocked on the door. It swung slightly open. Did nobody ever lock their bloody doors? 'Bri?' came a voice. 'Is that you?'

So at least Joey's dad wasn't there. 'It's me,' she called. 'Paula. Can I come in?' She did anyway.

'Paula, love,' Christine said, rising from where she'd been curled up on the sofa. She smoothed down her dressing gown. She was obviously all set for bed. She looked past Paula, with a confused half-smile. She looked *so* young. 'No Joey? I thought you and he were –'

'You're not going to like this,' Paula said.

'Oh, dear God!' Christine said, once Paula was done. 'Oh, dear God! You told him *that*? God, you stupid, stupid girl! What bloody possessed you? Why didn't you speak to me? Christ. You have no idea what you've done! All these years I've protected him and now you've bloody gone and done it …' She went to the window. 'Dear fucking God! Christ, what's he going to do? We have to stop him. We have to find him and we have to stop him …'

She turned back. 'I'll get some clothes on. We'll go and find him … you've got your car, right?'

'It's out of petrol.'

'Fuck,' Christine said. 'So don't just stand there – call a

bloody cab then!' She jabbed a finger towards the phone. 'While I go and dress!'

Paula went to the phone, dialled the number of the cab firm she knew, with shaking fingers. She'd been right then, Susie wrong. Absolutely right not to tell Christine first. She'd have done as she'd predicted. Try to talk her out of it. She breathed away her rising panic. They'd find him, they'd *find* him. They'd go straight to the club – that must surely be where he'd be headed. They'd find him and stop him from confronting Mo, and it would all be okay.

Christine reappeared only moments after Paula put the phone down. 'Five minutes,' she told her, while she lit a cigarette.

'Want one?' Christine said, proffering the pack.

'I don't smoke, thanks.'

'Course you don't,' Christine said. She puffed on hers hungrily. Like it could give her some magical bloody strength. 'I can't believe this,' she said, waving a plume of smoke into curling wisps. 'Josie *actually* said that? God, if Joey thinks that, fuck knows what he's going to do.'

'Course Mam said that,' Paula answered, feeling needled. Whose bloody fuck-up was this, after all? 'You think I'd say that if she hadn't?'

Christine walked to the window, then turned around and rolled her eyes. 'Yeah, you're right, she probably would. Anyway, here's the taxi.'

'So *didn't* he?' Paula was confused now, a dread forming inside her, only heightened by the look Christine was now giving her.

'It's not that black and white,' she said. 'Nothing ever fucking is in this world.'

It was a good twenty minutes before Joey got his bearings. The rain had stopped but too late – he was already soaked through. Though it did nothing to cool his fiery rage. He walked on, fast and furious, too short of breath to run now, down Manchester Road, under the footbridge and onwards towards town. He had no plan in his head yet, just a jangle of possibilities. One of which, he felt sure, would resolve into something concrete eventually. Just keep walking, and thinking, and hating, and hating – he didn't think he'd ever felt such intense hate in his life.

The Listers pub came into view, a gaggle of men clustered outside it, chatting, and – was he right? Was that his uncle Nicky's voice he could hear? Shit! He kept his head down, collar up – at least his hair hung in strings now – cursing himself not to have thought to go another way.

Too late. 'Joey, lad? That you?' Nicky peeled from the gaggle. 'Where you off to?' he called out. 'Wait up!'

For a moment Joey wondered if he should tell Nicky what he knew now, but dismissed the thought immediately – he was only just out of bloody prison.

'Alright, Nicky?' he called across, adding a wave. 'You doing afters?'

But Nicky had already crossed the road and was catching up with him.

'Nah, mate,' he said. 'Bunch of miserable bastards in there tonight.' He laughed. He was pissed. 'Proper kicked off. Tony lost it. Smacked toothless Mickey with a pool cue. So out comes fucking Jean, shaking her imaginary rolling pin – "Like, you lot can fuck off right out of here!" – the way she does.' Like Joey would have a clue. 'So we're heading into town now. You coming with us?'

He was talking as if Joey had the first idea who all these people even were. He considered again, thinking quickly, the thought of reinforcements appealing. But again dismissed it. Nicky was so pissed he'd probably fuck things up anyway. What things, though? An idea suddenly popped into his head.

'No, you're fine,' Joey told him. 'I'm off to Dicky's and that, actually ...'

Lame. And Nicky picked up on it straight away. 'Weren't you just there?' he said, grabbing his arm to slow him down a bit. 'You sure you're okay, Joey, mate? You don't look right. You alright?'

Joey carried on walking and Nicky, walking too, carried on looking at him. 'Oh, I get it,' he said finally. 'You've had another row with that bird of yours, haven't you? Bloody women, eh? Always messing with your fucking head, aren't they? Well –' he chuckled. 'Not in my case, more's the pity. Christ, what I'd give to get my leg over sometime soon! Anyway, you go and apologise – even if you did fuck-all wrong, you go right back and apologise ...' He seemed to be going off on his train of thought now, and Joey was happy to let him. 'If there's one thing you need to know when it comes to birds, it's that, son. Say sorry. Even if you've done fuck-all wrong. Bloody women.' He patted

Joey's back. 'But she's a good 'un. You'll be okay, kid. Nighty night.'

Joey turned to watch the men go, staggering along the bottom end of Manchester Road, variously on and off the pavement, planning to follow them into town as soon as they were comfortably far ahead. Then the idea that had been worming into his consciousness took better, sharper shape. He turned around and set off in the opposite direction.

Chapter 22

The whole street was in darkness, as it would be. It was almost one in the morning. And Joey's house was no exception. Which meant either his mam and dad were in bed, or they were out on the razz somewhere. He vaguely remembered that his dad was – wasn't his mam staying in tonight? She had an early shift tomorrow morning, didn't she?

Joey edged the iron gate open just enough to get past it, then walked silently up the path to the house. He then crept round the back, to the end of the garden, the shed a blacker shape against the charcoal of a cloudy, moonlit sky.

Here he knew he had at least one potential obstacle. The padlock was easy enough to deal with – it was a newish combination one, and his dad used WD-40 on it regularly – but the bolt itself was an enormous beast of a thing, more suited to a castle portcullis than a suburban back garden; the legacy of living in a place full of light-fingered kids. And, like a petulant kid itself, it usually resisted all attempts to shift it, a situation made harder because the shed door had dropped so much over the years.

It resisted Joey now, gripping on for grim death, till it finally gave up and slammed noisily back into place. Too noisily for comfort. Joey stood a moment, his heart thumping in his chest, before pulling the door back and stepping inside.

It was even blacker in the still-warm and compost-smelling interior. But, though he knew where the torch hung, he propped the door open instead, to make use of what little light there was. It was enough; he'd been in and out of this shed for half his life. And his dad kept it tidy – with Joey's help, often grudging down the years – so he knew exactly where everything lived.

His questing hands quickly found what he was looking for; the khaki-coloured twenty-litre Jerry can of petrol that his dad always kept half-filled for emergencies. But he also needed rags, and he knew those would be harder to lay hands on, mostly because Joey was usually in the habit of purloining any he could find – he got through them at a great rate because he used them on his round. And today, of all days, he knew he wouldn't find any on his cart. He'd taken them all in, and his mam – the thought angered him further, if that were possible – had given them a boil wash, in her giant saucepan, on the stove.

He climbed over the lawnmower, parked as ever in its allotted place, adjacent to the workbench, just to see if there were any others he could find. But he knew, even as he disturbed the webs and dining options of the resident spiders, that his only sensible option was to risk going in the house and grabbing his own – most of which were draped in a scratty row over the hall radiator.

He felt automatically in his jeans pocket for his door keys. If his mam had been long in bed, chances were that he could do that without detection. He'd just have to hope and pray, assuming that his dad was in too, that he'd be too pissed to stir either.

He backed out of the shed carefully, taking care not to let the door bang behind him, electing not to try and force the bolt back into place. Odds-on, he'd be the only one intent on crime tonight.

Joey put down the Jerry can and opted for going in through the back door; as his parents' bedroom was at the front, it would be safer, and, to his relief, the key slipped in and turned noiselessly. Picking up an old plastic bag from the pile at the bottom of the veg rack, he then padded through into the living room. It too was dark, bar the window-shaped squares on the carpet that had been conveniently placed there by the weak moonlight. Enough, he noted grimly, but not too much.

Glancing around, he took stock, and felt relieved. Like any other, his home had a recognisable signature and, tonight, all the signs pointed towards his parents *both* being out still. No cans on the coffee table, and his mam's hand-bag missing; even in the gloom he could see that it wasn't where it should be; hanging from the back of the chair by the door into the hall. There was also no light spilling down from the landing. Were they in, and him out, they would always leave it on, so that he wouldn't have to stumble quite so hazardously up to bed, or, indeed, his uncle Nicky, needing a piss.

Feeling more confident about noise, but newly anxious

that they might return at any moment, he hurried out into the hall and snatched the rags up from the radiator – they were dry and pleasingly crisp now – and stuffed them in the crumpled bag, before leaving them parked by the newel post while he headed up the stairs.

He took them two at a time, his mind now fully focussed. It was almost in lock-down – a fortress where thinking couldn't penetrate. He had decided what to do and he wasn't going to talk himself out of it. His rage was too powerful a force. Necessary items – that was all he must consider now. A lighter – he knew he still had one, in the drawer of his bedside table – and his thick black winter work coat. He shrugged off his damp leather jacket. Not so much because he cared about it getting damaged, but simply because it wouldn't do. He needed something with a hood.

The coat on, his sodden T-shirt feeling clammy underneath it, he then retraced his steps, grabbed the bag from the hallway, let himself out, locking the back door with more haste than stealth, picked up the Jerry can and headed back off into town.

It was well past one by the time Brian returned from the pub, so he wasn't surprised to find the house in darkness. He was surprised to find Christine wasn't in it, however – hadn't she said she was having a quiet night in? Only the most cursory look around suggested she wasn't there, quickly confirmed once he made his way up the stairs.

He came back down. Where the hell had she gone, then? There was no note – she wasn't the note-leaving type anyway, but then again, neither was she the stay-out-past-one type – not if she wasn't with him, anyway.

He took his coat off, put the kettle on, and poked around a little more. And, as was his way, seeing the smelly and overflowing bin in the corner – Nicky and his bloody stinking takeaways – pulled the bag out, and tied it, to put it outside the back door. It was high time Nicky moved on, and he'd be glad when he did. He was getting reasonably regular bits of work now, so there was no reason why he shouldn't. It would be nice to have their living room back.

It was then that Brian noticed that the shed door was slightly open. Fuck! Hadn't he bolted it earlier? Yes, he had. Bloody kids, he thought crossly, as he stomped down the garden. If his lawnmower was missing he'd be absolutely fucking furious. Thieving bastards on the estate, you couldn't trust fucking anyone anymore.

He pulled the door open. The lawnmower was exactly where he'd left it. As was his tool box, as was his small cherished collection of carefully maintained power tools. *What* then? He was just about to concede that either he had left the door unlocked, or – more likely – that bloody Nicky had been down here, when he saw the space on the floor where his Jerry can should be. Who the fuck would leave all this lot and take *that*?

He was scratching his head, his tea brewing, when he heard a noise from out front. A car door opening and shutting. So she was home then. But when he went into the living room, it was to see not just Christine coming up the path, but their Joey's Paula as well.

He felt a sinking sensation as they banged into the hall. A heavy parental whump. What the hell was going on?

'What's up?' he asked, properly frightened now. Christine was crying and Paula's face was mascara-streaked and puffy. 'What's going on, Chrissy?' he said. 'Christ, love – tell me!'

Christine couldn't speak, though – she was in too much of a state, so while she perched on the sofa, her head in her hands, it fell to Paula to try and fill him in.

Brian listened, his tea growing cold in the kitchen, as she burbled the events of the evening. 'God, love, what were you thinking?' he said, glancing at his snivelling wife. 'Why the hell didn't you come and speak to us first?'

Christine's head snapped up. 'Don't fucking blame her, Bri!' she barked at him. 'How was she supposed to know how much shit this would cause? It's not her fault – it's bloody Josie's – bloody Josie's and Eddie's! Mouthing off!' She slapped her hands down on her knees and stood up, looking at Paula apologetically. It seemed clear to Brian that the two had had words. 'And who can blame them frankly? They don't want their daughter in the middle of it, do they? Just like we don't want our Joey tangled up with our sorry fucking past either.' She grabbed Brian by the front of his jumper. 'Bri, you have to *do* something. We can't find him anywhere. We've been almost an hour now, hanging around outside that bloody club, trying not to be seen. And that fucking great lunk outside – and all the bloody shitbags on the street … so we thought – God.' She looked around her. '*Has* he been here? Have you seen him?'

Brian felt the whump in his stomach grow solid and scary. He was glad he'd yet to say anything about the Jerry can. But *shit*. Joey. Could he? *Would* he? Christ, if that was what he'd been told … He glanced out into the hall, knowing but hoping. His hope was dashed. The rags were gone. The rags he'd laid out there himself.

'Bri!' Christine was yelling at him. 'Bri, we have to stop him! *You* have to stop him. He'll fucking kill him!'

He'd say nothing about the rags. No point. They'd be hysterical. He turned to Paula. 'I'm sorry, love,' he said. 'I know you did what you thought best. And keep calm, okay? Our Joey's not stupid. He's rightly angry, I expect, but he's never been a hothead. He might have marched off intending to give someone a hiding, but it's not in his nature. He'll have calmed himself down now. Leave this to me,' he added, wondering if that was a hope he *could* cling to. In truth, was it likely that Joey *had* calmed down? When he'd clearly walked all the way home, which was a fair bloody distance, sneaked in, and helped himself to petrol and rags? He dredged up a reassuring smile and squeezed Paula's shoulder. 'I'll find him, love. Talk him down. Bring him back safe.'

'But where?' Christine shrieked. 'He's not at the club, he's not here, so where *is* he?'

Brian felt a jolt of clarity, and with it a kind of bleak optimism. 'Yes, but if he's still set on fronting it out with Mo' – Paula's hand flew to her mouth – 'then he's not going to do that with all the punters in there, is he? He'll wait till everyone's gone, won't he? Till Mo's on his own.'

A sob escaped from Paula now. 'But Mo'll *kill* him!'

'I doubt that,' Brian said. He scowled. 'What with everything.' What with that bastard Mo being his son's bastard flesh and blood. That must surely count for something. He hoped so.

'Nico, then. *Billy ... God ...*!'

Enough, he thought ... the pair of them ... they'd have him shitting himself as well soon.

'Not happening,' he said. 'I'll get him home, okay?' He went to get his coat.

Brian wished he felt as confident as he sounded. He couldn't take his car because he'd make himself too visible, and if Joey was set on doing something that bloody stupid, that was the last thing he needed. He'd discounted the idea of calling a cab for the same reason. So there was nothing for it but to walk.

But marching along the silent streets, his collar pulled tight and high against the already dewy chilly pre-dawn air, at least gave him something physical to do. He counted steps doggedly, pumping his legs, trying to fool himself into not feeling scared. He tried to think of anything but the confrontation he might well be having. Christ, he hoped he found Joey before they did. Because everything pointed towards him having told an untruth to Chrissy and Paula – Joey's actions made it clear he hadn't calmed down at all.

Nature versus nurture – the phrase wormed its way into his brain. He remembered it off a documentary he'd once seen. One he'd taken a special interest in because it meant so much to him. He'd been dad to Joey, always, but he wasn't that, was he? However much he might feel as if it did (that whump of pure parental love, the scariest kind, was a constant companion) not a drop of his blood ran in Joey's veins. And that was what the programme had been about – how much that mattered. Was the way you ended up, what kind of person you became, down to the way you were brought up, by *whom* you were brought up, or was it partly in your genes, inescapable? Brian had always been convinced, perhaps because that's what he wanted, that nurture, not nature, was usually the winner. Which wasn't just wishful thinking. It also made sense to him. Surely you took on the traits of whoever brought you up?

He walked on, growing fearful. Perhaps it wasn't so. Because if Joey was planning to do what Brian thought he was, then that was most definitely not a Brian thing to be doing. And very much a Mo thing. And Joey was bright – perhaps brighter than Chrissy and him together. Was he feeling Mo's blood running through his veins as well? And if so, how must Joey be feeling now he knew what he knew? Brian quickened his pace.

Chapter 23

It was almost three in the morning by the time Brian got to Silks. Once he'd got into town, he'd walked up every back alley he could find to avoid being seen. Though he'd risked checking the main road, popping his head out from round a wall, just to see if Mo's car could be seen anywhere.

Joey had bragged about it often enough, so he knew he'd be able to spot it, which he did, sitting outside the Indian – now shut, with just the glow of a rear light on – like a fat, malevolent toad. There was another car parked behind it – an equally flash Mercedes. Nico's. It had to be. So they were both still inside.

But where was Joey? He moved stealthily, keeping close to the wall. There seemed to be no one about – it was a weeknight after all – but this was town, full of all sorts, so you never knew.

He'd turned the corner, down the side-street, at the near end of the building, when he heard the faintest of sounds and then, across the road, caught a glimpse of a human silhouette. *Joey's* silhouette. He'd have recognised it anywhere. He was hunched closely against the wall at the side of the building, and unless Brian was mistaken – and he knew he probably wasn't – he was at this very moment dousing his cleaning cloths in petrol.

Brian swallowed, feeling relief washing over him. So no violent confrontation. Something he could deal with – something from which he could drag Joey away, hopefully before he'd done what he'd so obviously come to do. Then fear again. The fucking idiot could strike a match at any second. And then he realised Joey was already stuffing rags into something – something that resolved itself as he looked into what looked like a small window. Frosted. One of the toilets, he presumed.

So he'd thought it through. Chances were that the front would be locked up and securely bolted, making it difficult, in a panic, to get themselves out. Brian tried to think too. Would there be other people in the club too? He had to think fast. Maybe he should just run back round to the front and start yelling and banging on windows. With the sound of the disturbance, Joey would surely have the sense to run away. But as he watched his son, he could see that there would be no sense forthcoming. Joey was literally shaking with rage.

Decided, he emerged from the shadows – not that Joey had even glanced that way – and ran across the narrow road.

'Joey!' he hissed, causing him to spin round, startled. 'What the hell are you doing, son?' he asked, grabbing him by his coat sleeves. The fumes prickled sourly in his nostrils. 'This isn't the answer, lad. Come away now. Come away.' He bent to try and take the petrol can off him.

Joey shook his hand away. 'Get the fuck off me!' he growled. 'Go home, Dad. This has nothing to do with you.'

Knocked off balance for a moment, Brian reached out to the wall. And, regaining it, tried to grab Joey again. 'It's got *everything* to do with me, Joey,' he whispered urgently. 'Come away. *Leave* this. For now, at least. Come home. Mam's worried *sick*. You want to end up in the nick like your uncle?'

Joey looked at him in a way that made Brian start. Then pushed him, flat-handed, on the shoulder. 'This should have been you, Dad!' he spat, hitting out again. 'Should have been *you!*' This time Brian toppled and went crashing to the pavement. '*You* should have taken the bastard out!' he yelled down at Brian. 'You've known for all these fucking years!'

Brian heaved himself to one side, bent his legs, and scrabbled quickly to his feet. Joey had returned to piling the soaked rags through the tiny window. A window Brian realised he was too short to reach. He was no match for his son, either – not right now.

He tried even so, throwing himself against him and trying to wrestle him into a bear hug. 'It's not what you think, lad – it's *not* – you've been told wrong. Son, stop this – this will only make matters worse, believe me. There's more to it than you think!'

But his words were falling on deaf ears. Or perhaps not. Joey span around, his shoulders heaving and shaking. 'Don't fucking *lie to me!*' he screamed in Brian's face.

Joey's own face was filthy, streaked with petrol and tears. Brian took his chance, grabbing the rag Joey was holding and yanking it. And tried again, with all his might, to get him off his feet.

It was then, as they tussled, that Brian realised they weren't alone. Other silhouettes were now moving in the corner of his vision, and as he opened his mouth to speak, Joey once again pushed him to the ground. Threw him, almost, as if discarding him, to be all the more ready to face his own quarry.

Brian rolled over, his back protesting with stabs of intense pain, and saw three figures approaching – Mo, unmistakably, and two other, wider figures. Almost as fast as he'd been felled he pulled himself to his feet again; Joey was lunging towards Mo now, but one of the big men had blocked him, throwing a punch that sent Joey reeling.

Finding a strength he didn't know he had, Brian threw himself towards the big man, who growled and roared like he wasn't even human. He was flung against the wall though – like a doll – as the man piled in on Joey, who was still on his feet but staggering badly, as if stunned still from the punch.

Brian tried again – his pain dulled by his desperate need to get between them – but he simply couldn't get between the two wrestling men, and taking a blow to the side of his neck for his trouble. Which was when, panting and reeling, he saw the glint of something metal – something passed by the other big man to the one wrestling with Joey – a glint above his head, no more than a streak of silver. A knife – he was passing him a fucking knife!

'No, Nic.' Was that Mo's voice? So why the fuck wasn't he stopping it? But the glint in the man's piggy eyes made it clear that trying to stop him – or his brute – would be akin to stopping a runaway bloody train. But no one was stabbing Joey – not while he had breath in his body. He dived in again, arms flailing, unfeeling, uncaring – perhaps Joey was right. Perhaps it should have always come to this – feeling something crack in his cheek as a fist again connected, and then again, in his chest, before slumping, legless, to the ground again.

Joey fell as well, then, landing on top of him in a tangle of limbs, and the man roared again, piling onto him torso first, and now the other man – Brian registered his suit: a fucking suit! – swung a leg back, and hammered a foot into his head. The world seemed to explode, then, but it galvanised him too; made him heave his son off of him, scrabble up to his knees, try to form a barricade to protect him from whatever was coming – then just as he'd found the strength to raise his hands to defend his head, he saw the glint again, and felt something slam into his groin.

The pain wasn't instant. Just a heat, a searing heat – then, all at once, it came for him and pulled him back down to his knees. Then to the ground, where he curled into a pulsing ball of agony, only dimly aware now of the foot connecting again with his head, which lolled and rolled – roll with the punches, that was the way you did it, wasn't it? – and of Joey screaming blue bloody murder, while he vomited.

Chapter 24

In the midst of the maelstrom – he couldn't see straight, he had blood running in his eyes, and from his head – Joey found that, bizarrely, he was taking everything in. Not least the fact, that, as he struggled once again to his wayward feet, Big Billy wasn't trying to kill him anymore. Indeed, he'd stepped back – just like a dumper truck, slowly reversing – and something else, the sound of sirens, drawing nearer.

'You fucking animal!' he screamed, dropping to his knees again, by his dad, who was screaming as well.

But Billy kept on reversing. Big, lumbering bear-steps. 'You fucking animal!' he yelled again, trying to haul his dad into his lap. But that just made his dad scream all the more. He struggled to his feet again – he needed to go and flag down an ambulance. How the fuck did you flag down an ambulance anyway? Assuming it even was one – the sound of sirens was now close and loud. But would it even be an ambulance? 'You fucking cunts!' he yelled. 'Go and get some fucking help!'

There was shouting then, lots of it, and as Joey staggered forwards, he realised what he was seeing through his pink and filmy vision; or rather, what he *wasn't* seeing. There was no sign of the knife, no sign of the petrol can and rags, and Mo and Nico were calmly walking up the lane towards a police car that had screeched to a stop, its doors already open and spewing officers.

One made straight for him, at a run. Another made for his dad. 'Help him,' Joey sobbed. '*Please* help him. He's really hurt.'

'Don't worry, son,' he said briskly. 'The ambulance is on its way.' He then dropped to his knees, to check Joey's dad over, whose whole trouser leg now seemed to gleam with fresh blood. He was groaning incoherently, tears running from the sides of his eyes, a slick of vomit clinging to his left cheek.

Joey thought he might be sick too. He rubbed his eyes with the filthy sleeves of the thick winter coat. He could smell the petrol. Could anyone else? He could see a paramedic approaching and stepped back to let him through. The movement made him dizzy and he had to lean against the wall. Christ, he thought, as the paramedic calmly pulled kit from his bag, his dad could bleed to death! Couldn't they *see* that?

But within moments the man had cut and stripped off the front of his dad's trousers and clipped a strap around his thigh – a tourniquet, some part of his brain randomly informed him – and Joey dared to breathe out again.

The officer turned to him now. 'You hurt, lad?' Joey shook his head. Everything hurt but he knew nothing was broken. And if it was, so be it. Just as long as his dad was okay. 'I'll just help get this gentleman into the ambulance, then. Don't disappear.' He looked at Joey sharply.

It seemed inconceivable that Mo and Nico were just standing there a few feet away, calmly discussing what had happened – yeah, sure – to another of the officers, while a third started putting handcuffs on Billy. What the fuck? Feeling emboldened, while another paramedic with a stretcher headed towards them, Joey moved sufficiently to hear what was being said.

'I can't tell you exactly, officer,' Mo was saying, glancing benignly in Joey's direction, 'but that lad there, works for us.' He then pointed towards Big Billy. 'As does this man. My colleague and I were in the back office, cashing up, when we heard the disturbance – some shouting – out here. By the time we'd come out, the pair of them were brawling in the street. The man on the floor, I don't know.' He shrugged his suited shoulders. 'Maybe he stepped in to help, break it up – tried to intervene …'

Joey couldn't help it. 'The man on the floor is my dad, you cunt!' he yelled at Mo. He couldn't believe what he was hearing.

The officer talking to Mo turned and glared at him, lifting a reproving finger. 'Shut it. I'll get to you in a minute, boy,' he said coldly. Then looked at the officer who had just cuffed Big Billy. He pointed at Joey again. 'He's next for the bracelets, PC Carter.'

The officer led Big Billy away and Joey took the opportunity to check on his dad, who was being lifted on to the stretcher now, a mask over his face. His eyes were closed and he was silent now. Was he dying?

'Dad, *Dad*!' he said, trying to shake him awake. Wasn't

that what you had to do – try to keep unconscious people awake? But reason told him that they'd probably given him something. He jiggled his father's arm, even so, just wanting to see him open his eyes and look at him.

'He'll be okay, son,' the second paramedic said, while the first put his kit away. But wasn't that just what they always said, even when it wasn't true? The copper was approaching now as well, ready to cuff him. He wore a pained look that Joey recognised from every cop show he'd ever seen. It said 'You tedious bloody fuckers, giving us this shit to deal with at this hour'. He gestured with hand movements what Joey should do with his own. 'Give me a minute, mate, please,' Joey said. 'I'm not going anywhere. He's my dad. Just let me see him into the ambulance, yeah?'

The paramedic closest to Joey nodded, and he was allowed to go with his father into the ambulance, though not before the officer told him he'd be taking him in. And for a moment, Joey didn't register where he meant. To his police car? He recoiled. Not with Big Billy, surely? But at the head of the lane it all became clear – there was a meat wagon parked up as well.

The jolt up into the ambulance must have jerked his dad awake, at least. His eyes flickered open and he pawed the air, trying to grasp Joey's hand. Once he'd gripped it, he yanked on it, pulling Joey down, closer to his face.

'Go with it, Joey, do you hear me?' he whispered. 'Say fuck-all about fuck-all. Nothing. They won't, trust me. That halfwit will cop for it. Not a word, you hear me?'

Joey glanced beyond him to where one of the paramedics had already climbed into his cab, while the other was doing something by the rear doors. Might they have heard what his dad said? They showed no sign of having done so. 'Really, Dad?' he whispered. 'Why would I want to –'

'Do it!' his father hissed. 'Do as you're bloody told! I'm trying to save your fucking bacon here, you idiot!' But his dad gripped his hand again, squeezed it with surprising strength.

'But what am I supposed to say?' Joey hissed back. Too late. 'Come on, son,' said a voice from the back of the ambulance. 'We'll let you know how he's doing once he's safely in the infirmary. Chop-chop, we don't have all night. And the sooner we get you down to the station, the sooner you'll be out again, won't you?'

Joey did as instructed, while Mo and Nico stood by and watched, at just sufficient distance that Joey couldn't lash out and hit them. Which was just as well, as, once the officer had the cuffs round Joey's wrists, Mo turned to the one nearest him and shook his head sadly. 'I'm afraid this is what happens, you see, when you invite a boy into a man's world.' He sighed and met Joey's gaze. 'I'm assuming you won't be popping back for your P45, son. No worries, I'll pop it in the post instead.'

Joey had thought he was spent, but some force was unleashed within him. They had to wrestle him, screaming and kicking, into the purring police car.

Chapter 25

Joey had never even seen the inside of a cell before, let alone spent any time in one, so being roughly manhandled into one (which he knew he'd brought entirely on himself) came as something of a shock. It was not like the cells of his imaginings. For a start there were no bars – just a heavy steel door, with a viewing pane set in it, and a small window, set too high to reach. From somewhere outside he could hear birds chirruping gaily, while the darkness paled to grey. It must be dawn.

He'd been 'processed' and now left 'to calm himself down a bit', and try to get some rest before his interview. He'd been asked if he wanted a solicitor (he didn't know) or a doctor (he didn't think so) and, though they'd allowed him a cup of water, there'd been nothing else on offer. Now his nausea had gone, his stomach was rumbling, but it did so automatically – he had no part in that process. He might not feel sick, but he felt sickened to his stomach by what he'd done. He was desperate for news of his dad.

He tried to console himself by accepting what the paramedic had told him, and by the unexpected strength in his father's sudden grip. Though he still wasn't completely happy about what his dad had told him to say when interviewed!

Should he have demanded a solicitor? Was that what you were supposed to do? He'd asked the officer who'd come round – not the one who'd slung him so unceremoniously in the cell – but he didn't seem to know either.

'Your first offence, lad?' he'd asked him.

Joey had nodded. 'But it wasn't even an offence,' he said. 'So why would I need one anyway? It was' – he chose his words with care – 'just a scrap that got a bit lively.'

The policeman, who had a kind face, said it was up to Joey. 'But if it's as cut and dried as you say, then maybe you don't. But I can't say either way. All I know is that in the middle of this "scrap" a bloke got stabbed, so …' And then he shrugged again.

'But not by *me*,' Joey said, feeling even more anxious. 'It was my *dad* who got stabbed!'

'Well, there you go,' said the copper. But nothing else.

Joey lay on the narrow bed, which was actually a concrete block with a thin mattress on top of it, and listened to the birds singing – such a strange thing to hear in such a place. They made him mournful – he couldn't remember the last time he felt so much like crying. He knew the tiniest thing and he'd be sobbing his heart out, so when he thought of Paula – and his mam – but particularly Paula, he had to chase the thoughts away like they were enemies. Christ, what must she be thinking? Did she know? Did she know anything about what had happened? Where *was* she? He'd just left her – and, fuck, why hadn't he just done what she'd asked him to? Why hadn't he just done what she'd fucking asked of him, and driven far, far away?

Then he thought of his mam again, and how wretched and frightened she must be feeling. Wondering where he was – where his dad was. Would anyone have told her? He imagined her getting a phone call – at this hour – and how scared she'd be to take it. God, he hoped his dad was okay. He didn't, couldn't, wouldn't, mustn't let his mind stray to Mo. Bastard Mo. Rapist Mo. No, don't go there. He closed his eyes, and slept.

When he woke again, it was fully daylight, and the birds had stopped singing. He rubbed his eyes, which were gritty – what the hell must he look like? – and rolled onto his side, his joints protesting. There was nothing else in the cell, bar a low, unlidded toilet, barely concealed, presumably for privacy, by a low wall. It jutted out into the tiny space like a miniature room divider. The bare plaster walls had been painted magnolia – the same colour as the hall and stairs at home. And in the paint, very faint, was evidence of multiple other occupants, some painted over and old, some much newer; names of cons, he presumed – Terry, Gazzer, Desperate Danny. Fuck the establishment. All coppers are cunts.

He rolled onto his back and stared up at the ceiling. Then lifted his hands, which felt stiff, and were swollen. No gig tonight then – the thought came to him suddenly. And then another – that he could have hurt his hands badly. Broken fingers perhaps. Not be able to drum again. He had to sniff back a rush of self-pitying tears. And all he could do was lie here. For how long, he wondered. And then interviewed. And then he'd have to lie.

The door rattled noisily, keys and bolts and stuff, some half an hour later. 'Come on then, sunshine,' a voice said as it opened. It was the same officer who had cuffed him outside the club. Joey stood up and stretched, and the man led him out, and along a corridor to the interview room. It said so on a plaque on the door. There was another copper – at least he assumed so, he was in plain clothes – waiting for him at a long table. The man told him to sit on a chair opposite, so he did so, while the other policeman took a seat as well.

'I'm DS Cronin,' the plain-clothed man said, then pointed to a recording device on the table. 'Also present is PC Roberts and Joey Parker. I have explained to Mr Parker that this interview is to be recorded.' Even though he hadn't – he was doing that now. He then said the date and the time – it was apparently now mid-morning. He then, finally, turned and addressed Joey.

'I'm going to ask you some questions, Joey, and you must speak the answers. If you nod or shake your head I will have to indicate that on the tape. For the purposes of the tape can you confirm that you've been asked, and declined to have, a solicitor present?'

Joey answered yes. His nerves were really starting to jangle. This all seemed so serious.

'Can you tell us in your own words, Joey,' DS Cronin asked him, 'exactly what happened last night, please?'

'Like we all said at the time …' Joey began. DS Cronin held up his hand.

'Not what anyone else said, lad. Just from your point of view, please. We are in the process of taking statements from everyone else involved.'

Joey took a deep breath. He could do this. He had to. If he knew anything, he knew that. His dad had made that clear. 'Okay, well, I work at Silks,' he said. 'And so does that Big Billy. He's a bouncer, I think, and a workman on the building. He doesn't like me for some reason, never has. I'd gone down after closing tonight because I thought I'd left my pager in the office. I have that in case I get called in in an emergency.' Another breath. He'd rehearsed this. He could do this. 'Anyway, before I got the chance to, you know, get in, that Billy – Big Billy – came at me, telling me to fuck off, and that I'd have to come back and get it in the morning. I told him it had nothing to do with him and to get out of my way. Next thing, he started kicking the fuck out of me.' He looked from one officer to the other. Was that enough? Would that do? They remained silent. 'I don't know how we even ended up outside, to be honest,' he added. 'Must have been as we were fighting. That's what happened.'

DS Cronin's face was blank. 'And then?' he asked. 'Your dad. How did your dad end up there?'

Joey shrugged.

'Mr Parker shrugged his shoulders,' DS Cronin said. 'Joey, can you answer the question for the tape, please?'

What the fuck to say? 'I don't know how my dad ended up there,' Joey said, which was true. 'He must have been in town,' he said. 'I don't know. With his mates, or something. He was probably heading for the taxi rank, or a kebab. I don't know. The first I knew was him running over and wading in. He'll have thought Billy was out to kill me. He's twice my size,' he added. 'In case you didn't notice.'

'Right,' DS Cronin said. 'And the knife?'

Joey met his eye. 'The knife?'

'There was *obviously* a knife, Joey. Your dad was stabbed. Quite badly too. Who had the knife? Was it yours?'

His? Surely they wouldn't think that? 'No, it wasn't mine! I never even saw a knife,' he told them. 'First I knew about my dad being hurt was when you lot turned up. I didn't even *know* he'd been stabbed then. If he had then it must have been Big Billy. But I never saw a knife.' He kept his voice low and even, and as he lied, he knew that it wouldn't matter. His dad was right, wasn't he? The big bastard would happily admit to it, even if it meant jail. That's what Mo's 'boys' were paid to do. He suddenly felt very much what Mo had insinuated he was: a boy in a man's world. He hated that.

'Anything to add?' Cronin asked, his finger poised above a button on the recording device.

Joey shook his head and said no.

'Right then,' Cronin said, standing up. He was taller than Joey thought. 'Officer Roberts will take you back to your cell and get you a blanket. You'll be with us until after lunch now, because we can't take Billy's statement until his solicitor turns up.'

'But what about my dad?' Joey asked, anxious that nobody would know where he was. 'Someone needs to know about him. I promised him I'd be there.'

'Don't worry too much about that, Joey,' Officer Roberts said kindly. 'Your mam's been on the phone. She's up at the Bradford Royal Infirmary with your dad. He's doing well by the way,' he added. Then he smiled. The first smile he'd seen in such a long time. 'And she's told us she'll be down here as soon as she can, to give us hell till we release you to her care.'

Joey hung on till he'd been taken back to the cell again – just. Till the door shut behind him and the keys and bolts had rattled. Then he turned to face the wall and this time he did cry.

Chapter 26

Christine wondered if she'd ever understand motherhood. Not properly. As she watched her son being led out towards her, head down, in his stockinged feet, it was like she was two different people. One who wanted to leap on him and batter him for being such a fucking idiot, and the other who wanted to leap on him for entirely different reasons – to hug all the breath out of him and never let him go.

She took her vexation out on the police officer instead. 'So, is he being charged?' she demanded. 'Because from what I've been told, you'd no business even arresting him let alone banging him up in here. None of it was my Joey's fault! None of it!'

Joey, pale and tired-looking, took the pen he was proffered and signed the form that had been placed on the counter. 'Mam, shhh. They know, they *know*. I'm not getting charged with anything. I'm just getting a warning.'

'A warning?' Christine huffed, her voice rising sharply. 'What, a warning for you to keep away from arseholes that might beat you up?'

Joey frowned. And she could see that she was embarrassing him now, so she shut up and waited quietly as the copper on the desk read something out to him before giving him a paper bag with his trainers in. He shuffled over to the row of adjacent chairs and got the trainers out of the pointless bag, and she watched him wince as he bent down to tie the laces. He was hurt, and she wanted to hit someone for it. He looked haunted. And exhausted. And they'd a fair way to go. The walk from Toller Lane nick to the Bradford Royal Infirmary was really too much of an ask. She turned back to the copper on the desk. 'Any chance you could call us a taxi?' she asked him. 'We were going to walk, but as you can see, my boy's in a bit of a state.' She glared at him pointedly. Then let her gaze slip as it occurred to her that she did have a bit of a cheek. She'd called him an incompetent fuckwit only minutes earlier, after all.

'Be outside in five minutes,' he told her curtly.

They didn't speak much in the cab and that was fine by her. Joey didn't seem to want to – he seemed shell-shocked, closed-off – or maybe he didn't know where to start the conversation. Christ knew, she didn't either. Where did you begin to start a conversation like that anyway? That they had to have it – well, that was no longer up for debate, obviously. But not yet. Not with Brian lying there in the state he was in currently, with a broken cheekbone, a head wound and a pierced femoral artery, having to have blood transfusions and God knew what else.

She'd got the call just after five – she and Paula galvanised and terrified in equal measure – and with Paula refusing to be dropped back at home, and not allowed to go to the police station and see Joey, they'd both spent what was left of the night at the hospital, first in the waiting room and then, when Brian was finished in theatre, in a two-woman vigil round his bed. No, they hadn't told her he was in mortal danger or anything like that – but he'd certainly caused more than his fair share of crises – typical of Bri to manage to have a bloody complication.

But all was well. Well, as well as it could be, which was the best that could be hoped for. He'd be off work for a bit, obviously – he now sported a wire in his jaw, quite apart from anything else – but they'd said there was no reason why he shouldn't be home in a matter of days. And a matter of only a few more, no doubt, she thought affectionately, before he started driving her completely up the wall.

But one thing kept coming back to her. It was like a sore that kept weeping. That, if Brian was right – and though he'd been rambling, he'd managed to explain that much – Mo was just going to walk away. Again. Have his hired hand – Big Billy (even the name set her teeth on edge) – just step up and take the punishment for stabbing her husband, while Mo and his lowlife partner simply washed their hands of him. They must be paying him bloody well, she thought. *Too* bloody well.

And it didn't matter a jot that Billy *had* stabbed her husband. The wounds Mo had inflicted went so much fucking deeper. The way he'd played Joey, the way he'd bowled into his life and, seeing something he wanted, just breezed in and assumed he could take it. Same old, same old. No karma for Mo. At least, not right now. Maybe never.

Now wasn't the time to let that get to her, though. Mo didn't matter. Karma would come for him eventually, she was sure of it. And if karma dragged its heels, then someone else would take him out. And if she could be around to see it, she'd rejoice.

But karma had come for her, and it was time for her to face it. She knew her boy, sitting beside her, had a head full of questions. And the horrible truth, which she'd spent hours now going over and over, was that, in the end, the likes of Mo were of no consequence to her – not compared to the chilling realisation that she might have lost Bri and Joey, and there was no escaping it; every bit of it was her fault.

They pulled up outside the hospital and she peered up at the imposing 1930s building. It was altogether grander than St Luke's, where Joey had been born, and which day she still remembered so vividly. How could she ever explain to him how she'd felt bringing him into the world? How the moment she'd looked at him her heart had swelled in a way it had never done before? How she'd vowed to take care of him till her last breath on earth. And how, so soon after, it had all gone so wrong. How she'd thought she'd been so much better, so much stronger than she had been – the piece of rubbish her mother had told her she was. Not fit for purpose. Not fit to be a mother. Not fit to be *his* mother. She'd proved it, hadn't she? Mo, in the end, was just a side-issue. It had been *her* who had failed him so badly. She'd spent his entire life trying to make that right.

But how must he feel, now he knew what he knew? Or *thought* he knew. She wondered if she'd have acted less rashly than he had, thinking that. She certainly didn't blame him for what he'd tried to do. Feared for him, yes, of course – but understood it absolutely. How did it make him feel about *himself*? It was so important now that she set him straight.

After paying the taxi man, Christine climbed wearily out of the car. Joey was at her side moments later – always the gentleman – and linked arms with her as if it was her that needed helping rather than him who was so battered and bruised. She patted his hand. He was staring up at the building too.

'Mam, I'm so sorry,' he said, looking so young, so boyish. Not half the man he had seemed to be yesterday but, at the same time, much more of a man than he could ever know. A good man. Her heart swelled again. She could take comfort – and courage – from that.

'You don't need to apologise, Joey,' she told him.

'I don't know what I was *thinking*,' he said. 'I was just so *angry*.'

They'd been dropped off at a place where visitors often gathered – not to mention the odd dressing-gowned patient as well. An unofficial smoking area – no one had any tolerance for smoking in hospitals these days – and within it, for the sorts of days when you needed cover (which were many) there was a large Perspex shelter, clouded and scratched by age, with benches running the length of the back wall. No one else was in there, so she tugged on Joey's arm. 'Come on, love – let's have a quick ciggie before we go in and see him, eh?'

Reluctant at first – he was trying to give up smoking, for Paula – he eventually caved and took the cigarette she offered him. 'Joey, love, it's not your fault. You were acting out of love, I know that. But you have to know, absolutely no one blames you. If anyone's to blame, it's me. It's always been me. I should have told you who your father was when you were a little boy. Like your Paula said – and she talks sense, that girl – I was telling everyone, myself included, that I was protecting you from all the shit in the past, but really I was only looking out for myself.'

'How can you say that? How could Paula *think* that? Mam, I know how much you and Dad love me – how much I love *you*! Mam, I understand now. How could you begin to tell me something like that? "Oh, by the way, Joey, your real father is a rapist." Fuck's sake Mam! How on earth could you have told me *that* when I was a nipper?'

Christine drew on her cigarette. Where did she even start? So many lies. So much buried, and where had it got them? To this. To Joey – her baby – almost committing a fucking *murder*. Another life almost destroyed, and all because of her.

He spoke into the silence. 'How *could* you have, Mam?'

'I should have,' she said. 'I should have because if I had it wouldn't have come to this, ever.' She twisted on the bench. 'Joey, I know what Paula told you – and it was only what she heard from *her* mam, but …' God how to say this? God, she couldn't hate Mo more. But she had to make it clear, for Joey – because he needed to hear it, for his own peace of mind. 'He didn't rape me, Joey. I know that's how Josie's always put it, and I know why as well. To make me feel better. But she's wrong. He didn't rape me. He took advantage of me, yes, but –'

'So why the fuck would she say he *did* rape you, then? Christ, Mam – why would she lie about something like that?' His eyes narrowed. 'God, Mum, you're not trying to defend him, are you? Jesus –'

'No!' she said. 'Never. God, never in a million years! But it wasn't that simple. As far as Josie was concerned he as *good* as raped me, yes – he was with my mam, Joey – your gran –'

He stared. '*What?*'

'Not married or anything, not in that way.'

He looked appalled. And she loved him for it. Her sweet innocent Joey. 'God, that's disgusting!' he said. 'The *bastard.*'

She wanted to tell him he didn't know his gran. But that could sit. Running through all the ways in which her mam had failed her helped nothing. Besides, she'd made her peace with that. Done the right thing. Drawn a line. One she wasn't going to cross again, ever. 'I'm not even going to tell you that he forced me, because he didn't, Joey. I was young. I was stupid. I was seduced. I regretted it. Fuck knows, it didn't take long for me to work out what was bloody what. You tend to do that when you're sixteen and pregnant. But I never regretted having you, Joey. Never, never, never. Even when Mam threw me out –'

'*What?*'

No, he didn't know his gran. Nor would he. 'Things were different then, love. She … Look …'

'*How* different? Christ, *tell* me, Mam.' Insistent now. 'What the fuck else don't I know?'

Christine drew deeply on her cigarette before throwing it to the floor and grinding it out with her foot. Smoking on an empty stomach, off the back of no sleep, was a particularly sick-making combination. Perhaps she'd try to give it up too.

'A lot,' she said. 'And trust me, I will sit down and tell you everything, I promise. All of it. Some shit you wouldn't believe.'

'*What* shit?'

'Shit I've been too scared to ever let you know, Joey. I wanted you to have a good life. A different life. Different to the lives me and your dad had. And you have, haven't you?' Her voice cracked. 'We've done right by you, haven't we, me and your dad?'

'So *tell* me, then,' Joey pleaded. 'Yes, yes – you *know* you have. I've had the *best* life. But I need to know, Mam. I can't live like this. So messed up. So *angry*. I swear I would have killed Mo if Dad hadn't turned up.'

'Well, thank God he did, then,' Christine said, grabbing both of his poor, swollen hands in hers. 'Joey, my life would be meaningless without you, you know that, don't you? And that's what stopped me … the stuff from before … there's so much, Joey. Bad stuff. Things that I thought would make you hate me. Mo is just a part of it. That's the thing you have to understand. God, I hope the bastard rots in hell. Hope he gets there sooner rather than later, for that matter. But if it had just been about Mo, I'd have told you *years* ago, honestly. Christ, bastards like him are ten a bloody penny. You've seen that for yourself now. But not now, okay? Not today. Let's just go and see your dad, yes? See how he's doing. Save this for another day, okay?'

Joey pinged his own cigarette into the corner of the shelter, half-smoked, burnt down, already gone out. 'You promise? Mam, you've got to.'

'I promise, Joey,' she said solemnly.

He stood up, offered the crook of his arm again. She took it.

Then he smiled. 'It's okay, Mam. So stop that bloody crying. Seriously. Mam, I've known you all my life, haven't I? You're my mam and I love you.'

'Oh, stop it,' she said, slipping her hand free so she could spare it to bat him on the arm, while the other was busy wiping the tears from her face.

'No, I mean it, Mam – what could you possibly tell me that would make me *not* love you? Christ, I love uncle Nicky, don't I? And he's been in prison for bloody murder! And Paula's uncle Vinnie – Christ, some of the shit he's been up to! It was you taught me that, Mam – good people sometimes do bad things. It doesn't mean they're bad people. You've been saying it to me all my bloody life!'

'Well, I would, wouldn't I?' she said, as she went up the steps. And lighter of step, too, because it had finally hit her

261

that Joey – *her* Joey – would be the one to set her free. 'Speaking of which, let's go and see bloody Rambo,' she added, 'before he starts kicking off in here as well.'

Chapter 27

Anger, Joey decided, was a very strange emotion. So powerful, in the way it could completely take you over; make you think things and do things that you'd never do otherwise – such a violent unstoppable force. Yet it was also weak; in the face of so many other emotions, it could wither and die. Compared to other emotions, it had so little staying power. So little ability to endure.

He no longer felt angry, and he was glad. Now, though, he felt silly, immature, full of shame. The thoughts he'd had about his dad. The things he'd said – he *had*, hadn't he? The fact that his dad had risked his life both to stop him and protect him. The sheer folly of not only thinking he could do something about Mo, but that he even *had* to – that it would make him somehow a better man. When, in reality, all it did was make him a worse one.

He had more of an inkling about the things his mam had to tell him than she knew. Not much – who knew what terrible secrets she might have hidden from him? But given what he *did* know – that she'd had a bloody shitty upbringing, had no family bar him and Nicky, that she'd been so young when she'd had him, that his dad somehow 'saved' her – he was sure there was nothing she could tell him that would change how he felt. She was his mam, for God's sake. Who'd done right by him all his life. What could he ever set against that?

He was also desperate to see Paula. 'Is she here, Mam?' he asked as they walked down the wide corridor, his mam's little steps clicking and clacking beside him as she tried to match his stride with little jumps and jogs.

'Not now,' his mam said. 'But she was here all night, bless her. You've copped for a right little trouper there, Joey. But I told her to go home and get some rest while I got you – have a bath, have a sleep. I said you'd call her.'

And he would. The shame burned. When he'd cleaned up as well. Washed every trace of the idiot he'd been last night away. Start today as he meant to go on. Do whatever it was that she wanted him to do.

'If she doesn't hate me,' he said, thinking of all the reasons that she might do.

'You dozy fucker,' his mam said. '*Hate* you? You want your brains testing, you do! If you weren't in such a mess, I'd be minded to knock some bloody sense into you.' She sniffed. 'She'll have you off me, that one, before you can say Jack bloody Robinson.'

'Jack bloody Robinson,' he said, feeling better.

His mam stopped then. 'Here we go,' she said. 'He managed to get a side-room. Bribed someone, probably. Or blathered on so much that they wanted him tucked out the way. Brace yourself, Joey. He's not looking his best.'

Joey gasped, seeing his dad. He looked so small in the bed. He wasn't a big man, but he looked even smaller

– insubstantial and frail, pale and vulnerable, a muddle of leads and drips and God knew what else sticking in him, and out of, and all around him. There was a bag of blood – red and amber – that hung ghoulishly from a hook, going into a long tube that snaked into his arm.

His face, in contrast, was swollen up, almost like a beach ball, with what looked like a nappy bent round the bottom half, tied above his head, like an upside-down bonnet. Where had he seen that before? A Bugs Bunny cartoon came to mind.

'Don't laugh,' his dad mumbled through the wires and the stitches, still managing to fashion a ghost of a smile. He indicated with his eyes that Joey should sit on the closest chair, but he went straight to the bed and perched on the edge of that instead, anxious about touching him for fear of causing pain, but unable to be anywhere else.

'Fuck, Dad,' he said. 'Christ, what did they *do* to you?'

'What *didn't* they?' his mam said, sitting down.

'Christ, you could have *died*, Dad.' The enormity of it all finally hit him. Tears filled his eyes and started dripping down his cheeks. He didn't care.

His dad tried for a reassuring smile, but all he managed was a wince. 'Here, and I might have,' he mumbled. 'Mam tell you?'

Joey's mam shook her head.

'Mam, what happened?' asked Joey.

His dad tried to wriggle up.

'Will you stop *fidgeting*, Bri!' his mam snapped. 'You'll have all your bloody stitches popping!'

He batted a hand in her general direction. His fingers were even more like sausages than Joey's. 'Blood,' he said. 'Frigging hossie didn't have enough of my blood type in, did they? Running round like blue-arsed flies, they were, all night – trying to find the right stuff to top me up with. Proper panic stations here, by all accounts.'

Joey's mam leaned across and patted his dad's arm tenderly. 'But they got there in the end, thank God. How are you feeling now, love? Have they given you more painkillers?'

His dad nodded. 'I'm fine. I'm doped up to the bloody eyeballs. Mind you, I haven't seen a mirror yet. Ask me again when I do.'

'You don't want to,' Joey said, trying to stem the tide of tears with humour. 'You'd better brace yourself, Dad. The plastic surgery definitely didn't work. And if they're short of blood they should probably stick a needle in your eyeballs. They look like you've been on the cider for a fortnight.'

'I wish. State of me, I'll be on bloody soup for the next month. And pissing in a potty, to boot. I don't know what's going on under here –' He gestured down the bed. 'But I have a feeling that when I do, I'm not going to like it.'

Once again, Joey's dad tried to laugh as he said this, but only succeeded in causing himself pain. So much pain, Joey realised, and so much still to come. The stark fact was that for every blow Joey had suffered, his dad had suffered two, if not three.

'Christ, lad,' he said now. 'Don't keep blubbing all over me. You'll set me off, and I'm trying to play the hard man round here. Milk it while I can.' He looked at Joey's mam. 'It's not often I get the chance.'

'Ah,' said a voice, 'so the prodigal son is here.' Joey turned his head to see a nurse of the officious rotund variety, who bustled round to the other side of the bed, plumped his dad's pillows, then made an inspection of his drip stand of blood. 'So where were *you*, lad?' she said sternly, over a pair of wire glasses, as she grabbed a chart from the bed end and wrote something on it. 'Could have done with a drop of yours last night, did you hear? Might have had a match – your poor dad laid up here, gasping like a bloody vampire, and you down in the cells, too busy feeling sorry for yourself, by all accounts. Here –' she added, bumping him with her enormous bosom as she reached across to the bedside cabinet to grab the box of tissues. 'Mansize, these are. Now stop that bloody snivelling while I go and get you all a cup of tea.'

That did it. Joey tried his best, but a racking sob escaped him anyway. The one thing he could have done, and the one thing he probably couldn't. He might not know much about blood types, but he did know about blood. That the stuff in your veins didn't matter one bit – the man who was your father was the man who loved and raised you.

'Hey, you leave off him,' his dad said. 'Or you'll have me to deal with.'

The nurse grinned. 'You and whose army?' she said, with a wink.

'Seriously,' Brian persisted. 'You should have seen the other bloke.'

He wrapped a hand around Joey's then, and squeezed it, tight and hard. 'Honest, nurse. You just ask my son here.'

Acknowledgements

Many, many thanks to my wonderful editor, Vicky Eribo, and the whole team at HarperCollins, who continue to get the stories out there and remain loyal and supportive. Thanks also to the world's most fabulous literary agent, Andrew Lownie. Without his endless encouragement and hard work, my words wouldn't continue to find their way into your hearts. To Lynne Barrett-Lee, my beautiful friend and co-writer – you know how much I value the magic you bring, and long may it continue. I also want to thank my fellow writer friends, Kimberley Chambers, Mandasue Heller, DS Mitchell and Kerry Barnes, for being there to chat to late at night if I need it, and most of all for continuing to inspire me with your own wonderful words. All very talented and very lovely ladies, I salute you! Last but by no means least, thank you so much, my loyal readers – your feedback and your stories touch my heart, and I'm forever grateful.

Moving Memoirs

Stories of hope, courage and the power of love…

If you loved this book, then you will love our
Moving Memoirs eNewsletter

Sign up to…

- Be the first to hear about new books

- Get sneak previews from your favourite authors

- Read exclusive interviews

- Be entered into our monthly prize draw to win one
  of our latest releases before it's even hit the shops!

Sign up at

www.moving-memoirs.com